SM

LOVE in the
ASYLUM

ALSO BY LISA CAREY

In the Country of the Young

The Mermaids Singing

LOVE in the ASYLUM

lisa carey

WM

WILLIAM MORROW

An Imprint of HarperCollins*Publishers*

This book is a work of fiction. The characters, incidents, and dialogue are drawn from the author's imagination and are not to be construed as real. Any resemblance to actual events or persons, living or dead, is entirely coincidental.

HarperCollins books may be purchased for educational, business, or sales promotional use. For information please write: Special Markets Department, Harper-Collins Publishers Inc., 10 East 53rd Street, New York, NY 10022.

FIRST EDITION

Designed by Nicola Ferguson

Printed on acid-free paper

Library of Congress Cataloging-in-Publication Data

Carey, Lisa.
    Love in the asylum : a novel / Lisa Carey.—1st ed.
        p.   cm.
    ISBN 0-06-621288-X
    1. Psychiatric hospital patients—Fiction.   2. Substance abuse—
Treatment—Fiction.   3. Narcotic addicts—Fiction.   4. Letter-writing—
Fiction.   5. Women—Maine—Fiction.   6. Women authors—Fiction.
7. Alcoholics—Fiction.   8. Maine—Fiction.   I. Title.
PS3553.A66876L68 2004
813'.54–dc21

                                                                    2003051246

---

04 05 06 07 08 WBC/RRD 10 9 8 7 6 5 4 3 2 1

For my mother and father

Acknowledgments

I'd like to thank my agent, Elizabeth Ziemska, for her tough love; my editors, Jennifer Hershey and Jennifer Brehl, for their patience and talent; my family and friends, for forgiving my neglect; my best friend, Sascha, for telephone counseling; my dog, Axel, for relinquishing long walks; and my husband, Tim, for editing, errands, encouragement, and everything else.

Contents

CONTENTS

1

The Asylum

AN ASYLUM, ALBA BELIEVES, is where you are sent
when you want to die—a sanctuary for the prevention of
suicide.

Alba's asylum, Abenaki Hospital, sits, elegant as a
hotel, atop one hundred acres of land—devoted to farm-
ing in the days when inmates worked for their stay—now
grown over with fields of wildflowers and the occasional
wooded grove, blue-gray mountains skulking in the distance. To get there you must cross the Manasis River,
giving your name to the security guard in the hut that
waits before the covered bridge. The nearest town is
almost twenty miles down Rural Route 3—a sleepy
Maine village where the residents have the hospital's
phone number on speed dial, for when they spot a suspicious character on Pleasant Street. Though most of the

inmates these days are self-committed, leaving Abenaki is made so inconvenient that, once inside, the majority of patients, out of lethargy or comfort or discouragement, do not think of escaping. Except of course for the drug addicts, for whom special precautions are taken.

Abenaki is an Algonquin word meaning "People of the Dawn-land." In the eighteenth century, the land was occupied by a small tribe of Abenaki Indians, who had managed to save a scrap of their homeland by maintaining a neutral position between warring French and English colonists, and making themselves useful to both. There was a tradition—no one knew quite how it started—of sending white women off to live with these natives: wives, mothers and spinster daughters who had displayed behavior that could not be explained or cured by local doctors. Women who wept too copiously and often; women who walked or screamed in their sleep; women who attacked their husbands with sharp instruments, or defecated in their own kitchens; women who tried to take their own lives. The Abenaki were thought to be especially tolerant of the old, the sick and the insane; some believed they had secret, potent drugs that could cure things white medicine couldn't even diagnose. But mostly the women were sent there because they could be; the Indians took them in and saved the white families from shame and inconvenience. There were stories of husbands who, wracked with guilt, went riding out to see their wives and found them leather-skinned and toothless, dressed in native clothing, speaking a barbaric language, with no memory of their former lives or no desire to return to them. But generally, people did not visit the Abenaki; they were sent there to disappear.

Ultimately, most of the Abenaki men, lured by the promise of better land, became Revolutionary soldiers and were killed in the war. The women, both Indian and adopted white, died in a massacre in the winter of 1777, the details of which remain a mystery. In the aftermath of the war, the land was bought, despite the rumors of spells left behind by grudge-hungry Indians, by a doctor who had controversial theories about the origins and treatment of insanity.

A mental asylum, retreat, center or hospital—depending on the politically correct terminology of the day—has existed on the Abenaki land ever since. The name has been changed a number of times. At the beginning of the twentieth century, when it was run by the Catholic Church, it was called Saint Dymphna's Asylum, after the Irish patroness of nervous illness, and resembled a convent, with halls full of stealthy nuns. Nowadays it is one of the most renowned and expensive hospitals in New England, and includes adult and adolescent wards, as well as a drug rehab program with a highly publicized success rate. Famous people come here, and praise the staff in interviews in *People* magazine; movies have been filmed among the half-dozen Georgian buildings, where only a close-up lens reveals heavy gridiron lining the glass windows. Behind the main buildings are a few log cabins, left over from when the hospital housed both staff and patients in a pavilion plan. Though they should be torn down, there are some who feel the out-buildings give the place a sense of history—as if those native women are still there, tending pots over a fire. Of course, the cabins were built long after the Native Americans were gone, but this is conveniently forgotten. The movie directors love them.

No one disputes that the hospital has saved lives, though it has also lost a few—in bathrooms, the river, on tree limbs in the woods, and, once, in one of the historical shacks—but these episodes are rare, not to mention hushed up. In 1983, the name of the hospital was changed back to Abenaki, partly because of the inspiring translation—the doctors think *dawn* is a hopeful word—but mostly

because it validated a new plaque endowed with the words ESTAB-
LISHED, 1789.

When Alba Elliot was still in high school, she traveled with her
father to San Francisco. They took a boat tour to Alcatraz, and
when Alba stood in the concrete prison yard and saw the city's sky-
line across the water—looking like life held captive and miniatur-
ized in a confetti-filled dome—she thought immediately of
Abenaki. She'd already been a guest there twice, and remembered
that, late at night, through certain hospital windows, she could see
the faint glow of real life beyond the borders of that unused cush-
ion of land. Prison, she thought, would be similar to a mental asylum. Not as comfortable, but operating under the same dichotomy
of rehabilitation and punishment. A place where you watched your
life tick by. Alcatraz became her nickname for the hospital, and she
always says it with a biting, almost furious humor, which her father
refuses to find amusing.

Alba knows Abenaki's history not because she has been there so
many times that the nurses remember her birthday, but because she
read about it in a book she found while organizing the hospital's
new library. She initially volunteered for this job out of nervous
energy, and kept it to relieve her boredom and the persistent fear
that she is of no use in the world. The hospital hasn't had a library
since after World War II, when the books were crated and stored
away to make room for its first male ward, occupied primarily by
traumatized soldiers. Now there is a new building—donated by a
former patient whose memoir about overcoming obsessive-
compulsive disorder spent 154 weeks on the *New York Times* best-
seller list—with walls of floor-to-ceiling oak bookcases, sliding
ladders, and masculine, green leather armchairs. Just-born books
have been delivered by the truckload, but Alba prefers salvaging the
old ones. She thinks of these musty volumes as having been buried

alive; she digs them up, slaps off the dust, and returns them to the shelves of the living. One book she found, *History of a Mental Reservation*, was not a properly published book, but something released privately, most likely by the author. It was written in 1943 by Nathan Stockwell, chief of staff at the time, and has chapters praising shock therapy and cold-water submersion tanks. She read it all one night in her room during a stretch of insomnia. After the nurses caught her with her light on and gave her a sedative, she fell asleep and dreamed she was dressed in animal pelts, wearing war paint instead of scars, dancing to the beat of a manic drum, on the same lawn where she has spent her mornings—almost every sum-mer for the last ten years—smoking, watching the river change, and trying to stir up some enthusiasm for rejoining the world.

This morning she watches a new patient arrive. This is not nor-mally something she would witness, as the admissions building is a separate cottage hidden behind the main ward, which most patients see only once, unless they are readmitted. But the thin road that leads in from the countryside winds between the widest, most benign section of the river and the sloping front lawn, and Alba has a balcony view of the baby-blue Mercedes as it glides by. The pas-senger door opens and, while the car is still in motion, a man tries to step out, but ends up tumbling, clown fashion, onto the tarmac. By the time the car stops, and the driver gets out, holding his hands up in a plea, the escapee has already gained his feet and, weaving con-siderably, begun walking back the way they've come. The driver, his tie flying up in his face, has to jog a few steps to catch up. He tries to put his hand on the man's shoulder, but is shrugged off. Alba hears the rustle and buzz of walkie-talkies behind her, and soon two staff members are making their way down the hill. One is a nurse with a syringe, Alba knows, hidden in the pocket of his starched white jacket. The other is a rehab counselor, which means that the thin, messily dressed man changing his mind by the banks of the river is a drug addict.

The syringe proves unnecessary. In a few minutes the man is sitting on a log by the water, his forehead pressed against his shaking knees. The counselor squats next to him, murmuring encouragement and patting his shoulder. The driver stands back awkwardly, checking around to see if anyone is watching. Seeing that every patient on the lawn is riveted, he turns back toward the water. After a while the counselor poses a question and the addict looks up, wipes his nose with his shirtsleeve, and nods. The four of them get into the car, the counselor in back with her new patient, the nurse, just in case, up front with the driver. The car makes its way around the hill and out of sight, and people begin milling around the lawn again, their conversations resume; the next drama is already brewing.

Alba knows what comes next; she can picture the man sitting long-legged and wide-eyed in a mauve armchair, clipboard and pen in his lap. For the next few hours he will be interviewed by staff and students who all look suspiciously alike, and made to fill out so many forms that, by the time he is done, he won't care where he is as long as he can lie down. Alba has a theory about entrance paperwork—the forms are like bedtime stories, uninspiring and ritualistic, intended to lull you to sleep, so that it is morning before you realize that you've signed yourself away to an insane asylum.

The first time Alba was admitted to Abenaki she was a minor, so her father was given the paperwork. He filled out forms about her medical history and psychological symptoms while Alba rocked back and forth in the armchair. The hospital had been recommended by the emergency room after Alba, who hadn't slept in twenty-six days, set a lighter to her bedroom curtains. By the time her father woke up, wrestled her outside (she had fought him, saying she needed to keep an eye on the flames), and called 911, most of the upstairs of their house had been burned or damaged by smoke. All of Alba's eyebrows and most of her formerly long, dark hair had been singed off, so, in the admissions office of the mental hospital, she would have looked comical if it wasn't for the jumpy, determined glare of her eyes.

They did ask a few questions of Alba herself, privately, after they'd gleaned all they could from her frightened but poised father. They brought her to a separate room where four psychiatrists, two counselors, and five medical students were lined up at a table that could have been set for dinner. Alba sat alone, set back from the table and exposed, wondering what to do with her knees. One of them—a woman—asked her why she had set the fire.

Because I was tired, she said.

Tired of what?

Tired of trying to remember all of the things I would have to save if the house caught on fire.

I see, the woman said, but Alba didn't think she really did.

The students scribbled furiously on their clipboards long after she refused to answer any more questions. At one point she yelled—*What the fuck are you writing, I haven't said anything*—and that was the end of the interview.

Her first diagnosis—Bipolar Disorder—stuck, though she has collected additional variant disorders since then. She seems to develop new symptoms soon after she has the last ones under control. In her massive chart are labels like Agoraphobia, Anorexia, PTSD, SAD and, the latest one, Panic Disorder. Now, at twenty-five, Alba has been in that admitting cottage ten times. For years her father believed—despite all contrary medical opinion and a genetic predisposition—that she was merely going through a "bad stage," and would grow out of it. Sometimes, she seemed to. Months would accumulate where her days were not measured by levels of mania or depression, but simply lived. She would appear, even to her father, like a normal young woman. Medication, once life-saving, would seem genuinely unnecessary, until she ended up back at Abenaki. When she was eighteen, in her first year of college, and she slit her wrist to the bone during spring break, her father stopped believing in his bad-stage theory. Alba never believed it anyway; she knew who she was, knew even before the symptoms started that there was something elementally wrong with her. More wrong than other children—disturbed in their own ways—from single-parent homes in the privileged Cambridge she grew up in. What Alba often forgot were the details of her illness, and how quickly they took control. When she abandoned her medication, she did so under the delusion that the next time she fell apart, she would be able to handle it. Stop it before she lost herself.

When she sees that drug addict, as she watches his resigned shoulders ducking back into the car, she envies him. She would like to be here for the first time. The first time is when you believe that all you need is a rest from the world, a transition before your life kicks into gear. Something that will turn into anecdotal material in later years—when your life is organized by details and ambition rather than symptoms and a plastic days-of-the-week pill case—when it becomes "that time I went away for a while." Before you start to suspect, after three or four returns, that it is you—not the world—that is deranged.

This time, she has a plan. She hasn't always had one; on most visits she is so drained she decides merely to surrender, live out her life as an inmate. She is almost always here in the spring or summer, the seasons that feed her mania, or in November, after daylight savings nose-dives her into depression. Her latest abandonment of medication led to the inspiration to drive across the country. Her father had to bail her out of jail in a small town in Iowa, after she refused to pull over for speeding and led the local sheriff in his first real car chase. She came back to Abenaki and, once the lithium got the mania under control, she began having panic attacks, which require additional medication. Her father has accused her of playing Russian roulette with her pills, and her doctor, though not inclined to use such suggestive terms, thinks the same. Alba has recently calculated that she has lost a third of her life to illness and hospitalization. Another third has gone to of starting over.

Her plan is this: she will take her medication every day for the rest of her life; she will live mentally muzzled and stop wishing for something more exciting. Excitement, her father insists, lasts for about six weeks, in that hypomanic stage, where she is brilliant and creative—alive—and anything seems possible. It is always, without fail, followed by chaos, and then darkness.

Of course, none of this is what she really wants. What she secretly hopes for is a miracle—mental health without the dependence on drugs that snuff out her soul. The drugs buffer so many sensations, flatten all but the most benign feelings, that she wonders if death would be all that different. No one, not her doctor or her boyfriends or, when she's sick, even Alba herself, believes that it is possible for her to live without drugs.

And though she keeps thinking about that drug addict for the next few days, though she'll be sorting books in the library and suddenly remember his face—blotched, desperate and defiant—she believes he is merely a symbol, a reminder that she is face to face with her final chance. She doesn't realize that it is the man himself, and not what he represents, that will change her; doesn't know that he will throw an unexpected twist into a journey she seems fated to repeat, over and over, with little hope of ever getting it right.

2

Paperwork

ABENAKI HOSPITAL

ALCOHOL AND DRUG ABUSE TREATMENT PROGRAM

PERSONAL BACKGROUND QUESTIONNAIRE

Name: *Oscar Jameson*
Date of birth: *3/22/73*
Today's date: *5/15/2003*

1. How old were you when you had your first experience with alcohol? *9*
2. How old were you when you had your first experience with drugs? *9*
3. How old were you when you first began having problems from alcohol or drugs? *9. Just kidding. That depends. Define <u>problems</u>.*

4. Please indicate from the following all drugs you have used and frequency of use (e.g., times daily, weekly, monthly, etc.):

    a. Alcohol: *Almost daily.*

    b. Heroin: *Sometimes daily.*

    c. Methadone: *I wish.*

    d. Other opiates/narcotics: *It varies.*

    e. Benzodiazepines: (Xanax, Klonopin, Valium, etc.) *No more than your average housewife.*

    f. Other sedatives/hypnotics/tranquilizers: *Fairly often, to fall asleep.*

    g. Cocaine: *Daily in the 80s, of course.*

    h. Amphetamines: *They helped in college.*

    i. Marijuana: *With my coffee in the morning.*

    j. Hallucinogens: *Limited to social gatherings.*

    k. Other (please specify): *Alka-Seltzer, Pepto-Bismol, hairs of the dog. Don't ask me to remember their frequency.*

5. Recently, which drugs have caused you the most problems? *Heroin.*

6. Among the following alcohol- or drug-related problems, please rate how serious these problems have been for you over your lifetime. 0 = not at all, 1 = mild, 2 = moderate, 3 = serious, 4 = very serious.

    a. Medical problems: *0*

    b. Legal problems: *0*

    c. Family problems: *4*

    d. School/work problems: *1*

    e. Psychological problems: *0*

    f. Loss of control over use: *1*

    g. Relapses: *1*

    h. Physical dependence: *I should think that would be obvious.*

    i. Constantly thinking about drugs: *Of course I am, especially while filling out such a questionnaire.*

7. How serious do you think your substance problem is?

_____Very serious

_____Serious

___x__Not very serious

_____Not serious at all

8. How strongly do you believe that you need to stop alcohol and drug use?

_____I know I need to stop completely

_____I think I need to stop completely

_____I'm not sure if I need to stop completely

___x__I don't think I need to stop completely

_____I have no intention of stopping completely

9. How supportive is your home environment and/or family for your recovery?

___x__Very supportive

_____Somewhat supportive

_____Not supportive but it won't make recovery harder

___x__It will make recovery harder

10. Do you believe in God or the idea of a Higher Power? *Sometimes weekly.*

11. Do you have any experience with twelve-step meetings and/or SMART or Rational Recovery meetings? If so, do you have a preference between their spiritual and non-spiritual philosophies? *Yes. I don't find either "philosophy" particularly enlightening.*

12. Do you feel that any of the following may affect your use of substances or your recovery?

   a. Work or school: *No.*

   b. Leisure-time activities or recreational interests: *Do drugs count as a recreational interest?*

   c. Sexual orientation or behavior: *Let me think about that one.*

   d. Physical abuse in past or present: *Irrelevant.*

13. Have you ever been in the military? *I assume this is a joke, but no.*

14. Please feel free to give further details in the space provided. *If you know anything about me after this ludicrous interview, aside from what you have already assumed, kudos to you.*

3

Lawn Therapy

THE FIRST TIME I SAW ALBA was on the hospital lawn where they let the junkies and the lunatics mingle. A massive, manicured body of green that dipped toward a river, with small, tree-thronged islands that made me, a former Boy Scout, think immediately of escape, camouflage and refuge. No canoes, however, and swimming was discouraged by the white-uniformed attendants patrolling the shore.

Actually, almost every time I saw her during my six weeks at Abenaki was on that lawn—under the willow tree, poured into a plastic lounge chair, looking pale, mean and beautiful, though neglectfully so—but the first time sticks out. First times always do, not just because our lives are organized by them (first step, word, sex, drug, love, need I go on?) but because, before you know someone, the first time you see them is when all possibilities still exist. When you have yet to make a fool of yourself by pretending you're someone you're not, or let the only wonderful thing that ever happened to you walk away as if they are nothing.

I was not at my best that morning. It was my first time outside since arriving, and the spring sun on a lawn so recently cut you could smell your childhood in it struck me as insulting. The three-week binge I'd stolen between promising my brother I'd commit myself and actually doing it, combined with ten days of detox, not to mention twenty years of not-so-recreational drug use, had left me with a body that was no joy to be trapped in. I was surprised the machine still worked, to be honest, though its only function seemed to be excretion. In the panic of bodily flood, my brain had leaked from my pores alongside the chemicals, so that even the decision between toast and bagel at breakfast had left me nauseous and half-blind, as though I had come unprepared and hungover to a multiple-choice test.

Later I found out that Alba was not at her best either (also that her best was a matter of opinion and some contention). But that morning, even with the lithium gluing solid the normally swift parts of her brain, she was too much for me. I was not equipped for a conversation with her. But, from the moment she first spoke, I wanted to be.

People who drink water make me feel guilty, she said.

I was standing about fifteen feet away, pretending to look at the lake, though really I could not focus on anything so large, and I had my purple sport water bottle with me—the one they give to all the drug addicts at check-in, like a party favor, to encourage the flushing of the system. The sun was in my eyes; I had to turn and put a hand to my forehead to look at her. I stumbled a bit; I was tripping a lot over nothing those first weeks. Her voice had something to do with my imbalance—a low, ravaged voice which, even when saying something sarcastic, sounded like a seduction. It was a voice, in every inflection, that I wanted to impress.

Huh? said I. For an educated man (I was stoned for all of my college years but I do have a B.A. in English and like to think it counts for something) you'd be surprised how often this wordless grunt comes out of my mouth, most often in the presence of women. My response raised her eyebrows; even my imagination couldn't convince me she felt anything but scorn.

Wa-ter, she said in a convincing imitation of a speech therapist, pointing to my purple pal. Can't get it down. I try, every once in while, to do the six to eight glasses a day. But I can barely manage one, which leads me to think, if I can't do a simple thing like drink water—our bodies are *made* of water, it makes no sense that it's repulsive to me—how am I ever going to do the rest? Quit smoking, eat vegetables, meditate, *ex-er-cise*. Hopeless. That's what I think when I see people with water. That I'm so far behind it's hopeless, and I might as well stop worrying, which I would if I didn't feel so guilty.

She had short hair, dark and heavily straight across her forehead, the kind of hair that made you notice her white, graceful neck and unpierced earlobes; like Scout from *To Kill a Mockingbird*, grown-up and no longer virginal.

She looked up at me, clearly waiting for a response.

Yeah . . . well, I said, making a dismissive motion with my purple bottle. Keep in mind the detox, that I'd just emerged from group therapy whose purpose seemed to be finding creative ways to declare oneself a loser, not to mention my repeated confrontations with the charge nurse whom I believed was parsimonious with sedatives. I had nothing left in the communication bag. I was reduced to single syllables—a sentence seemed more arduous than anything I'd attempted in my life so far. But that voice, and her eyes—I didn't know what color yet, she was wearing red-tinted sunglasses, but I was sure they were riveting—presented an invitation, a challenge. My first sober human contact not counting other addicts and staff. I wanted her, from day one, to never be able to forget me.

So I threw my purple bottle into the river. It was a good throw—hard and high—and carried within it the sensation of a perfect boyhood baseball pitch, the kind that bathes you with temporary invincibility. We both watched it whip through the air and connect with a splash, then pop up again, and bob its way to freedom with the current. For a second I felt discouraged; I dreaded having to ask for another—water bottles, like drugs, were given out stingily—but when I turned back I saw what I thought was a smile, a smile she was fighting, just as it faded from her face.

It was a beautiful moment, and she ruined it.

Are you a junkie? she said.

I know it sounds silly, but in the last few seconds I had forgotten my status, misplaced my chronic shame, even ceased the compulsive counting of the hours before I was free to indulge again, and I was not happy to be reminded of it all.

Why? I said, finding my voice, though it was an ugly, defensive voice, one that I believed belonged to someone else, despite the fact that I'd been using it for years. Are you a lunatic?

Obviously, she snorted. She sounded bored, but her hands shook as she pinched a cigarette from the soft pack of American Spirits in her lap. She flicked the lighter a number of times before managing a flame. My anger lowered a notch—I thought I'd affected her—though later I found out the shaking of her hands was from her medication.

It's not so obvious, I said, though it was. Even my swimmy,

detoxing vision could see she was too thin, too shadowed in the face for someone so young, and that she gave the impression, with all that dark clothing on a warm day, of hidden scars. Do I look like a junkie? I added.

She inhaled so hard on the cigarette it actually crackled.

I guessed because I haven't seen you on the ward, she said. And the purple bottle is a big clue, but yes, now that you mention it, you could be a poster child for the war against drugs.

My momentary sympathy fled with her hackneyed phrase.

You have something against drugs? I said.

Everything, she sneered.

They claim nicotine is as addictive as heroin, I said. I'm sure my wince was noticeable. Now *I* was resorting to clichés.

She inhaled again, savoring the smoke, teasing, the way I've seen dealers shoot up in front of someone who is almost dead from need, making them wait that one more minute which is longer than a lifetime.

Get the doctor, she said, so loud it startled me. I've been misdiagnosed.

I didn't think she was the slightest bit amusing, and arranged my face to say so.

Want one? she said, offering the pack. It had an American Indian on a blue background, smoking from a long pipe which I thought was more likely to contain peyote than additive-free tobacco. I suspected this was her attempt at a truce, but I was still rankling from the junkie remark, and not willing to make it easier for either of us just yet.

Never touch them, I said.

Her expression switched from conciliatory to mocking without a snag. What *are* you detoxing from, then? she said.

I'm just here for a rest, I mumbled.

What a coincidence, she said. So am I. Who's your sponsor?

I assumed she was using AA terminology (I'd been to AA before, and NA and ACOA, all the letters). In twelve-step programs you were designated a sponsor, usually an older, reformed addict, now obsessed with gardening, whose job it was to answer three A.M. phone calls with preapproved slogans.

I don't have one yet, I said.

No, she said. I was amazed she could fit so much impatience in two letters. Your *benefactor*. Who's paying for you to be on this cruise? You don't look like the corporate-health-insurance type.

Abenaki was a notoriously expensive hospital, so everyone wondered the same thing about each other, though most were too polite to ask. It was none of her business, not to mention a source of great embarrassment for me, but, perhaps to keep hearing that voice, I answered her anyway.

My brother, I said.

Family money, she assumed.

No, I blurted. He's rich now. We grew up poor.

Congratulations, she said, scraping her cigarette out in a bald spot she'd already made on the lawn.

I did that too often—toted out my childhood poverty as though it were an asset, something that had driven me to success, when really, there I was, thirty years old, back in detox, the most notable thing on my résumé that I'd never kept a job longer than one year. Most people with whom I burdened the Oliver Twist analogy either didn't pick up on it or glossed it over. But Alba made it a point to grab on to such absurdities and throw them back in your face.

So your brother's the genius and you're the failure, she said.

Did you learn that theory from your shrink? I said, blushing. If you're the lunatic, who's the genius?

Lucky me, Alba said. I'm both.

There we were—less than five minutes and we couldn't stand each other. But even then I knew that this was not a dismissive dislike. It was the kind of dislike that would follow me afterward, when I was alone, thinking up sentences stunning in their vocabulary and eloquence, the ones I might have (though probably wouldn't have) formed had I not been working with a brain of noodles. The kind of dislike where I would try to remember an unflattering version of her face even as she became more striking in my memory. An infatuated dislike. Attraction, in other words.

Even so, I probably would have left the lawn—who needed this, depleting sunshine *and* antagonistic psychiatric patients—had I been able to storm off at that point with a shred of dignity. (I'd lost my dignity sometime in my early twenties, but I was faithfully expecting its return at any moment.) Instead, I had what my new caretakers referred to as an episode.

It knocked me from behind, like being hit with a baseball, except the ball didn't crack off but entered, embedded itself, still spinning, in my skull. I believe I managed a stilted, *Sorry . . . must . . . sit,* before I dropped to the lawn and went blind. I started to sweat, not in droplets but an instant, unhindered gushing from my skin. It was the way I imagined bleeding to death must feel.

I wanted to cry, though this was impossible. I could never cry enough—it would not do this justice, nor would it help. The only thing that could possibly help me, that could keep everything that made me real from spurting outward, irretrievable, into a hellish void, had been taken away. And that's how I thought of it in these moments—that drugs had been stolen from me. It was like being denied oxygen or food, just for spite. Impossible that I could have checked myself into this—that would be suicide. I didn't want to kill myself; I wanted to live and I couldn't live, I couldn't even breathe, without drugs, and nobody, not my brother, not the overly trained nurses and counselors, not even the other addicts, believed me when I told them this. They thought that I was lying, and worse, thought they understood why.

I may have screamed, it wouldn't have been the first time. Perhaps I only moaned. There was an almost imperceptible part of me that stood back and watched it all happening. I thought of it as the me I could never get to again—the person who existed before anything went wrong. Before I made it wrong. This Oscar had healthy veins, clear skin, a future. He had nothing to do with the man who appeared to be dying on freshly mown grass.

Then Alba touched me. Her hand, pressed firmly against the back of my neck, was freezing. She didn't stroke, did not try to insult me with nursing platitudes, just kept her hand there. The lake turned right side up, my body calmed to an occasional twitch—I could breathe again. In and out. It seemed so easy, yet miraculous, now that I was doing it.

Even as I stood up to leave, shooing her away in the same moment I grumbled my thanks; while I saw her shrug with contempt, as if tending to junkies were a daily chore, and settle into her chair again, putting on the sunglasses that must have slipped off during my spell; even as I walked back up the lawn, sick now, wanting only to make it to the dark privacy of my bathroom, I was already imagining—with the cunning torment that distinguishes the addict—when she would touch me again.

Her eyes, I knew now, were gray—almost silver—as cold and soothing as her hand.

4

Rounds

WHEN ALBA LOOKS BACKWARD, her memories are not organized by age, year, school or job, like her acquaintances, or even by mood (manic, depressed and, rarely, level), which is how her father monitors her. She includes these things, but they are subcategories. Instead, the stages of her life are filed under good and bad luck.

Birth to age four, though she remembers little about it, was lucky. Then her mother died, and Alba learned, during one week of shocked voices, formal clothing and every room packed tight with grown-ups' knees, that death was not just something that happened to you; it was something you could bring upon yourself. Between accusatory whispers of neglected motherhood, her father's awkward explanation that her mother had been ill—not bodily but in her mind—and his assurance that it was all right to be angry but blame would be unfair, Alba began to understand something. In the same way that her mother had not wanted to get out of bed, eat dinner, leave the house, or, once out, come home, she also had not wanted to live. She had chosen to die. Alba, who had always been told she was the image of her mother, decided that vigilance would be necessary to prevent the same decision from tempting her.

Ages four to twelve, though shadowed by the bad luck of being half an orphan, were fairly happy years. Alba had always been closer to her father, and once her mother was gone, they became inseparable. She spent her after-school hours at the Elliot House, a museum of which her father was the curator. The mansion had belonged to his great-great-great-grandfather, whose ancestors came over on the *Mayflower*. In school projects involving ancestry, Alba not only had more detailed information than any of her classmates; she had props. Her father told her she was lucky to come from such a rich heritage. Her mother's family, a melting pot of dark-haired immigrants with rumors of Indian blood, was rarely mentioned.

During puberty, her luck changed again. She began to experience symptoms—the most alarming of which were obsessive thoughts about her own death—that she feared were the inheritance of her mother's disease. She hid them, the same way she camouflaged the changes occurring in her body, because she wanted her father to believe that she was still his little girl. This deception brought about a number of disasters, culminating in her first visit to Abenaki, and a diagnosis that proved she was most definitely her mother's child. Her father took the news with initial despair, then quickly turned to determination. He began to resemble a combination of nurse and football coach, monitoring her medications and pushing her into "healthy activities" with forceful cheer.

In high school, luck was divided into semesters; fall was lucky, by spring things had usually fallen apart. College was similar, except for the complete wash of a year that saw her wrists sliced. When she was twenty-three, and the first in her series of children's books was published, she was so happy she didn't recognize herself.

Alba has superstitious theories about her luck—for instance, bad things happen in threes. A depressive episode will be followed by writer's block, then an uncommon, undiagnosable physical ailment. Mania segues into a car accident, panic attacks, sudden paralyzing agoraphobia while traveling in Europe. Good luck is recognizable from the beginning, and is usually associated with a person. A new boyfriend—those generally warp into disaster—her first real writing teacher, meeting her agent. There is a magic surrounding certain people that makes her believe that, for those particular moments of her life, she is not merely herself. She occupies a strange, dizzy, not always comfortable, but thrilling space with each of these people, and these spaces, like the ladder of moods she has careened up and down since she was a child, define her.

Which is why, even before she knows his name, she begins to think of spring 2003 as belonging to the Junkie.

Names come on the second day—first names only, the inmate's etiquette—when he walks purposefully, wobbling a bit, over to her chair on the lawn.

I'm Oscar, he says, holding out his hand. He is not looking at her, but at his palm, as though by watching it he can stop its tremor. It is only after she scoots forward and captures his hand with her own that he lifts his gaze.

Alba, she says, and neither of them can help their little smiles. Are you starting over?

Always, Oscar says. He gestures a question—*May I sit?*—and she shrugs in agreement. There are no other chairs nearby so he drops stiffly to the lawn, the knees of his long legs filling the worn patches in his jeans.

She takes him in quickly, reinforming her impression of the day before. He is wearing surprisingly white socks, black sneakers gone gray at the toes, a flannel shirt, opened at the neck but buttoned at the cuffs, far too big for his bony frame. His hair is dark, in need of a trim, curled boyishly over his ears. Cheekbones that look vulnerable and prone to sunburn, slightly chapped lips, the sliver of a gap between his two front teeth, and brown eyes that are, temporarily she hopes, having difficulty focusing on her.

Oscar's eyes are so solidly brown—no chips of green, no starry ring of yellow around the pupil, like eyes colored in by a child—that Alba can't decide whether or not they are attractive. Every man she's ever kissed has been blue-eyed. It is one of her weaknesses.

They sit for a moment, pretending to look at the lake, snatching glances at one another, and every movement—Oscar's scratching, Alba's cigarette-lighting—seems clumsy and far too loud. She wonders if he regrets sitting down.

I see you've given up the water, she says.

Oscar smiles, in the way that most of the patients smile, slightly, as if any show of pleasure must be metered out in careful portions, so that it will last.

Can't you hear me dehydrating? he says.

I was wondering what that noise was.

Actually, they won't give me another bottle. I fear I'm being punished.

Maybe next time you won't be so careless with hospital property, Alba says, imitating the staff voice—condescending, put out, almost to the point of being pleased.

After all, Oscar adds, mimicking her tone, I am privileged to be here. Prison would not be so accommodating.

Not to mention entertaining, Alba says.

I haven't noticed much in the way of entertainment, Oscar says.

Not the variety you're used to, Alba says. We make our own entertainment. Try patient-watching.

Oscar smiles blankly at her, not sure if she's putting him on. Alba's voice has a natural tendency toward mockery, and she's used to people looking at her with half-bewildered, half-defiant expressions.

For instance, she says, observe Marta—the woman over there wearing a smock. She is a painter and is convinced Abenaki is an exclusive artists' colony, which, from what I know about artists' colonies, isn't as delusional as you might think.

Alba waves to Marta, who begins moving across the lawn toward them.

Good *morning*, Alba dear, Marta yodels. She is a heavy woman, with features so bulbous they look masculine, wearing white slippers, a loudly printed dress, and a painter's smock, so clean it is obvious it has never been introduced to a palette.

Are you our Alba's latest beau? Marta says to Oscar, standing so close to him that he has to lean back on the lawn to avoid her billowing dress. He is blushing, his freshly shaved cheeks aflame with irregular patches of red.

This is Oscar, Marta, Alba says, though Marta isn't looking at her; she is too busy mooning at Oscar. He's a new patient.

Oh, a new *resident*, Marta squeals. What are you working on?

Pardon me? Oscar says, his voice, though alarmed, primly polite the way some men become when faced with women who look like housewives.

What is your medium, dear? Marta says.

Oscar clears his throat. I'm sorry? he says.

Your material. Inspiration. Marta's voice is growing louder; she is afraid her world is about to be contradicted.

Oscar looks from one woman to the other and back to Alba, who shrugs and dares him with a smile.

Um. Oscar rearranges the mischief in his face to solemnity. Needles and spoons.

Ooo, Marta says, a sculptor! It's been a while since we've had one. She shuffles off then, abruptly and without explanation, muttering about a misplaced easel.

Is she for real? Oscar laughs when Marta is gone.

Of course, says Alba. That's Charles, the fellow in the tweed. He thinks this is his summer home, he asks only black attendants to bring him a martini. We're all waiting for one of them to haul off and hit him. Laura, over there, is always offering me money for my lighter—she wants to burn the palms of her hands. There are no lines left on them. Jonathan has giggling fits—he believes he's being tickled by his mother—and he'll laugh until he screams and needs to be medicated. I don't know what it's like on your ward, but mine is very entertaining.

I see you know all the regulars, he says, with a bit too much scorn for Alba's liking.

I *am* a regular, she says.

Oh, he mutters. Does she hear disappointment there?

How do you afford that? he says.

It's not a problem, Alba says.

I see. His shoulders, if it is possible, are even stiffer than before.

You don't like people with money, Alba says.

Oscar squints at the lake. It's not—he starts. No. No, I suppose I don't.

Do you like your brother?

Oscar laughs. Not as much as I used to.

Well, I despise people who do drugs, so we're even.

Not so fast, Oscar says. I am a reformed man. I will never

indulge again. His voice mocks the booming, self-conscious tone of a person in group therapy.

Really, Alba says with obvious doubt.

Oscar slouches, chuckles, pulls grass from its roots.

I don't know, he sighs softly. I'm the last person to know what I may do next.

They are both quiet for a minute. Alba has a shiver of déjà vu; she thinks she said the same thing once. To a boyfriend. Or was it her father?

Are you going to tell me why you're here? Oscar says. Alba looks away. It's only fair, he says, since you're privy to my secrets.

By this point your drug abuse is definitely out of the bag, Alba says. I hope you have other secrets.

Yes, well, Oscar grins. We'll see.

He is flirting with her now, and she isn't quite sure, though she's been waiting for it, how she feels about this. She sighs; underneath the fear that she will have to explain too much, this part always bores her.

I'm unlucky, she says. He smiles again, full force this time, and the intensity of it startles her. She has a history with dangerous grins.

Too easy, he says. Join the club. What else?

I'm bipolar, she says, the same way she might say, I'm twenty-five, or, I'm allergic to nuts.

Oscar nods. At least he knows what this means. Isn't there something you can take for that? he says.

Yes, Alba sneers. A number of things.

But you, Oscar says, don't take drugs.

That's right, she says. She is a bit startled by his eyes, which have cleared up like the river after clouds blow away; they are flashing at her. I take them sometimes, she says. I'm taking them now. But I always stop.

Because you'd rather stay in this palace than swallow your daily pill?

Here we go, Alba thinks. It's not that simple, she says.

No, Oscar says softly, I'm sure it's not.

He is looking at her arm. Her sleeve, probably while lighting her last cigarette, has slid up to reveal three raised, purple scars, like huge, embedded caterpillars, reaching almost to her elbow. She rearranges her cuff, but it is too late—he is almost imperceptibly cringing, but she catches it; she's seen people do this before.

There was a time when Alba didn't bother to cover her scars. She believed they awarded her a special privacy, a martyr's force field. They are so raw—they look painful, though they actually have no sensation at all—so revolting, she thought that only people who truly understood what could lead to such cutting would attempt to get close to it. She was wrong. She attracted Christians, scolding old women, cheery people named after flowers who asked about her suicidal tendencies with barely camouflaged glee. Now she wears long sleeves even in the oppressive heat of summer, skirting do-gooders.

But no one has ever come out and said to her, without guile or pity or scorn, but casually, as if it hardly mattered, what Oscar says to her now.

Right arm. You must be left-handed.

She opens her mouth, but nothing comes out. She can't speak because what she wants to say, what she has already whispered in her mind, is preposterous. It is this: *I love you.*

I'm sure you floored them, she says instead, shivering in the sunlight, on the entrance IQ test.

Just then, a slight breeze from the lake fills her nose and mouth with the particular promise of summer. This is a smell she usually finds mournful—summers have always been disastrous—but for a moment, sitting next to this man, who is smiling at the same sarcasm that often repels others, she feels an uncomplicated excitement. What is it she is smitten by? The remark about her arm was almost rude, but its originality, its *precision*, caught her breath. Of course she does not love him—that was a twitch, a chemical misfire in her beleaguered brain—but she is looking forward rather than backward again, if only to what he might say next.

That afternoon, in the library, Alba finds the first letter—written in blotchy ink on the blank back pages of a book about New England bird-watching.

She has found things written in the books before. Graffiti, for the most part: initials paired within the borders of crooked hearts, the occasional free association of a paranoid schizophrenic. But what she discovers this time is not random scribbling, it is a letter, dated, addressed, written in the kind of formal, old-fashioned cursive no one bothers with anymore. A letter left bound in the book, never intended to be mailed.

———————

Saint Dymphna's Asylum
March 5, 1941

Peter Doherty
85 Squantum St.
Quincy, Massachusetts

Dear Peter,

Today is your eighteenth birthday; you are officially a man, though I can't imagine you as one. I often think that time, though it drags on in here, has stopped on the outside; that you are still that dark-eyed boy who barely reaches to my shoulder. If by some miracle you were here, now, you would most certainly smile down at me, and with far less worship than when you once smiled up.

It hardly matters. I no longer hope to be released, and you likely think me dead.

Once I planned for this day, thought out what I might say to you, my oldest child and my only son, the man I raised. What I say now is different from the words I thought once were wise.

Trust no one.

Think only of your own survival.

Never believe that love can save you; it is more likely to lock you up.

But, then again, perhaps this new advice is inappropriate. It may not apply, because you are a man, not a woman, and thus will be allowed to choose your own world.

Perhaps, like your father, you will be the one locking others up.

Alba turns the yellowed pages, but that is the end.

The bird book was the first in a box from the nature section of the former library. Alba pulls out the others, flipping open the back covers first. The end pages of all the books are filled with the same writing, all letters addressed to Peter, some dated as far back as 1933.

Alba is supposed to be under the supervision of the new librarian, but Karen leaves her alone most of the time. By the time a nurse comes to escort her to therapy, Alba has arranged the books in the chronological order of the letters. She asks Karen if she can return early the next day. There are four more boxes marked "Nature" that she hasn't opened yet.

Leave those for me, Alba says to Karen, rolling her eyes. They're a nightmare.

5

Visiting Hours

MY DAYS AT ABENAKI soon fell into a routine. Organization in a rehab hospital is a funny thing; because you no longer occupy the real world, the hours that were once taken up by work, errands, and social engagements, not to mention drug acquisition, need to be parceled into some semblance of purpose. At Abenaki, everything—bathing, recreation, therapy, meals—had its time and place, and the staff adhered so maniacally to the schedule (God forbid you took a notion to shower in the afternoon) that my time there began to feel like the self-indulgent, enthusiastically run, but essentially boring summers I'd spent at charity camp as a boy. I noticed other inmates, those further along in the six-week program, who were married to this habitude—so much so that they seemed more like staff than patients, eager to explain the ropes to newcomers—and they reminded me of those boys who had looked betrayed and not a little panicked when camp ended midway through August. Boys who believed that without archery and color wars and campfire songs, there would be no design to the world. Those were the boys who were relieved when school started again. My brother was one of those boys. I was the one sneaking into the woods with older girls, to guzzle beer I'd pilfered from the counselors.

After my ten-day detox was deemed successful, and I emerged as I imagine Lazarus must have stumbled out of his tomb—brain rotted, limbs half-working, the smell of recent death stubborn in his clothes—a schedule was slapped upon me under the guise of rehabilitation. They didn't want us moping around in armchairs, thinking of how much more rewarding a life of crime would be. They didn't seem to want us alone at all. Even my nights were punctuated by the quarter-hourly swish of my door, followed by a nurse checking that I was still in the land of the soberly living.

My mornings began at four A.M., with an altercation at the ward desk with the charge nurse. It usually went something like this:

I can't breathe.

You seem to be breathing just fine to me, Oscar.

I'm not. Air refuses to go below here (pointing to my neck). *I need something, Ativan maybe.*

You know you can't have anything. Try meditating.

I think I should have gone the methadone route. I could die from withdrawal, are you aware of that?

The doctors agree that your detox has gone smoothly without methadone. (That was the killer—smoothly for whom?) *Relax, Oscar, and try to go back to sleep.*

How can I go to sleep? I can't breathe. *Are you deaf as well as incompetent?*

Watch it, Oscar. You'll be all right. In and out. Look, you're doing it now.

I want to speak to the doctor.

He won't be in till five. Go back to your room.

Isn't there someone on call?

Only for emergencies.

You don't consider respiratory arrest an emergency?

Go to bed, Oscar.

What about a Valium?

Bed.

As you can see, these confrontations involved fairly repetitive dismissals from the nurse. I would have wondered if she even knew it was me—she rarely looked up from her paperwork—if she hadn't used my name, albeit in a syrupy, patronizing tone.

This scene was repeated, with the same failed conclusion, at five A.M. with the resident, and at seven when a fresh batch of nurses arrived for the day shift. By the time the morning officially started, I was exhausted, but by then I was not allowed to lie down. I had to shower (my private bathroom only accommodated vomiting and tooth-brushing), locker-room style: a line of men shivering in lukewarm spray, our penises limp and sad-looking—uninterested in sex for so long that they seemed to have forgotten their roles.

Then breakfast, coed, men and women with dripping hair and gleaming, scrubbed faces. The food, I'll admit, was not bad, and generously doled out, overeating being a vice the staff believed was not under their jurisdiction. This was a relief as, once out of detox, for the first time in months, I was ravenous. (A full stomach slows the absorption of heroin, so for a long while I had considered nutrition optional.) I piled my plate with the high-cholesterol choices—the made-to-order omelets were ecstasy. Breakfast inevitably made me even more desperate for a nap, but next on the divine schedule was Group.

Group Therapy, in my opinion, though nobody asked for it, was nothing but a farce. A circle of plastic chairs in an otherwise bare and far too bright room, occupied by men (we parted ways with the girls again) who fidgeted constantly, whether from need or boredom was hard to distinguish. First we went around the room announcing our names, the premise being we were too stupid to remember each other from the day before. (Okay, maybe they had a point.) Then our addictions (just in case someone had wandered into a drug rehab program thinking it was Weight Watchers). After that launch, the men took turns whining. They whined about their childhoods (drunk fathers, battered mothers, a lack of physical affection, or so much ardor it bordered on incest); about their wives and children (their new families were, of course, as repulsive as the families they'd grown up in); about craving drugs. I rarely spoke, a fact that was stamped, I'm sure, somewhere in my mound of hospital records.

The truth is, I had nothing to contribute. The procedure for these "discussions" was as follows: a patient recognized something in another patient's whining and added to it with his own similar, pathetic story. I didn't intervene because I had nothing in common with these people; they were, for the most part, losers, harsh as that may sound. I had never hit a woman, never been scraped off the bathroom floor by my own child, never spent the winter homeless and moving between crack houses in the city. My childhood wasn't *The Brady Bunch*, but I could hardly blame my parents for how I'd turned out. My brother's never done a drug in his life, and he had the same parents, as far as we know. Yes, I was an addict, but different from these men. Drugs for me had been largely a private and harmless experience—at least where others were concerned, almost to the end. I was not indulging all the time; I went on binges, and even then, most of my friends had no idea I was under the influence. I never shared a needle, didn't worry about AIDS any more than the normal, heterosexually active, twenty-first century male. Less, actually, since sex took a backseat to heroin.

Group stories tended toward the violent and melodramatic— death threats from dealers, armed theft to support a habit, a mother-in-law breaking up a marriage over the disappearance of the family silver. None of this ever happened to me. (Not to suggest there was never trouble, but it was of a different, slightly more respectable variety.)

Our group leader, Mitch, couldn't have been more than twenty-five years old; a nervous, geeky guy, with slickly combed hair, starched shirts, and a permanent startled expression. He had no control, could barely raise his voice to be heard over the cacophony of wailing addicts, and the meetings sometimes got out of hand— patients accusing each other in that ridiculous nose-to-nose posture that we males seem to believe is threatening. There was the occasional punch (some excitement at last!) that would send the more muscular attendants rushing to Mitch's rescue. Unfortunately, even in chaos, the meeting always went the full ninety minutes.

So I sat back, tuning it out when I could, feeling more and more irritated, but mostly alone, as the minutes clicked by. By the time Group was over, I was near to exploding with demands that I be released on the grounds of misdiagnosis. Not that anyone, even eager-to-please Mitch, would have listened to me.

In the afternoons, I had fifty-minute private therapy sessions. I lack the energy to describe them just yet.

The best part of my day (the only good part, besides the three meals and snack) was the recreational hour; the hour during which other men engaged in tension-relieving basketball or chain-smoking—the hour that I spent, and began to look forward to more and more, with Alba.

In the first two days of our meeting, Alba had managed to confuse me, embarrass me, and not occasionally enrage me, but she was, already, the only aspect of Abenaki I thought of as real. We could have been in a public park, a café, or on a date, if it weren't for the intrusion of a few details: her scars, my episodes, and of course the frequent "checks" we were both required to endure.

I forgot to mention the checks. Both Alba and I were under supervision; while on the ward, if not in therapy, we had to check in with a staff member every fifteen minutes. Alba was watched, I assumed, because she was suicidal; I was monitored like all new addicts, to keep me from slipping off to the woods to pick up drugs delivered in the carcasses of birds. (This had been known to happen, and don't think I was never tempted.) On the lawn, neither of us was required to get up and find a nurse. We were shadowed by designated attendants, who reported back to the ward via walkie-talkie. Our first conversations, until I learned to tune it out, were accompanied by the background music of low-level static and our names murmured in militaristic voices. Eventually, I graduated to half-hour, then hourly, then twice-a-day checks, but Alba always remained at fifteen minutes. Her cigarette lighter, a potential weapon of self-mutilation, was confiscated when she went inside. She was either unaware of or immune to these indignities. We never spoke of them.

So, I was more than a little disappointed when, on the third day of our acquaintance, just as I was making my way to the lawn (the heart palpitations were unrelated to detox), I was told that my brother had arrived for a visit.

Grouch! David said when he saw me, initiating a stiff embrace. Ever since our *Sesame Street* days, this has been his nickname for me, and it never fails to make me surly.

Dave, I said through clenched teeth. Checking up on me already?

Something wrong with wanting to visit my little brother? You're looking good, by the way.

This was a blatant lie; I'd never looked worse. I'd been trying to avoid my skeletal visage in the mirror. But David is always giving false compliments; appearance is important to him. Another thing: I am not his little brother, I am eleven months older than he is. David just happens to be taller—six three to my barely six—and thinks it amusing to diminish me.

How are you feeling, buddy? David said. I'm sometimes forced to hand it to him: he never stops trying.

Like Lazarus, I said. Let's go out on the lawn. I could see his brain searching for the reference; David is a numbers man, allusions are not his forte.

I chose two reclining chairs halfway down the slope; close enough to Alba that she would notice me (if she ever looked up from her book), but far enough away that she couldn't hear our conversation.

Posh place, David whistled.

Get the bill yet? I was sneering, but he ignored it.

Don't worry about that. We just want you back at the end.

We referred to him and his wife, Bethany. Our parents were dead, there was no one else to include in that familial phrase. David and Bethany were married two years before, just after David's Portland-based software company went public, and he became a millionaire. They met through me, though I'd had no intention of introducing them. I can say nothing slanderous about Bethany except this: she is even more optimistic and charming than David. They are an insufferable, or delightful, couple, depending on whom you ask. They could blind you with their blue eyes and gleaming teeth (our parents could not afford braces, but David paid to have his mouth wired with clear plastic for a full year after he finished college). And boy do they look fabulous in bathing suits.

So, really, how are you? David tried again.

Alba had not yet turned her head in my direction. Perhaps I should have chosen closer chairs.

Detox was jolly, I said. Sweats, projectile vomiting, and, oh, hallucinations. At one point Mom was slapping my arm looking for a vein to shoot into. Regretfully, she didn't find one.

I'd gone too far. David's face was rigid, pale beneath his J. Crew suntan. He always crumpled over any blasphemy of Mom.

I know you probably hate me right now, he said softly. (David did not release his anger often enough; it was one of his failings.) But I had to do this, Oscar. *You* had to do this. Things couldn't go on like that forever.

Like what? I said. I was handling it fine.

No, David said firmly. You were far from handling anything and you know it.

Alba was combing her cropped hair with her fingers like it was the only task she had left before she died.

So, I said jovially, changing to a safer subject, how's the old ball and chain? This was my nickname for Bethany, allowed by her only because she was so unlike the cliché, she actually thought it funny.

David shifted in his chair—no doubt worried about his Armani suit wrinkling between the slats.

Actually, that's part of the reason I'm here, he said. He was attempting to look solemn, but could barely contain his glee. Bethie's pregnant.

Good for her; right on schedule, I said. Alba noticed us finally; I could tell because she looked away too quickly, pretending she hadn't seen me.

We didn't tell you before because, well, that's pretty obvious. She's due in November.

Congratulations, I said. Scorn leaked out, I couldn't help it.

Knock it off, Oscar.

No, I'm being completely sincere. You'll have the happiest kid in the world. Blue eyes and a Ferrari for his sixteenth birthday. Who could ask for more?

You can be such a bastard sometimes, David said. He sounded tired. What *he* could possibly have to be tired about was beyond me.

Dave, I said, I'm always a bastard, and you know it.

Alba's chin jerked up. For one paralyzing moment I thought she could hear us, but then I saw her wave to a passing patient. I was not proud of the person I became around my brother. But for more years than I could count, I hadn't known who else to be.

David tried to salvage it, of course; that's always been his role. He chatted for twenty minutes—stocks were up, Bethany had finally stopped puking, they'd gone to the grave on the anniversary of Mom's death. Oh, and he might have a job for me when I got out, more my kind of thing than the last time—something about inter-active classic literature on CD-ROM. Alba smoked six cigarettes, cleaned her sunglasses on her sleeve twice, grinned a couple of times, apparently at what she was reading. All I wanted was to be sitting on her portion of the lawn, pretending that my brother, and thus myself as a brother, did not exist.

When David got up to leave, and I walked him toward the glass (shatterproof, of course) patio doors, I sensed rather than saw her come up behind me. I slowed down, letting David step inside alone.

Your brother, she said, in that titillating growl of hers, is the better-looking one.

You're not the first woman to think so, I said. I could see David through the glass; he'd just noticed that he was talking to himself and was looking back for me.

I turned to face her. I'd never seen her upright, and she was taller than I'd thought—five ten even though she slouched, tall enough to look me straight in the eyes. She was standing very close; I hoped it was on purpose.

Did I hurt your feelings? she said, with half a charming smile.

Did you want to? I said. I resisted the urge to put a hand out and grasp her, gently, around that ravaged wrist. I wondered if, next to her coolness, my hand would feel like a flame.

What I want, she whispered—and the effect of this on my body was surely visible, possibly audible—is to know if you have any feelings at all.

That's when I knew that I hadn't been paranoid. I was the victim of crosswinds: she'd heard every word I'd said.

6

Meds

WHEN THE NURSE COMES in with a breakfast tray at seven-thirty A.M., Alba jolts out of a headachy sleep. Taking meals in her room is something Dr. Miller insists on. Alba's appetite is a clear indication of her mood: when she's manic, food seems unnecessary, when depressed it becomes revolting. The nurses monitor her food intake along with her meds. Though the supervision irritates her, Alba doesn't mind eating alone; she finds the dining hall, with its shuffling lines and zombie-like chewing, unappetizing. On her breakfast tray, next to the small boxes of cereal and milk are two plastic cups—one of water, the other crowded with a variety of capsules and tablets. The nurse lingers, watching as Alba tosses the pills down, gagging even after she drains the water. This nurse is new—Ginny, her nametag reads—younger than Alba with a Maine accent and far too much lipstick. She smiles and murmurs an enthusiastic *Good girl,* ignoring Alba's sneer. Alba mentally files Ginny under the "Coddler" section of nursing staff.

Even after she eats her Lucky Charms, the chalky, saliva-inducing taste of the pills still clings to the back of her throat. She will gag on and off all morning with the memory. More often than not, this is the reason that Alba has abandoned her lithium in the past; arguments about side effects and fear of losing herself aside, sometimes she simply can't get it down.

She showers quickly and gets dressed. She missed the library the day before—Karen called in sick—and now she intends to go straight there to sort through the rest of the letters so she can begin to read them. While Alba is putting on her boots, Ginny pops her head in the door.

Phone for you, she chirps. Alba follows her out of the room, trying to warm her fingers in the thin pockets of her jeans.

She picks up the pay phone receiver and wipes it on her sleeve. The patients' phone disgusts her; the earpiece is always slightly greasy, the mouthpiece smells of medicine and dental plaque. She listens for a few seconds to her father's quiet, expectant breath on the other end.

Hi, Daddy, she says finally.

Morning, Baba, her father says, using the nickname she gave herself as a baby, before her tongue was able to manage *Alba.*

How's my favorite girl?

Great, Alba says. Well, okay. The same.

You still sound beautiful. Wish I could see you, kiddo, her father says. Normally he is a frequent visitor at Abenaki, but this week he is in D.C. touring exhibits at historical museums.

They keeping you busy? he says.

I'm working at the library a lot, Alba says, her voice, before she can curb it, growing excited. I found something written in one of the old books, Daddy—a letter, by some woman who was here in 1941. There are more—years' worth. I'm going to sort them out and—

Whoa there, her father says in the forced joking tone that never fails to stifle her. Slow down, he says. What about your time with Dr. Miller? Aren't you seeing her every day?

Yes, Daddy, she says slowly. She shouldn't have sounded so excited. She thought the subject matter would interest him, but her illness interests him more.

I'm not missing anything, Alba says. I go to the library in the afternoons.

I just don't want you taxing yourself, Baba, her father says. You're supposed to be resting up, getting well.

I am resting, Dad, Alba says fiercely.

Don't get upset, now.

I'm not upset.

How are the meds? her father says.

Fine. Dr. M. is adjusting my dosage. I'm supposed to have fewer side effects.

And is it working?

I guess. I can't tell yet. Alba can hear her own voice—it is squashed flat. Her father doesn't seem to notice this; or perhaps he doesn't believe it merits the same concern he showed for her fervor.

How many hours you sleeping? he says. He always asks this; it is the most obvious clue to her moods. For some reason she cannot fathom, he assumes she won't lie about it.

Around eight, she says.

Good. I miss you, sweetheart, he says. She knows he is about to hang up, and she feels both relieved and guilty.

Miss you too, Daddy.

I'll call you tonight, okay? I'm collecting quite a few goodies for you out here.

Alba has a brief image of her father strolling across the lawn, laden with impeccably wrapped packages. They will be time-eating presents: playing cards, paperback best-sellers with cheerful, harmless themes, pedicure kits without the nail clippers. The kind of gifts one might give to a sickly, prepubescent girl.

Okay, Daddy, she says. Bye.

Bye, bye, darling girl.

After he clicks off she stands there, the dial tone pulsing in her ear. She considers talking to it (Irrational Thought, she is supposed to write these down), but it is droning on, and she doesn't really believe it will listen to her.

Alba doesn't make it to the library because she spends the next hour convincing the nurses she is not—despite the acting-out behavior of slamming the phone—upset. By the time she calms them down, she is due for therapy. An hour later, when she emerges from Dr. Miller's office, there is nothing she'd rather do than go back to sleep. As this would be noted by the nurses, she trudges her way to the lawn instead. It isn't until the sunshine slaps her face that she remembers Oscar.

He is already there, sitting on the ground next to her empty chair. He stands up when he spots her coming, his grin lopsided and sheepish. Yesterday, Alba decided he was an asshole, but now her pulse skips a few beats under her scars.

Hello, he says. He's worried, she thinks. Well, he should be.

You didn't have to sit on the ground, Alba says, noticing, as she lowers herself into the chair, that her knees are jumping. She wonders if this is a side effect to one of her new meds. She presses her knees together and takes out her cigarettes.

That's okay, Oscar says, still standing. Since everything here is common property, I figured the least I could do is leave you your chair. Especially since I didn't know if you'd want to talk to me today.

Alba shrugs. Oscar hesitates, perhaps hoping for a more encouraging response, then decides to settle himself back on the grass.

Alba lights a cigarette, exhaling into the air between them. So, she says, inhaling again, tell me why you hate your brother.

Oscar clears his throat, looking as if he regrets sitting down. This is both how she wants him to feel and not how she wants him to feel at the same time.

Sorry, he says after a pause. I didn't see Lawn Therapy listed on the schedule.

This is a mental hospital, Oscar. Everything is therapy.

I see, he says, squinting and waving the smoke from his eyes. Ever notice how cigarette smoke always goes directly to the faces of nonsmokers? he says.

That's because smokers have a personal haze barrier. But you're changing the subject.

Oscar sighs. I don't hate my brother, he says. And I'd rather not talk about it, if you don't mind.

Come on, Oscar, Alba says. Haven't they told you yet, *I don't want to talk about it* is not an acceptable answer. You acted like you couldn't stand him.

Why in the world would you want to talk about my brother? he says. I'm sure you heard enough yesterday.

I don't know, Alba says. I'd like to talk about something besides myself for a change.

Oscar looks as if he is about to smile, but he coughs instead. Fair enough, he says. Fire away.

How can you treat your own brother that way? Alba says. Like he's your enemy.

Do you have siblings? Oscar says.

Nope, only child.

Well, sometimes my brother and I turn into twelve-year-olds when we're together. I can't explain it.

He wasn't acting like a twelve-year-old, Alba says. He seemed like he was trying to help you.

He's trying to *fix* me, Oscar says. He massages his shoulder, digging at the joint as though testing it for pain.

I'd say you could use a little fixing.

I knew you were mad at me, Oscar says. I should go.

I'm not *mad,* Alba says, too quickly. I'm just curious.

Oscar pauses. Don't you have anybody in your life who overreacts? he says. Who tries too hard, who tiptoes around you like you're a time bomb, even when you're doing fine?

Alba looks toward the river. No, she says.

Well, David worries too much. He thinks, because I don't have his money, his supermodel wife, his overly waxed luxury cars, that I'm floundering. Sending me here was overreacting. I don't belong in this place.

Aha, Alba says, lighting a new cigarette. The prisoner who didn't do it. I thought you said you were a drug addict.

I never said that. You merely assumed.

Pardon me, Alba says. My mistake. If you're not an addict, why do you fall to your knees with need?

That's just from the last month. I had a bit of a binge. It happens sometimes, but it's not a regular thing. It's not as if I *need* drugs. Not like some people.

Why do you do them, then?

Oscar straightens up a bit. They're *fun,* Alba. Like any recreation—an escape. They take the edge off of life.

Recreation? Alba laughs. Oh, please. Drug abuse is merely a slower, hipper form of suicide.

She can sense it coming, their anger, like the smell of ozone before a thunderstorm. Her throat feels unyielding, flattened by psychosomatic pressure on her neck.

You wouldn't know anything about it, Oscar sneers. Why would you need to relax when you have rich parents who cater to your every whim and tuck you into hospital sheets if you so much as get a hangnail?

Shut up. Alba whispers.

Did I hit a nerve?

You, Alba says, speaking as low as she can to keep her voice steady, are like every other addict that breezes through here. An angry loser who thinks he's on top of the world. Who the fuck died and made you so *entitled?*

I'm not the entitled one, Miss Queen of Abenaki. I'm surprised they don't have your portrait hanging in the entrance hall.

I'm here because I'm ill, Alba says, standing up. This *happened* to me, and will probably keep happening for the rest of my life. You're here because you did something stupid *to yourself.*

Oscar stands up, looking as if he is about to bite her, but instead he speaks, slowly and quietly, his brown eyes shadowed to black.

I suppose it was someone else then, he says, who branded your arm.

Alba blinks, horrified, but also slightly elated, that he has managed to sink so low. This, after all, is what she was pushing for.

Fuck you, she says.

Oscar merely smiles, sheepishness replaced by scorn. I may be angry, he says, but you eat livid for breakfast. Good day.

He turns on his heel and walks off, carrying the last word with him, clutching it in his fists, like something illicit he plans to enjoy later, when he is alone.

7

Saint Dymphna's Asylum

May 3, 1933

Dear Peter,

You are most likely concerned with my hasty, secretive departure. Your father did not want to frighten you by waking you up so far into the night. There may be rumors that I was arrested, but the sheriff simply gave me a ride. I am sorry I was not there in the morning to explain to you.

I have come here to rest up from a nervous condition that has greatly concerned your father and his family. They felt it was best that I regain my strength away from home, so I will not be a burden. Your father plans to tell you I have gone on a visiting tour, but I do not feel that his lies are necessary. He told

me he would tend to my garden, but I would like you to do it.
Volunteer as if I hadn't asked you. I need not tell you to keep an
eye on your sisters—you always have.

I am not allowed to write anyone as yet, but hope to be given
the privilege soon. I plan to write you letters as if I could mail
them, and then you will have a whole stack from me all at once.
Though correspondence may not be necessary. With a little rest I
should be able to convince your father to fetch me before the
breeze round the house catches the lilacs in full bloom.

All my love,
Mama

May 14, 1933

Dear Peter,

Lately I have been pretending that I am on that visiting tour your
father made up. The countryside here is beautiful, though I miss
the sea. The asylum has what they call a pavilion plan: a series of
detached cabins set up like dormitories. My ward is nestled in the
woods, and I can often hear crickets at night if the screaming
doesn't get too loud. I can block out most of the distractions in
this place except for the sound of keys. There are keys ringing out
in my dreams. Remember when your sister Annabelle found that
box of old keys in the attic? I dreamed she was here last night,
jangling her little toys on a ribbon.

When I arrived here they took away my clothes and my
purse. They won't even let me keep my rosary, as if I am a child
who might choke on the beads. But I can still say the round of
prayers by heart, though I was not raised a Catholic. I converted
to marry your father.

It is really not as bad here as I make it sound. There are a lot of very ill women, and though I am sad for them, they give me hope; for I am not ill, and so the doctors will soon send me home. The doctor who interviewed me upon my arrival seemed confident that I answered his questions correctly. He wanted to know if I'd ever experienced a yearning for my life to be something other than it is. Of course I told him no, though I thought it was a somewhat silly question. As if an imagination or a hopeful disposition in a woman dissatisfied with her situation indicates a sickness of the soul. I think it would be just the opposite.

I do miss you all very much. I am often close to tears, but I hide them, as I have heard that the nuns are liable to drug your breakfast if they think you are too emotional. Many women shuffle through the day in a dazed trance. I want to be fully alert for the day they send me home.

Don't forget to press some lilacs in a page of my Bible. I do it every year.

Love,
Mama

July 24, 1933

Dear Peter,

I think it is mealtime that is the saddest time in this place. It is in the cafeteria where women from all the cabins converge; women who are seriously ill as well as women like myself. Many women refuse to eat, and the nuns do not show much kindness or patience in these situations. I have seen women hit across the face, dragged across the cafeteria floor by their arms; sometimes the nuns force porridge into patients' mouths. I do not want to alarm you; no one has harmed me here. But it is distressing to witness such behavior in a hospital.

I have made some friends, some ladies with whom I play cards in the afternoons. We leave our cabins every morning and spend our days, a combination of therapy and recreation, in the main building. I have discovered that there are quite a few women who feel unfairly diagnosed. Theresa claims that her husband had her committed by accusing her of adultery, and then ran off with his mistress. The doctors say she suffers from paranoid delusion. But I find her a bright, articulate, reasonable woman, whose sadness, I believe, is only a result of her being here. This frightens me. I think you are old enough to know these things now, Peter. I don't believe any longer that all doctors can be trusted.

They have given me a job: I am in charge of the hospital library. They noticed that I spend time there; I have been writing to you in the wasted pages at the backs of books, as I am not allowed stationery. It is a nice diversion to be among books, although the library is limited because a lot of classic and contemporary works have been banned by the doctors.

It is the appointment of this job that worries me. I am beginning to suspect that they intend to keep me here for an extended period.

Love, Mama

September 3, 1933

Dear Peter,

We are made to walk in lines here. Lines of naked women shuffling toward the showers, lines marching over the fenced-in grounds for daily exercise. A circus procession of exhausted women, constantly moving in one straight line.

I keep the key to the library with me at all times, in the pocket of my robe. I stow it under my pillow at night, and it makes me feel better. It is the only thing I have now that is my own; everything else has been stripped away.

I do not think I am crazy. But sometimes, often in the morning when I wake and see the metal rails on my bed, it seems it would be easy to let my melancholy slip into the madness.

Mama

8

Paperwork

I. DRUGS AND ALCOHOL

1. It is expected that during your stay here you will not use drugs or alcohol or bring them onto the ward. Any drug or alcohol use will most likely lead to discharge.
2. Random, supervised urine screens will be performed during your stay. Urine must be given within 4 hours of request or will be considered positive for drugs. Room, belongings and body searches will be conducted on a random basis. A positive urine test or

confiscation of drugs or alcohol will most likely lead to discharge.

3. All medications, including over-the-counter medications (aspirin, Tylenol, cold remedies, vitamins, etc.) must be prescribed by your ward doctor.
4. No products containing alcohol are allowed on the unit (mouthwash, hairspray, inhalants).
5. Patients are asked not to wear clothing with alcohol/drug/gambling names, references or logos.
6. Patients of the Drug Abuse Treatment Program are not allowed to wear sunglasses while on the ward.

II. SHARPS

1. Sharp objects (razors, scissors, tools, etc.) are stored in the nurses' station.
2. If a patient is on Supervised Sharps by a doctor's order, a staff member must be present while he/she uses the sharp.

III. PHONE CALLS AND VISITORS

1. All cell phones will be confiscated and returned to you upon your release.
2. The red phone in the hall is for patient use. From midnight to 7 A.M. calls come through the nurses' station.
3. During groups, the ringer is shut off.
4. Please limit your calls to 10 minutes.
5. Please be considerate of others' privacy when answering the phone. Answer with a *hello*, take a brief message, and leave it in the patient's mailbox. *Never identify this as a hospital.*

6. Visiting hours are between 11 A.M. and 7 P.M. Visits should not be scheduled during the times you are expected in meetings.

7. Visiting privileges may be suspended if your doctor thinks it beneficial to your recovery.

8. You have the right to refuse visits at any time.

9. Supervised visits may be prescribed by a doctor's order.

10. Staff must inspect any packages brought by visitors before they are given to patients.

11. Patients may go into another patient's room only if invited. The door must remain open. Patients should not sit or lie down on the bed of another patient.

12. No sexual activity is permitted on hospital grounds.

9

Sharp Objects

THE MORNING AFTER ALBA and I started to hate each other, I took a marker and, on the laminated sheet of Ward Rules taped above my bureau, I wrote:

Any sexual activity will most likely lead to discharge.

I chuckled over it while getting dressed, but wiped it off before leaving my room. I was beginning to get paranoid about Privileges and Restrictions (another sheet) and didn't want to lose my time on the lawn.

Sex was on my mind again (from the looks of things in the shower room, I wasn't the only one); longing had begun fizzling up in the cells I'd so relentlessly flushed clean with water. This reawakening was familiar enough (with heroin in my veins, the last thing I want is a woman's hands on my body—without heroin, it's the first), but this time my desire seemed oddly discriminatory. Usually, coming off a binge, it would be any and every woman I coveted; this time, much to my annoyance, I was plagued with fantasies of Alba alone. The fact that I was ferociously attracted to a woman I thought of as a spoiled, raving bitch made me so angry even the other addicts noticed. A feat, as our ward was backstroking in anger.

I was determined to get hold of myself. If she came to me with an apology, I'd consider it, but I wasn't about to go parading across the lawn again. (This sounds immature, perhaps, but I believe we've already established that I'm a bit of a late bloomer.) I had enough on my back—my brother, an army of staff, a full schedule of camp activities—and I certainly didn't need Alba screaming alongside the various monkeys already parked there. Not that I was proud of my own behavior (I cringed whenever I remembered the things I had said and tried to focus on her insults to make myself feel better), but I had the distinct suspicion that our confrontation had not been accidental. She seemed to *want* me to feel bad, whereas I had merely been defending myself. Who needs her, I said in my mind, so often it occasionally escaped from my mouth, startling my already agitated companions.

Resolved: not until she came to me. Why wasn't she coming?

I spent day five on the lawn with a spillover of groupies from the morning NA meeting. One of them was Max, a girl barely eighteen, too thin and a bit yellow around the eyes, but seductive nonetheless—with one of those swollen mouths that make you wish you had a breath mint. Max was a tough little thing; she'd been in and out of jail and hospitals since the age of thirteen, and was enthusiastic about showing me the tattoos on her hip and lower back. Normally, just the act of her peeling away her jeans for display—she had that skin like white soapstone that young women take for granted—would have set me panting, but I was more interested (still, I hate to admit it) in whether Alba was watching us.

She didn't seem to be. For one thing, she was reading and not looking up except to fish out cigarettes. At one point I said something witty about the camp counselors that made my little enclave laugh, and Alba looked up, as if annoyed at the interruption. She missed entirely Max's wide-eyed devotion, the heavily ringed hand she put on my thigh, not to mention the whispered offer of oral pleasure in a janitor's closet she inexplicably possessed the key to. (I declined gracefully. Randy I was, but I still had my romantic ideals. Max was far too unhygienic to take seriously while sober.)

When the hour was up, I hung back, but Alba, rather than walking toward me, went off to another building, white-sneakered attendant in tow.

The afternoon was sucked away by Relapse Prevention, a farcical exercise where we identified "triggers" that would tempt us toward drugs once we'd regained our freedom. To my horror I was assigned homework. *Write your life story, including pertinent childhood and adolescent trauma. Be brief.* I tried to be a model pupil, sitting down after dinner with my yellow lined pad, but the "brief" clause gave me trouble, and I was becoming weary of defending myself. Even to me, I was starting to sound, especially when I thought of Alba, *defensive.* I was rescued by a solicitous phone call from my sister-in-law, and spent the rest of the evening watching sitcoms with a roomful of fidgety comrades.

The next day, Alba had a visitor. I was sitting with Max again on the patio (she was becoming tedious—I'd heard her none-too-brief life story and was almost to the point of swatting her hands away) when I saw him walk by. I'd already learned to spot visitors. For one thing, their clothes were ironed, but the real clue was the way they moved across that lawn—trying to appear casual, but with anxious, disapproving expressions, the way teachers used to look making their way through the delinquent-thronged quadrangle at my high school.

This man appeared to be in his late forties, as tall as my brother, sporting a lush blond ponytail in stark contradiction to his expensive, professional-on-the-weekend clothes. He looked like a winker, the confident sort of man I despise instantly, the type my brother plays tennis with. He kissed Alba on the cheek; she smiled shyly at him. When I saw him pull a chair over, I swallowed my urge to swat and allowed Max to twiddle her fingers on my neck. After ten minutes of listening to Alba laugh, I excused myself and went to my room for a nap. This was like being back in high school—my room had the same medicinal odor as the nurse's office I once fled to when I was too drunk to sit upright in class.

I lay on my bed thinking how familiar this all was. This was how I felt whenever I was enamored of a woman: glorious one moment, deflated the next. For the first time, it occurred to me that other people, normal people, only felt glorious, never dismayed, while falling in love. (Did I know, then, that it was love? *Please.* I knew the first time I saw her.)

And on the seventh day . . . I can't say we rested, but I certainly felt rescued. Later, Alba and I would argue, about who gave in first. You talked to me, she would say, to which I always replied: You invited me to.

I was with Max again (give me a break, she was my only ally), to whom I had confessed in a whisper that I thought I might be gay. For some reason, this made her inclined to molest me all the more. Luckily, she had turned to say something to another groupie, and I was hands-free when Alba stepped out on the patio.

I was encouraged to see her gaze flit over the crowd and pause in my direction. She had no choice but to walk by me, but rather than storming, she moved slowly, actually releasing a shy little smile. It was that smile, combined with her outfit, that conquered me. She was wearing a tight red shirt, long-sleeved, that revealed the full breasts I had been guessing at, and denim overalls a size too large. There's something about a woman in overalls that drives me wild; always has. It has to do with the buckles, and the fact that I always want to pull her onto my lap and place my hand just under the crosspiece on her slim, vulnerable back. Even Max would have gotten further with Oshkosh.

So, when Alba tiptoed by, hands burrowed in her voluminous pockets, I caught her eye and smiled.

How's the lawn therapy going? I said softly. Though she paused, frowning, she couldn't hide her relief. We let out the same heavy breath in unison.

Bit slow, lately, she said, looking at Max, who had turned back and was sizing up the two of us.

Alba walked on, and I waited as long as I could (about twenty seconds) before I made my apologies and went after her. You see, she hadn't bothered to get rid of the second chair under the willow tree. That chair ripped something open in me; I knew now what I was going to say.

I sat down to her right, putting my elbow on the wide armrest, unbuttoned my cuff and rolled up my sleeve. The crease of my elbow was measled with marks—familiar scars, newer scabs, long, mustardy bruises, and one angry infection that refused to respond to antibiotics. Alba looked, but she did not cringe.

My brother's given me a lot of money the last few years, I said, instinctively clenching my fist. My veins no longer rose beneath the skin; they were hibernating, collapsed and exhausted. Most of it has gone straight into this arm, I said. Whenever I see him, it's the first thing I think of, and it makes me hate. Not him. Me.

Alba nodded. Why are you telling me this? she said quietly. Her arm, the scarred one, hidden under ruby cotton, was resting in the same position, only inches from mine.

Because you're the first person I've met in years whom I don't want to lie to, I said. (Did I hear her breath catch? I believe so.) And because I shouldn't have said what I did the other day. It was cruel. I meant it to be, and I shouldn't have said it.

That's okay, Alba said. I asked for it.

No reason for me to comply, I said. Why did you though? Ask for it?

Alba grinned. Nobody fights with me, she said. I thought you'd be good at it.

And was I? I focused my eyes, willing her to glance up. I was so relieved by the look I saw in her now soft gray irises that I swear I almost sang.

Merciless, she said. Her gaze flickered back and forth, from my left eye to my right, as if they were doors she was watching, wondering which would open first.

She looked away. I could see the pulse point, throbbing fast, on the side of her neck. I rolled my sleeve back down. My breathing was labored again. Any more talk like this and I'd be throwing myself in the river.

Bird-watching? I said after a minute. She looked confused, so I nudged the book in her lap with my fingers. You'd think I'd slid my hands between those overalled thighs, the way my body flared up. She had to clear her throat, I noticed, before answering.

Oh, she said. Not really. I work at the library sometimes; I picked this up by mistake. She wasn't a very good liar. She took the book and slid it onto the lawn, beneath her chair. I couldn't imagine what was so secretive about bird-watching, but I didn't pursue it. There was something else I wanted to know.

That guy who visited you yesterday, I said, feeling proud and a little silly at how casual I'd managed to sound. Doesn't he fight with you?

My father? she said. No. Never. Well, it's more like he's impossible to fight with, so I don't bother.

That was your father? My voice must have wavered, because she looked at me with a touch of glee.

Who did you think it was? she said, smiling now.

Your boyfriend, I said, and my smile, though I wanted it to look amused, was actually one of relief.

How disturbing, Alba said. She took out a cigarette and, acting fast, I picked up her lighter.

Thanks, she said, both of us concentrating on the act of lighting that cigarette as if it were our most important test yet.

Do you have a boyfriend? I said. Boy, was I beginning to sound like an idiot.

Nope, she said. The hospital address repels most of the applicants from the dating service. Plus, lately, they all seem so *young*.

How old are you?

Twenty-five, she said. Ridiculous, but her inflection did make that paltry number sound old.

You look younger, I said. Her eyebrows flinched at this, which proved how young she really was, though I thought I wouldn't point that out just yet.

How old are you?

Thirty.

Are you married?

Me? No. I have the relationship skills of a fourteen-year-old.

That doesn't stop most men from getting married, Alba said. Her voice, when she was amused, was less self-conscious but still effective. I wanted so badly to put my hand on the throat that produced such gruff seduction, that I had to rub my palms along the thighs of my jeans, to distract myself.

My brother is married to a woman I used to date, I said suddenly, surprising myself. Why was I bringing this up?

Alba paused. Your brother stole your girlfriend? she said.

Well, not exactly, I said. It was our first and only date, and after dinner I made the fatal error of bringing her to a party David was at. I think we'd already decided we were all wrong for each other, or at least that I was wrong for *her*. I was still hopeful though. Bethany is unfettered. Happy. Almost *pure*. I guess I thought it might rub off.

I knew immediately, by the way she stiffened, that I'd said the wrong thing. I'm sorry—I didn't mean, I started, but she wouldn't look at me.

What are you talking about? Alba said, grinding out her cigarette.

Alba, I said, shifting, meaning to touch her, but just then my head exploded.

The sweats, the convulsions, the brick in my throat that kept me from drawing breath . . . why was this still happening to me? I was supposed to be past the withdrawal, yet these episodes plagued me daily. I shouldn't have said so much, I thought, putting my head between my knees. What's the point of confessions when you're not wasted? There's no cushioning. I no longer wanted truth, or even contact. I wanted a full needle and one minute when no one was watching me.

I couldn't see anything, but I felt those fingers instantly—they seemed almost as familiar as the drug rush I so desired. Alba was saying something, I couldn't make it out over the siren blaring in my ears. I sat up again, fumbling, and even as I did what I did next, I was waiting for her to pull away.

I took her hand from the back of my neck and pushed her sleeve up. Blindly, I traced the miniature mountain ranges on her arm, and as I stroked, as I felt her go from rigid to resigned, I began to breathe again; inhale, exhale, along with the rhythm of my fingers on her skin. When she finally pulled away, she did so reluctantly.

Oscar, she breathed into my ear; such a beautiful sound, my name caressed by that voice. In the background, I heard mumbles, questioning but professionally unconcerned, and I knew there were nurses lurking nearby.

Oscar, Alba said again, putting her hand lightly on my shoulder. They want to know if you're okay.

Tell them, I said, my vision sharpening on the angles of her face. Tell them I'm glorious.

10

Saint Dymphna's Asylum

November 4, 1933

Dear Peter,

The book I am defacing is a fairly monotonous field guide to hibernating mammals. I'd like to know who donated this volume, and whether they realized the humor in their gift.

The one thing I have always been able to do with any sustained success is sleep. I have never tossed and turned and kicked at the sheets, never felt that my mind could not stop running long enough to lie down and rest. I don't remember ever missing a night's sleep unless I meant to. The doctors here find this hard to believe. Apparently, a woman in my condition is supposed to go for weeks without shutting her eyes.

Lack of sleep is both a symptom and a cause of insanity. I have
told them not to waste their time on this diagnosis. Even here, in
a roomful of cots whose inhabitants shriek and moan through the
night, I sleep like a baby.

Your father resented it. He was one to sit up half the night
wringing the sheets in his hands, worrying about whatever it is
men worry about that they think belongs to them alone. When we
were first married I tried to stay up, keep him company in his
sleeplessness. But he would never tell me what he was fretting
about, and eventually he began to hint, in those snide, eruptive
comments that mean he's overtired, that his worry was for my
benefit, and thus my fault. I thought this was ridiculously unfair,
but rarely said so. There's no defending oneself when your father
is fatigued.

For all my life, sleeping has been a simple joy. I lay my head
down—where does not seem to matter, strange beds do not affect
me—and I fall, slowly but firmly, away from the world. When I
was a child, I believed that I left my body when I slept. I could
feel it, the sensation of separating from my heavy limbs on the
mattress. I seemed to fall out of myself, through the bed and into
the land of my dreams, which, though sometimes frightening,
were always spectacular, and seemed to make more sense to me
than the world I stumbled through while awake.

I think the fear of this falling is the reason people are troubled
in sleep. They hold on too tightly to their bodies as they press
against the sheets. Your sister, Maggie, was like this from birth. As
a little baby in my arms, she would struggle to keep her heavy lids
open, and in the moment she began to drift off, she would jerk
herself awake with such violence it would make her cry. She
fussed through every day and by nighttime only slept because her
little mind was too weary to fight it. Even then, you could see her,

poised under a thin layer of dreams, ready to bolt awake at any disturbance that reminded her she was sleeping. No amount of singing or soothing ever made a difference. For a while, when she was first old enough to climb out of her crib, hers was the first face I saw in the morning. When I woke to my little girl she was usually scowling—I suspect it took a while to stare me out of peaceful slumber—and her first words were ones of admonishment, as though my sleeping were some sort of insult as well as neglectful parenting. She takes after your father, Maggie does. It is the same way he looks at me if I wake smiling in the morning. Sometimes whiskey, in sufficient quantities, allows him some sleep, but the headache makes him less grateful for it.

You, on the other hand, my little Pete-nut, take after me. You sleep with a smile on your face, as if you are plotting mischief in the land of dreams. The only time sleeping ever worried me was when you were born. I was barely nineteen, ten months into my marriage with no mother to advise me on the duties of a wife. Every mother on our block seemed vigilant, weary-eyed, running on some strange reserve fuel that kept them from falling asleep on their feet. "I haven't slept more than two hours together in six years," I heard mothers say, with more pride than self-pity, as though lack of sleep were a war wound they showed off to other women, but kept covered up in front of the men. I was sure I would fail as a mother; either I wouldn't sleep and the absence of my dream life would drive me insane, or I would sleep regardless and God knows what would happen to you when I wasn't watching.

Oddly enough, it was never a problem. When I first brought you home I assumed you were sleeping through the night. But then your father began to make comments in the mornings before he left for work, comments he delivered with a little smirk even as his voice dropped in sympathy.

"You must be wrecked," he'd say. "You were up with that boy every hour last night." I could only blink at him, and he would take this as agreement, bestowing a husbandly kiss on my forehead. I wondered if he was hallucinating. (He was under a lot of stress; his father had died of apoplexy just before your birth.) I was sure I'd been sleeping eight hours without interruption. Although during the day your mouth sought my breast every two hours, I assumed you just weren't hungry at night. I didn't realize the truth until the night your father woke me with yelling.

He often did this if he couldn't sleep, bellowed until I woke up and tended to him. Only on this night, when his voice dragged me back to my body, I was not in our bed. I was sitting upright in a rocking chair, and the window I opened my eyes upon was not my bedroom window but a small glass pane in the nursery I had painted with stars. I was holding you and you were suckling my breast, my nightgown was unbuttoned to the waist and I had a diaper draped on my shoulder. I was so confused I surely would have blurted it out, had your father given me a moment to speak. But he was raving—he hadn't slept well in over a week and his mood lowered exponentially with every hour he was awake.

"Stop that infernal singing! It's all fine and good for you to be tired when you lie around all day doing nothing, but I have to go to work! I'm due in court for closing arguments in four hours and if I don't get some sleep I won't be able to string two sentences together!" I murmured that I would try to be quieter and he stormed off back to the bedroom. I realized then, as I put you back in your crib, that since bringing you home I hadn't once woken in the morning with the swollen, leaking breasts that come with irregular feeding. I'd been tending to you all along, feeding and changing and singing to you, *without ever waking up*.

Even in my limited experience I knew this wasn't normal. I wanted to confess to your father, but when I returned to him a conversation was not what he was expecting. Your father often wanted me because it affected him like drink—he passed out for hours afterward. I'd refused him for too long—my body still sore after your birth—and that night his pent-up frustration led him to be even more athletic than usual. His goal seemed not to be pleasure as much as exhaustion.

I wonder, Peter, as I read over what I have written, if I would be so forthcoming if I was allowed to mail these letters. I am mentioning subjects that I believe are better kept from a boy your age. Then again, more often I wonder that I did not tell you everything sooner.

When I woke in the morning the bleeding from the delivery had returned. Your father left for work whistling and I spent the day fretting over my discovery. I considered asking one of the other mothers—the frazzled, glassy-eyed women who compared their sleep-deprivation while pushing their strollers—for advice. But I didn't think any of them would be sympathetic. I was already considered odd in the neighborhood—my dark eyes and hair caused speculation about my heritage—and I didn't want to give them any more reason to whisper about me. So I said nothing. And it turned out all right after all. I tended to you and your four sisters while sleeping—there were even a few instances where I took temperatures and called the doctor without ever leaving my dream. There was never an accident that I could have avoided by being awake.

Except for the night they took me away from you. I know I told you otherwise, but the truth is, I was committed without warning. I was unprepared and barely awake, otherwise I might have been able to convince the sheriff that he was making a mistake. Then again, your father's signature was on the commitment papers. His name is usually the last word in such matters.

Even so, had the sheriff come during the day I would have had the dignity of being decently clothed and the opportunity to comfort you children and promise you I'd return. As it was I left wearing only a coat over my nightgown—your father had packed me a bag—and the last thing I saw were Maggie's dark eyes at the banister, staring as if I were being carted away for murder.

I raged with disbelief right afterward, but the scene makes sense to me now. Dignity and opportunity are the first things they take from you when they put you in a place like this.

Mama

11

Field Trip

YOU'RE TALKING ABOUT OSCAR a lot today, Dr. Miller says.

Am I? Alba says, trying not to smile. I must be bored.

What is it you find so attractive about him?

The buffet of friends here is limited, Alba says scornfully, narrowing her eyes in blame. She does this a lot, tries to make Dr. Miller feel guilty about the hospital, the drugs, even Alba's setbacks. It has never been very effective. Dr. Miller merely smiles placidly, waiting for Alba's answer.

I'm not *attracted* to him, Alba says. I find him more entertaining than the others.

Because he's honest? Dr. Miller says.

Honest? Alba snorts. He's a *drug addict.*

Yes. But it's not a secret, is it?

What's your point?

I think we've agreed that the men you've been attracted to in the past have had a tendency to keep things from you.

Not all of them, Alba mumbles. Dr. Miller's gaze never falters. Okay, but I always know. I know when they're lying to me.

Always?

Yes. When Alba lets her voice drop to its meanest, Dr. Miller backs off. Alba inevitably feels guilty about it, though she would like to feel it's some sort of accomplishment.

Today Dr. Miller raises her eyebrows, settles back against the chair, picks up a yellow notepad and writes something down. These are all signs that she is about to change the subject, which allows Alba to breathe easier. She uses the momentary release from eye contact to study her psychiatrist. Dr. Miller is a beautiful woman, with clothes that Alba thinks most women would have neither the courage, the money, nor the poise to wear. Her outfits don't call attention to themselves, and it is only after you watch her for a while that you notice the fine fabric, the carefully chosen accessory—a scarf as vibrant as oil on canvas, or a shimmering necklace. Dr. Miller doesn't seem to care if anyone notices—if complimented she shrugs it off as unnecessary. Alba thinks all of this defines Dr. Miller as a woman with style, and she is envious. Most of the time she couldn't care less, but when she's around people like Dr. Miller, Alba wishes she had her own style. The only things notable about her wardrobe are the consistency of sleeve length, the repetition of one color for months at a time, and ill-fitting garments, because Alba, from going on and off her medications, sheds a size with alarming speed only to gain it back. She buys all of her clothes a little too large.

Are you writing? Dr. Miller says. Much better subject, Alba thinks, and feels her face go mean again.

Of course not, she says.

Yesterday you were going to give it a try, Dr. Miller says. It's her reminder voice, sharpened with a slight parental edge, as if she's repeating something to a child who refuses to pay attention.

What's the point? Alba says. It won't work. I can barely read. I have to read slowly or I get lost. I read a sentence and it doesn't seem to have anything to do with the one before or after it.

Not for the first time, Alba considers telling Dr. Miller about the letters. How, though she has to slog through them, they seem more interesting—more important—than anything she could write herself. But she is afraid that reading the letters is breaking some confidentiality rule, and she will not risk losing them.

Dr. Miller narrows her eyes in genuine concern. This always makes Alba want to crack a joke—seeing her doctor concerned frightens her.

Dr. Miller opens her file and looks at the drug sheet.

The confusion should be lessening by now, she says. We could add some Topamax. See how you tolerate it.

No. No more adding. Please. That's all new side effects that may or may not disappear in two to six weeks.

Dr. Miller's eyes soften, which means Alba's voice is ringing desperate.

Why don't we knock off a little Klonopin? she says. Your panic symptoms are lessening.

What about less lithium too? Alba tries.

Dr. Miller squints at her notes. I think we should leave that as is for now, she says.

Fine, Alba says. She blinks, trying not to cry.

We'll figure this out, Alba, Dr. Miller says, and her voice is enough to start the tears. You'll write again. These rough patches never last.

Alba resents Dr. Miller's encouraging voice more than any-thing. She wants so much to believe it.

No, they never last, Alba says, accepting a tissue from the lovely, discreetly jeweled hand of her doctor. But they always come back.

The smells of hay and horse manure always make Alba feel that there is a certain kind of life, a life of simple, chemical-free happi-ness, that she is missing out on.

This is her third visit to the state fair. Every summer, patients with enough privileges are allowed to go, but Alba has avoided the trip for her last few visits. The diversionary benefits are outweighed by the stress she feels watching her fellow inmates try to adjust themselves to the larger world. On the ward, when they are not in Therapy or Group or Art, the women of Abenaki gather in the common room, every inch of which is visible from the circular nurses' station. They are watched constantly. Everything they do, each emotion they express, all the words they speak, interesting or mundane, mean something. More often than not, it is written down. Some of the women are so depressed or delusional that they do not react to this attention. But a lot of them, and Alba is one, strut through their days as if they are on stage, improvising behavior just to see what reaction it provokes. It is difficult for these women, when they venture beyond the hospital walls, to readjust to a world that is not all about them.

The last time she went, three years ago, the fair had driven Alba into self-conscious overload. It's not good for her to have too many stimuli when she's just crawled back from the edge of psychosis, suicide or mania. Boredom is much more therapeutic. The routine of the hospital lulls her into believing she can find a safer routine for her life. She imagines the same must be true for the other patients—someone always loses it at the fair. But the field trip, because of what it promises—the illusion of freedom, not to mention rides and junk food—is hard for most patients to resist.

Alba is here only because she knows that Oscar earned the privilege and has been looking forward to it.

Dr. Miller is often right, even when she seems obviously wrong. Alba does not think herself attracted to Oscar as much as physically ransacked by him. Her libido (Dr. Miller's word; to Alba it sounds suggestively reptilian) for years now has been, at best, unreliable. Depression renders sex unimaginable, mania leaves it unsatisfying, medication makes it impossible. Alba has come to think of her sex drive as a visitor who knocks so infrequently, she often doesn't think to open the door.

Attraction, for Alba, has become something that occurs only in her mind. Most of the crushes she's had on men have been based on some movement in her brain—a prod they manage to elicit in a formerly untouched portion of her crowded head. Men have been known to say things to Alba that cause small, savory explosions in her thoughts—a mental version of an orgasm. Oscar did this at first, but now, for some reason she can attribute to neither medication nor mood, he is affecting her body.

She noticed it the day he touched her scars. His fingers on her wrist had caused a sudden, thrilling pull in her abdomen. It was as if a throng of formerly paralyzed nerves rushed downward, creating a sore heaviness between her hips. Her pulse quickened until it thudded in her ears, her breath caught, and it had been so long since these symptoms were associated with pleasure, she thought for a moment she was having a panic attack.

Luckily, Oscar had been the one having an attack, so he

couldn't see the look on her face: astonishment mingled with something she was embarrassingly sure resembled hunger. After the
nurses took him away, Alba had lowered herself, weak, shaking
and—she was sure—feverish, into her lawn chair. She did not trust
herself to stir for the next half an hour—her whole body felt deli-
cate, vulnerable, as if any more sensation might crack something
necessary inside her. It was only when the attendant called her in for
Group that she understood what she had felt; it had been so long
since her body had been jolted, except in the throes of fear or
mania. It was Oscar's word that came to her mind, his voice along
with a corresponding yank that buckled her thighs: *glorious.*

Since then, anything Oscar does is liable to tug at her insides—
if he smiles, squints, scratches his head, even yawns, her body
seems to be on the verge of combustion. She is sure this is obvious
to him—she can feel her skin warming as he walks toward her. This
is mortifying, so she tries to camouflage it by talking too much. She
harangues him in a slightly too loud voice, peppered with unattrac-
tive, insincere laughter. She smokes so much that the air around his
head is tinged with blue. She has extreme difficulty looking him in
the eye—the color of his irises is so dense she may as well be pressing against naked skin.

They haven't stopped arguing. She knows she is cruel to him,
not just sarcastic or insulting, but brutal in the way she is only with
someone who has a hold on her. Every day she expects she'll drive
him away for good, and can't decide if she will feel relief or devas-
tation when it finally happens.

He does not let her get away with abuse, as her father and Dr.
Miller sometimes do. He fights her, more than occasionally storms
off with the last word. But he keeps coming back; every morning
that his brother or her father is not intruding, he sidles across the

grass with a sheepish, slightly insinuating smile, as though their last altercation were some sexual innuendo only the two of them understand. It is this smile that alters her the most—like a thrust inside her, not rough but not gentle either—and by the time he sits down in the other chair, she is often wet and fascinated by the sensation— flesh living in a place she had thought was dead.

Alba stays awake most of the night before the trip, nervous about seeing Oscar outside the familiar landscape of the lawn. The addicts and the lunatics are transported to the fair in separate buses, so she doesn't spot him until her third time in line for the roller coaster. The drop in her stomach puts the upside-down loop to shame. He is standing apart from the crowd, eating popcorn, refilling his mouth so quickly he never stops chewing. When he sees her he halts, popcorn-fisted hand halfway to his mouth. He smiles as much as his lumpy cheeks will allow and lifts his hand in a wave, forgetting the popcorn, which flutters down his arm to join the thick litter at his feet. The gesture is dorky, boyishly sweet, which is not usually something she finds attractive, so she is surprised by the rush of warmth to her face. She leaves her spot in line and walks toward him, trying not to smile as he brushes clinging kernels off his shirtfront.

'Lo, he says, swallowing too soon, with obvious effort.

Hello. She reaches instinctively for the cigarettes in her overall pocket.

I can't stop eating, he says, grinning with feigned embarrassment. I've had fried dough, ice cream, cotton candy, chicken kabobs and four slushies.

Alba shakes her head when he offers the popcorn.

When I leave Abenaki, I'll be sober but bulimic, Oscar says.

Alba merely blinks at him. She has made it clear that she doesn't enjoy his careless comments about mental afflictions. This doesn't stop him—he seems to find her sensitivity to it all the more reason to continue with the jokes.

A wave of screaming falls from the roller coaster, causing them both to look up.

Have you been on yet? Alba says.

Nope. Not going either, Oscar says. He seems to have decided to give the popcorn a rest, but she knows he's craving it by the impatient way he is jiggling the box.

You'll stick needles in your arm but won't go on a roller coaster? Alba says.

That's right, Oscar smiles. Summed me up again.

Are you afraid of heights?

No. I don't particularly relish being thrown upside down, but that's not the reason. I grew up with this fair—we lived in St. Francis, a couple of hours from here. I used to get high with the ride operators—I never associated them with safety.

Oh, Alba says. She must look concerned because Oscar laughs and gently elbows her, which unsteadies her enough that she has to step away from him.

I'm joking, he says. Sort of.

Alba spies Ginny looking fearfully up and down the roller coaster line. Alba catches her eye and waves at her, irritated by the feeling that she needs to look out for the nurse who's supposed to be watching her.

Oscar takes her elbow, leading her to a bench recently vacated by ice-cream-dripping toddlers. He drops the popcorn box in the trash, with a regretful last glance. He sits cross-legged on the bench facing her, eager, attentive, and Alba has an awkward moment trying to decide how to sit. She settles on mirroring him, their knees close enough to bump if they stop paying attention.

I was hoping you'd be here, Oscar says, and Alba has to look away. She wonders if it is because he is older, or if it is some fundamental earnestness in his character that allows him to say things like that with such painless grace.

He sees that he's embarrassed her and he sighs, as if to suggest that it's silly, then leans back enough to let her breathe again.

I should really be working, she says, without thinking, immediately regretting it. She has avoided this subject before.

In the library? Oscar says, looking confused.

No, Alba says. Well, that too. I meant real work.

You have a job? Oscar says. Alba feels her face redden.

Of course I do, she says. Did you think I put *mental patient* on my résumé?

Sort of, Oscar says. Don't be sensitive. I've lost every job I've ever tried. I thought, since your family has money . . . Look, if I could live off an inheritance, I would. 'Course I'd probably blow it all on smack.

Alba squirms. She wishes they would both stop reminding each other that he's a junkie and she's nuts. But it has become their yardstick.

So, what do you do then? Oscar says. He's sheepish now, sorry.

I'm a writer, she says. She sees the familiar response—he raises his eyebrows doubtfully, and she wonders again why she never remembers to lie about this. She could tell people she's a house painter or a dog walker and avoid the inevitable conversation.

I should have guessed, Oscar says. Published anything?

Uh-huh, Alba says, picking at the frayed cuffs on the ankles of her overalls.

Poems? Short stories?

Um, children's books. Oscar looks surprised, as she expected.

Really? he says. Alba nods. Picture books?

No. Chapter books. A series for eight- to twelve-year-olds.

What are they about?

Alba shrugs. They're not that interesting.

I think it's interesting, Oscar says. Unexpected, but interesting.

Unexpected?

Don't take this the wrong way.

He is looking at her mouth, which causes it to go immediately dry. She peels her lips apart.

Okay, she says.

You don't really seem . . . *warm* enough to write children's books.

Alba almost laughs. Her father considers her writing a time-eating hobby; Dr. Miller believes it's therapeutic; her publisher, after a few initial disasters, decided to waive her book tour duties, claiming she'd alarm her young readers. No one thinks she has the personality of a children's writer.

They're not very warm books, she says.

Can I read them? He smiles.

Absolutely not.

Oscar laughs and turns his head, looking toward the roller coaster.

Your baby-sitter is flirting with my baby-sitter, he says. Alba has an urge to cup his neck with her hand, hold him so he can't lean away again. But she follows his eyes instead.

Ginny is indeed giggling at something one of the drug attendants is saying. She looks so naturally pretty, flushed and laughing like that, and Alba is amazed at how most women find it so easy to occupy their own faces. Before she can comment, Oscar has grabbed her hand and is leading her away, under tent poles and around mammoth stuffed animals, until they are hidden from view, where the litter is less pervasive, and the sounds of the fair are sleepy.

She is breathing audibly in surprise, trying to hide it because Oscar is now standing extremely close to her. She didn't expect such action from him; Oscar struck her as the sort who could drag flirtatious games on indefinitely. Like herself.

Hello, he says, a greeting. She understands why. This is the first time they are together without supervision, and it is startling, self-conscious, like the first time you stand naked in front of someone.

Hi, she whispers, leaning back, hoping vaguely that there is something solid behind her. There is. Then he is kissing her and she has a familiar, suspended feeling. It takes a moment before she can move from the anticipation of his kiss into the feeling of his lips on hers. She is kissing him for a while before she consciously starts kissing him. He tastes both salty and thirst quenching at the same time.

In one of their conversations on the lawn, Oscar had asked her why she was so reluctant to take her medication. Didn't it work?

It stops me from being crazy, Alba had said. But sometimes I worry I'll stop feeling anything.

Oscar had laughed. I worry that I won't feel anything without them, he said.

Alba is not the only one remembering this, because after Oscar kisses her, so long and unrelenting that a whimper escapes her throat before she can stifle it, he pulls his mouth away, still hovering, and smiles like he's won a little contest of wills.

Did you feel that? he says.

Alba nods. She does not trust her voice after that unseemly whimper.

Good, Oscar says, kissing her again.

They settle into serious kissing, mouths softening, initial tension vanishing into determination. Oscar has his hands on her face, sometimes guiding, mostly just resting lightly by her ears. Occasionally, he presses with his palms, as if he enjoys touching her face as much as he might some other, not so innocent part of her. He is not pushing his groin against her, or letting his hands wander the way she expected him to. This is the way she usually wishes men would kiss her—with care and reverence, rather than as foreplay to pawing which only makes her aware of how numb her body is. Oscar is concentrating on her mouth and, oddly, it is not enough. She wants him everywhere.

She pulls him closer, then pushes him away, suddenly suspicious of his expertise, and embarrassed at how young, how easy she must appear.

I shouldn't, she says, and Oscar gives her a look that says he is not fooled.

Yes, yes, he says. But you are. His attempt at another kiss is halted by a voice beside them.

Hey, lovebirds, someone says, and they both jump, expecting the disapproving stance of a nurse or attendant. But the voice comes from someone hardly tall enough to pose a threat. It takes a moment for Alba to understand that it is a boy.

I've got X, he says, shaking a miniature plastic bag, the kind cheap earrings come in, two yellow pills nestled in its corner. The boy is so small she thinks at first he is about six years old, but realizes he's probably older, suspended in the last gasp of boyhood that lingers before puberty.

Thirty bucks, he says, looking at Oscar now, as if he knows he's the more likely customer.

Get lost, kid, Oscar says, but Alba sees his eyes narrow on the little bag, and he licks his lips with the same urgency with which he fed himself popcorn.

The boy shrugs and winks at Alba, walking away. Alba sees that his hair is overgrown, curling delicately on his thin, baby-skinned neck.

Wait, she calls out, and the boy turns around, with an adult expression of impatience. What's your name? she says, her voice practically a whisper. The boy smiles wickedly, shaking his head. Then, as if reacting to her face or tone, he grows younger, serious with concern.

Joey, he says, and waits for her nod before he turns and leaves them.

Alba looks back at Oscar. He has stepped away from her, shoving his hands into his jean pockets. Still, she can see that he is shaking. She is bombarded with fury.

I hope that abstinence wasn't for my benefit, Alba says.

Oscar looks annoyed. No, he says. It was for mine.

You wanted to say yes, Alba insists.

Brilliant, Oscar says, the joking smile returning. Such an eye for detail. He steps forward, reaching a hand toward her face, obviously hoping to fix everything with more kissing. Alba slaps his hand away harder than she intends to.

What? Oscar says, then looks closely at her.

Are you all right? he says, his voice rising. Are you in pain?

She puts a hand up to keep him away—if he touches her now she'll scream—and tries to concentrate on her breathing. This time it has appeared without warning, the constriction in her neck, as though something inside it is broken, like a word or a bone or a scream is lodged in her throat, and if she moves even slightly, it will slip and choke her until she's dead.

Alba? Oscar says, panicked now. What is it? She crouches to avoid looking at him, darting her eyes from one object to the next— a crushed drink box, multicolored swirls of game tickets, an abandoned slab of taffy, Oscar's ragged sneaker laces. Everything she focuses her eyes on seems to bark at her. Closing her eyes is worse, though she tries it for long enough that Oscar's sneakers disappear and are replaced by the thickly polished white clogs of a nurse.

It's all right, a voice says, not Ginny, thank God, but an older, take-charge type of nurse. I've got you. She knows enough not to touch Alba, but merely guide her with hovering hands.

You . . . have to . . . give me . . . something, Alba says, every word jarring the mass in her throat and spinning her vision to dangerous speeds.

I know, dear. I've got Klonopin lining my pockets. Let's just get you some water.

Alba is concentrating so hard on walking that she barely hears Oscar's fading voice. Later, when she can think again, smothered in medicated calm, she will remember that what he was saying was: I'm sorry. He thinks it was something he did that sent her reeling into a panic attack.

It had nothing to do with Oscar, or kissing, or the offer of drugs and his weakness showing, or the overstimulation of the fair and physical desire.

It was all from seeing that boy.

12

Saint Dymphna's Asylum

October 28, 1933

Dear Peter,

Today I found Dymphna in an old volume of patron
saints. The book was misfiled because the spine has
completely worn through. I imagine there have been
quite a few patients over the years who have searched
for a savior in these pages. She is an Irish saint, which
may be why your father chose this place rather than
one closer to home. As much as he resembles a
Yankee, your father is still a superstitious Irishman.
His father, your grandfather, emigrated during the
famine and had the brogue until the day he died. Many
people find the Irish accent a charming one; I can
honestly say I never did.

Dymphna is the patroness of those suffering from nervous and mental afflictions, though she herself was never ill. It was her father who went mad from grief after his wife's death. He was determined to replace her and sent his servants out to look for a woman who resembled his once striking wife. When no one suitable could be found, he decided to marry his daughter, Dymphna, who at fourteen was the spitting image of her mother. Dymphna ran away to Belgium under the protection of a priest, but her father tracked them down and murdered them both— cutting off their heads with his sword.

Dymphna's portrait is haunting—the artist has made her into a pale, unsmiling girl, her beauty withered already at the age of fourteen, with the glazed, sunken eyes of an insomniac. I can imagine her lying awake at night, both alert and resigned, waiting for her father to visit her with his heavy breath obscuring the unthinkable. It is the way many of the women here spend their nights—strapped to their beds, helpless against the horrors that return with the regularity of the nuns' candles.

I would have painted her differently—plumper, more defiant, with short hair and a dangerous, vibrant mouth. As if she had managed to escape rather than been saddled for eternity by God knows how many mentally afflicted souls.

Love,
Mama

November 15, 1933

Dear Peter,

Have I told you about the baths? If the nuns consider you too nervous or agitated, if you're pacing or twitching or muttering, or even if you bob your foot up and down while waiting for your gin partner to discard, you may be carted off to the Hydrotherapy Room. Inside this huge, white-tiled room are six water tanks—basically wooden bathtubs with a door and latch—like a ship's hold—fastened on top. All you can see of the women is their heads—small, damp and either beet-red with perspiration or blue-lipped, depending on the water temperature prescribed. There is a nun sitting by each of the tanks, whose job it is to replenish the water if it gets too comfortable. I have not yet had a hot bath, but I like to imagine it is far more bearable than the cold one. After a few hours in one of these tanks, it takes you days to warm up again. I am not sure which behavior determines which bath—it seems to me that the same offenses are treated differently. For a while I thought the nuns—for it is the nuns who are in charge here, despite what the doctors think—simply decided that a patient was a cold-water woman or a hot-water one and bathed her accordingly. But Theresa told me that the nuns often alternate. She was once transferred from cold to hot to cold again, one directly after the other, until she could no longer distinguish the temperature—she was sweating through her goose pimples—and felt only a continuous, watery pain.

When I was in the cold tank, shivering so hard it rattled the lock, all I could think about was the time Annabelle had such a high fever we had to bathe her in snow. You might not remember this, you were only five, but even then you had a tendency to become a small, determined man in a crisis, and insisted on helping me. We kept moving her around the yard, burying her under the ice-crusted snow until her body temperature burned through to the mud, and we had to start again in a fresh spot. She was screaming—screaming in a way that did not seem possible for a baby, because we like to imagine that babies never know such misery. I can't recall where your father was, I only remember you, yelling encouragement to be heard over your sister's siren. It was only afterward, when the fever broke, the doctor had come and gone, and Annabelle was asleep, that you seemed like a five-year-old boy again. I was tucking you in for the night and you put a hand to my forehead, asking if I was sick as well. I assured you I was fine, and you started to cry.

"Then why," you said, and your voice seemed almost too small to reach me, "were you screaming too?"

To this day I am not sure if you imagined this. When I told this story to Dr. Winthrop he seemed unduly excited and scribbled it down in his notebook. He keeps his pen poised for all our meetings, though often he is just doodling, trying to appear to be taking notes—he thinks I cannot tell the difference. "Can you remember other times you had an inappropriate emotional response?" he said. I decided to think twice before telling him another story. Dr. Winthrop is a scientist, not a mother, and he has different tools—smaller ones, I think—for measuring the world.

He now says it is only a matter of weeks before I can come home. He will not say how many. I can't imagine they'll keep me over Christmas.

Love,
Mama

December 23, 1933

Dear Peter,

Your father is a liar.

For years he has kept my past a secret, tucked discreetly away like a soiled handkerchief, and now it seems he intends to keep me locked up as well. He has refused the request for my release. Dr. Winthrop seems to think this means I am sicker than I let on, and he is determined to mine me for evidence. I'll tell him nothing—like your father he hears only what he wants to and I will no longer risk my story with these men.

But you, Peter, to you I will tell everything. I will tell you who I once was, who I truly am, and of the people you and your sisters come from.

As soon as I figure out where to begin.

Your Mother

13

Restricted to Ward

IN THE CONFUSION THAT FOLLOWED after they took Alba away, everyone forgot to watch me, so I went after that kid and bought the X.

I considered finding Max and offering her one—Ecstasy loses some appeal when you have no one to share it with—but then I decided I'd better swallow both of them while I still had the chance—body checks were always imminent.

The first feeling I have when I fall off the wagon is never guilt—it's relief. Swallowing those pills was like the plunge of a syringe, the hiss of marijuana smoke between my teeth, the burning of tequila in my throat—there was no regret, only the easy breath of safety. All I could think was: Ahhh. There I am.

My resurrection was short-lived.

Due to the ban on sunglasses, my baby-sitter noticed my pupils immediately. He locked me in the bus, then rounded up the rest of the addicts, who all blamed me for cutting the day short and did not appreciate my rendition of camp songs on the drive home.

Back at the hospital I was squirreled into the isolation room, where I was interrogated, first by the nurses, then by the resident, and finally by my own counselor, Dennis. None of them got very far, as I was feeling so benevolent I kept complimenting them on their fine work.

Eventually they left me alone, and my mood plummeted exponentially. If you're locked in a padded room where the lights never go out and the only distraction is trying to identify the stains on the mattress, Ecstasy can only take you so far.

By midnight the last of the serotonin overdose had slithered away, leaving me with the residue of a headache and an intense, crippling misery. My cheeks were sagging so profoundly with remorse, I became convinced I needed to hold them in place with my hands. My palms were sticky and smelled like salt, yeast, spun sugar, and the expensively subtle odor of Alba's shampoo. I wondered for the first time (admitting that it was the first time made me nauseous with guilt) if she was all right. Of course, she was allowed medication, so I assumed she was safe enough on the brain level, if not the soul. Trying to think back on what I had done to upset her didn't get me very far. The whole incident struck me now as shamefully inappropriate—I could picture it written up in my mound of paperwork: ADDICT APPREHENDED SEXUALLY HARASSING MENTALLY ILL CHILDREN'S NOVELIST. I usually require intoxication to act so forcefully against better judgment. What did they put in cotton candy these days?

By the time they let me out at dawn, after an extended session of stomach-cramping tears, I was rallying a bit. I'd begun to plan in detail what I was going to do with my early release. I'd been here three weeks already—plenty of time to get the physical crutch out of the way. Now I was free to indulge in a pleasurable but controlled manner. I would keep track this time—meter out my hits, vary my substances so that I wouldn't get addicted again. I would return to recreational drug use—rewarding and much less dangerous than a professional commitment. I would need money, but it would be easy enough to persuade David for a get-back-on-my-feet loan. Perhaps I'd even take that job he mentioned, along with an advance on my paycheck. This kind of planning had gone awry in the past—I was shocked that David was even offering me employment after the last fiasco—but there's nothing like being institutionalized to add a new perspective to moderation. If I wanted to use drugs at all, I was going to have to do it reasonably and without abandon. Of course, if it didn't work, I'd have to seriously consider quitting.

By the time they unlocked the door I was already planning a bus ride to Boston, David pushed to the back burner because I remembered a friend in Dorchester who would gladly set me up on credit if I agreed to return the favor soon enough. I could picture myself in her apartment—in my fantasy it was cleaner than I remembered it—with my feet up, a beer sweating in my hand, letting her do the honors of cooking up my first hit on the road to recovery. The nurse considered shutting me back up again, until I showed her I was perfectly able to wipe the smile off my face.

Excuse me, I said, trying to appear composed while surreptitiously wiping the sweat off my lip, but this doesn't sound like you're tossing me out. Dennis actually smiled—the bastard. I was even less in the mood for him than I usually am.

No, Oscar. We've decided to let you stay on.

I see. I was having periodic difficulty focusing on him—my brain was still burping residual chemicals. Do you really think that's wise?

I think this episode could be a pivotal point in your recovery, Dennis droned. I could be wrong, but whenever Dennis spoke recoveryese, his voice grew bored, as if he didn't buy the platitudes any more than I did.

But I broke the first commandment, I said. How much authority do you think you'll have over these junkies if you don't follow your own rules?

It was never a promise that we would kick you out for drug use, Oscar. It was a possibility. Most people I'd be tempted to send packing—but there's something about you that makes me want to dole out a second chance. I get the feeling you want to change.

I don't, I said abruptly, and Dennis raised his eyebrows. I mean I have, I said. Changed, that is. This has been good for me; I've put a lot of things in perspective. I'm just not ready to go the whole way yet.

If you really believed that, Oscar, or any of the shit you try to fly in here, you wouldn't have to try so hard to convince me.

Prick, I hissed, flopping back in my chair.

You see, that's why you're staying, Oscar. I'd miss these touching moments of honesty.

You can't keep me here. I'm self-committed. All I have to do is call a cab.

True, Dennis said, tilting his ergonomic chair to a dangerous angle. Though the local cabs don't like to come out here, you could certainly give it a try. But if you did, I'd call your brother and tell him the conditions of your discharge, and I do believe this was the last in his string of ultimatums. You'll have a hard job getting any cash out of him this time. He's been to codependence meetings, remember?

You're bluffing. There's some sort of confidentiality rule you guys have to bow to.

Normally, there is, yes. I'm riding on the unlikelihood that you'll ever be sober enough to sue.

You're enjoying this, I said, rubbing my stiff shoulder.

No, Oscar. Not really. I don't enjoy watching one of my patients make an ass out of himself because he can't stand to be sober. Your life should be more important to you; I'm not quite sure why it isn't. But I've made it my mission to find out.

There's nothing more humiliating than being someone else's mission. The guarantee that you will disappoint them is almost, but not quite, more torturous than the realization that you are their mission precisely because you're too pathetic to undertake your own.

Can you let me go for the weekend, at least? I said. I could use a furlough.

Do you even hear yourself? Dennis said.

I try not to, I admitted.

I was Restricted to Ward for a week. According to my freshly photocopied guidelines, this meant no field trips, no visitors, no leaving my sterile hallway except for meals.

It also meant no Alba. I was denied that meeting after a first kiss—with all its nervous smiles and hopeful posture, where you can barely speak through the anticipation of kissing again. And if I know anything about women, I knew this—every day I did not show up on that lawn would make her hate me a little more, until she was wincing rather than tingling at the memory of our kiss. I've done this to women I've regretted sleeping with, but somehow it never made me feel as low as doing it to Alba unintentionally.

Of course, there was still the possibility that Alba was cringing from the beginning. She did have a panic attack right after kissing me, which doesn't exactly say much for my technique. Thinking about that look on her face was enough to make *me* wince.

Dennis beefed up our daily meetings to 120 minutes and gave me homework—the same assignment I'd been given before, no longer optional. Write Your Life. He actually gave me an outline, and those little wide-ruled blue books I'd used for college finals.

As spice sprinkled on top of my humiliation, Mitch hosted an additional Group to discuss everyone's "feelings about Oscar staying." I won't repeat it except to say that for fifty minutes I was made responsible for every other junkie's pathetic life. I wasn't allowed to defend myself until the end, and by then I was seething and incoherent and unable to respond. Afterward, Mitch came over for a pep talk I was hardly in the mood for.

Don't feel too bad, Oscar, he said. They'll get over it.

I don't feel bad, I said. I didn't do anything to them. They're just jealous. They resent me because they didn't get the chance themselves.

Mitch narrowed his eyes at me—he looked like a parent trying to decide between anger and disappointment.

That's not why they're mad, Oscar. Most of them want to quit, and this place is supposed to be safe. You bring drugs in, you take that safety away.

I never *brought drugs in,* I said. Let's not make me into a dealer as well as a rule breaker.

All most of these guys are trying to do is make themselves ready, Oscar. They've been offered a better life and they intend to take it.

That's not my problem, I said. I didn't betray anyone—no one's offering *me* a new life.

No one has to, Mitch said. I was struck by his tone—who knew that little Mitch could be so decisive and firm? If he did this in Group he'd get a lot farther with them. Not that I would be the one to tell him that.

Maybe I should drop out of Group, I said. It seems I've become an emotional trigger.

Nice try, Mitch said.

I went back to my cell and tried to lie down, but my brain wouldn't allow me any rest. I was nervous, twitchy, and overwrought with critical voices. I was tired of trying to defend myself. The truth is, between Alba and Dennis and Mitch and the glares from the other junkies, I hadn't felt this bad about myself since my last birthday. And I was pretty pissed off about it.

14

Paperwork

ABENAKI HOSPITAL

ALCOHOL AND DRUG ABUSE TREATMENT PROGRAM

WRITE YOUR LIFE

Name: *Oscar Jameson*
Date of birth: *3/22/73*
Today's date: *6/8/2003*

1. CHILDHOOD

A. FAMILY—Briefly describe family members. Note any substance abuse.

I was the first child: Oscar, Jr. Then my brother, David, born eleven months later, better looking—he took after Mom—and easily upset. My mother, Helen, who was very young—married at nineteen—but she always seemed old to me. My father, the senior Oscar, lobsterman and seasonal alcoholic (he fished all summer, drank all winter). Also, there was my mother's father—we all, even Mom, called him Sir—whom we moved in with when I was nine, after my father died. Dad passed out behind Saint's Tavern and either suffocated or froze in a snowbank. We never knew which, because my mother refused the offer of an autopsy. "It's not as if either one is a better option," was what she said.

B. HOUSEHOLD—Briefly describe your living situation as a child. Did you consider it safe/supportive/nurturing?

We lived in a trailer at the back corner of my grandfather's land. After my father died, we moved to the house, which was dark and cavernous and small, slanted doors leading to attic space. My grandfather slept in the master bedroom on the ground floor, where there was a woodstove, and we had the second floor to ourselves. My mother slept in her old bedroom, which still had teddy-bear curtains and a dollhouse. David and I were down the hall in our uncles' old room, which was kept like a shrine in case they came home, except they were dead—Vietnam—so that was unlikely. It was cold, but not as cold as the trailer and, I suppose, fairly safe. We were poor, but so were most families in St. Francis. The only job my mother could find was waitressing at Saint's Tavern, so most nights she was not home. On the nights she was, she sat up in her room watching television and popping the bubble wrap she took from liquor shipments. She had to keep her hands busy. I would listen to the snapping from my bedroom, satisfied when she found a loud one, restless when she came upon a patch of duds. I couldn't sleep until the cracking stopped. David could sleep through anything.

My mother did what she could. There isn't much time in real life to be supportive/nurturing.

2. ADOLESCENCE

A. What was your experience at home and in school during adolescence?

My grandfather was not an amiable man—after we moved in he often glared at us as if unsure where we came from and irritated that we seemed to be staying. He was massive—he'd been a logger in Vermont as well as a deep-sea fisherman in Maine—with hands that made his place-setting at dinner look as small as my mother's dollhouse set. David was afraid of him. He was only occasionally dangerous, but David was the type to never forget a bad scene, and in truth, my grandfather picked on him more. It was so easy to make my brother cry; people often pushed his buttons. At school, it was my job to stick up for him, but at home I kept quiet most of the time. The job required more subtlety.

My grandfather didn't imbibe often, but when he did it was serious drinking. Once every couple of months he would come home with two bottles of cheap whiskey, and they would be empty by the next morning. Though he always looked mean, it was only when he drank that he actually was. He hit my mother a few times and I knew, by the way she curled into herself like she was waiting, that he'd probably done it when she was a girl. He threw David around a bit, for minor infractions or just for looking "smart." Neither of them could do anything right when my grandfather was drinking. I was the only one who could handle him.

We played chess. My grandfather had learned it as a young fisherman and once told me it was a matter of honor not to lose your temper in chess. It was meant to be a battle of the mind alone. So, most of the time, if I stayed up all night and played chess with him until the bottles were empty and he was asleep (he never passed out, just put himself to bed at dawn), then no one was hurt. I didn't mind these nights as much as you'd think. Of course, I despised him for hitting my mother and David, but when we were playing chess I felt almost sorry for him. Since everyone was afraid of him, he was always alone, and sometimes, as I watched him crouching over the chessboard contemplating his next move, I thought he would have liked to have a family that loved him. He didn't even have any friends. I can't remember anyone who was not suspicious and on guard, even when exchanging friendly talk with my grandfather. Somehow, I didn't think this was his fault. When I was nine I still believed that people were born with their personalities—that my grandfather was mean the same way he was tall, and there wasn't anything he could do about it.

B. When was your first drug or drink (describe the event and circumstances) and how did your use progress?

My father used to let me suck the ice cubes after he'd drained his scotch. I don't know if this counts, but I loved it. I would roll the ice around in my mouth, trying to get the fiery, medicinal taste into every crevice. I always spat the ice out when the residue of scotch was gone. Those ice cubes were like a hint; my throat burned, my stomach warmed, and my constantly alert brain seemed to stretch and pop, make a tiny but notable readjustment toward repose.

My first real drink was pretty standard. I was in the fourth grade, at recess, and an older boy, whom I'd once stood up to in defense of David, offered me a swig from the paper-wrapped bottle in his jacket. It was some sort of liqueur—far too sweet—but three swigs and I was feeling what the ice cubes had hinted at. My brain seemed to sigh with relief. I sought out that bottle every day until I started carting my own.

There were specified hangouts in my small town, and I'd always known that Waban Cove was where the druggies went. I was the youngest one to venture there for a while, and the high school kids thought I was cute, treated me like a mascot, tousling my hair as I tried to hold pot in my virginal lungs. I loved it at Waban Cove, and to tell you the truth, I often miss it. Things were easy there—you never had to hide your need or your high, because everyone else was either wasted or looking to get there fast. The drugs were ample and everyone was generous. It was easy to belong. I lost my virginity there, when I was fifteen, to a seventeen-year-old punk girl who decided to take me on as an experiment. She was gentle and instructive and that, combined with the calm, absent feeling brought on by a cocktail of Valium, marijuana and tequila, left me with the impression that sex was enjoyable, but not very serious. I was not responsible for any of it, the way my mother had once warned me I would have to be. (Whistling and catcalling, popular recreation for the young men in our small town, were strictly forbidden by my mother. It was first on a long list of behaviors she considered disrespectful—the last and most vital being sex without the proposal of marriage.) This was how I often felt when I was high—that nothing I did mattered, that I could go through life leaving no impressions, not even on myself. Waban was the safest place I'd ever known. I tried a few times to get David to come with me, but he didn't approve. I was secretly relieved, as his presence would have required a certain amount of vigilance from me—and I left vigilance behind whenever I went to that beach.

(We learned Abenaki place names in school. I just remembered that *waban* means dawn or morning, possibly even beginning. Ironic.)

By the time we were in high school (David had been advanced to my grade, even offered a grade above me, but he refused), my brother became obsessed with going to college. He latched on to the romantic ideal of education as a savior—he thought it was the only way we would escape St. Francis. Though I had little motivation toward escaping, I humored him. Our school was not exactly competitive—half the students never graduated—so not much work was required to get good grades. David studied all the time and resented my ability to knock off assignments on the bus ride to school, either sleep-deprived from a night of chess or hungover from a session at Waban Cove. My brother always put his best into everything; I put in only what I had to. We both received full scholarships to Boston University. I wasn't planning to go—I didn't want to leave the cove and couldn't imagine my mother alone in that house with my grandfather. She didn't know how to play chess.

But then she died. One night at work the waitress who usually drove her home called in sick; we were asleep, so my grandfather went to fetch her. He was drunk, and on the drive home they got behind a snowplow he decided to pass. They collided almost head-on with another car, both drivers turning away from the rock face and toward the snowplow. The plow ended up in a ditch, and both cars were totaled.

Everyone walked away except for my mother, who hadn't been wearing her seat belt. Later, while drunk, after the charges against him were dropped by the local police, my grandfather admitted to me that she'd unlatched her belt trying to take over the wheel and keep him from the other lane.

Four months later, David and I left for Boston. There was a bit of a scene and we took off a week earlier than we'd planned, so we brought almost nothing with us. I liked it immediately, being able to carry my whole life in a bag on my back, and I continued to live this way for years afterward. David, as soon as he had the money to do so, started collecting things. He's loaded now, and his house is like a shrine to yuppie catalogues.

3. EARLY ADULTHOOD (20–29)

Describe progression of drug and alcohol use, and how this paralleled life direction and choices.

I'd always loved to read, so I majored in English at B.U., which qualified me to do exactly nothing. After graduation, when David went to New York—he was recruited out of the business department directly into an executive-track position at a software company—I decided to write a novel. My problem was I couldn't decide on a setting. My one creative writing teacher had instructed us to "write what you know," but since all I knew were St. Francis, Maine, and the college bars in Boston, I didn't think this was pertinent advice. Besides, I thought it would be much more interesting writing about something I didn't know—at least I wouldn't get bored.

I traveled, hitchhiking across the country, taking odd jobs whenever I ran out of money. I ended up working in a fishery in Alaska. I was second on the line; right after an Irish woman—Emer—used a knife to slit the fish, it was my job to scoop the guts out with a special sharp-edged spoon. By mid-morning we were up to our knees in bloody fish innards. Between the ten-hour days and late nights in the pub with my Irish coworkers, there wasn't much time left for writing. I thought up descriptive sentences of the Alaskan landscape while I spooned fish guts, but I never wrote them down. I was making a ridiculous amount of money—why else would I take such a job?—and I figured I'd save up for a sabbatical where I did nothing but write.

You never save as much as you think you will. Most things were cheap there, but some of the necessities, like pot (you try slaloming through fish guts without medicinal help) cost a fortune. Plus there was Emer's abortion (her decision—I offered to do the honorable thing but it only seemed to make her more determined) and my plane ticket home after I was fired. By the time I got to NYC, I was broke and had to sleep on David's couch for a month.

David's girlfriend at the time worked in publishing and hooked me up with a job writing flap copy for cheesy novels. It was a slightly humiliating job, and after a day of summarizing other people's work you're not exactly inspired to wrestle with your own. I met a lot of interesting people, and there's really no place like New York for entertainment. I suppose that was where I went the furthest in experimenting with drugs, but then, so did everyone I knew, except for David. NYC was where I first tried heroin, which I sometimes regret. I wish I didn't know how unequivocally wonderful it makes me feel, then I wouldn't be tempted to keep going back to it. But I was twenty-five and I tried everything, so I don't see how I could have avoided it for long.

Somehow, I was promoted to assistant editor, and a year later my boss was transferred to the UK division in London. She invited me to come along. (I like to think it was my copy-editing skills and not the fact that I was sleeping with her that gained me this opportunity.) I was a little burned out on New York, and thought the change of scenery would inspire me to write. (I'd abandoned the novels set in Anchorage and the East Village and thought London would be a fresh muse.) Of course, I had no idea that London, with the right crowd, can be even wilder than New York. There are no alcoholics in Britain—just Great Drinkers.

London was the first time I had a problem with heroin. I had a girlfriend whose brother was a dealer and I ended up on a complimentary binge I never would have been able to afford on my own. By the time it ran out—when she broke up with me and her brother cut me off—I was ill. I'd already been fired after my boss found out I was cheating on her, and couldn't pay my rent. David flew out to take care of me, though to this day I don't remember calling him. I'll spare you the gory details. By the time I emerged from the David Detox Program, I'd lost twenty pounds, come down with a pneumonia that would recur for a year, and was positive I'd never touch heroin again. David wanted me to come back to New York, but I thought I needed a break from the city. I wanted to go somewhere quiet where drugs weren't everywhere I turned, somewhere I could think about writing again.

I ended up on the Isle of Skye, off the coast of Scotland. I got a job running the local hostel and for a while things were good. I was relaxed, almost happy, and occasionally convinced I was leading an interesting life. At least the tourists thought so. Though it was easy to drink too much on a Scottish island, I tried not to be too hard on myself—at least I wasn't shooting up. I filled notebooks with ideas but nothing ever seemed to get written. This was the first time it occurred to me that I might never write a novel—I was twenty-seven and beginning to feel old, especially when cleaning up after nineteen-year-olds on their tours of Europe. I vowed to write something significant before I was thirty.

I went back to Maine. David was in Portland, having left New York to start his own company, and I stayed with him while I looked for a job. In retrospect, my next employment choice was not the best. I took a position with a drug company, pedaling antidepressants to New England psychiatrists. It sounds idiotic, but at the time I thought it would be good for me—like that recovering alcoholic on TV who owned a bar. Plus, antidepressants weren't exactly a tempting high. The training program was pretty rigorous, long hours and tests on the biology of mental illness, but I had plenty of recovery ambition so I made it through with honors. After all the buildup, my job basically consisted of driving and charging the corporate credit card with restaurant and bar tabs. Psychiatrists are wilder than you'd imagine. The standard sales dinner often warped into an all-night party at some divorced doctor's beach house. Their bathrooms were veritable pharmacies. There exists a different pill for every bodily function—sleeping, waking, concentration, excretion, you name it—and I tried them all. I was still off heroin even though I was making more money than I ever had before, and had access to boxes full of insulin needles.

I was fired after a DWI charge on company time. (I still don't understand how they expected me to wine and dine those shrinks and remain sober enough to drive home.) At the time I knew it was for the best. I was always on the road, constantly hungover, and my novel about the mental institution in the Scottish moors was going nowhere. David offered me a job writing software manuals, and I took it.

The next year was probably the happiest of my life. David's company was growing fast, getting lots of press and making ridiculous profits, and it was exciting to work there. David had a way of making us all feel like we were all essential cogs in the wheel, even those of us who didn't work very hard and coasted on the free ride of nepotism.

No longer partying, I used the extra time to finish a few short stories I had in a drawer. One of them was published in a small New England journal. It sounds silly, but that—more than any job I'd ever had—made me imagine myself a success.

Contentment was my downfall. Everything was going so well that, when I was offered a line of heroin at a coworker's bachelor party, I thought it would be safe enough. If you're depressed, a little smack and you never want to stop. I thought happiness would relegate heroin to recreational. I was wrong.

Though I thought I'd done a fair job of hiding it, David found out fairly soon after I started shooting up again. It probably tipped him off when I came down with bronchitis and missed a week of work. He demanded that I enter a rehab program, which I thought was absurd, since I wasn't even physically addicted yet. Plus I still had $400 worth of heroin under the bathroom sink (a Christmas gift to myself with my bonus check) and it would have been counterproductive to consider quitting before it was gone. David gave me an ultimatum—rehab or I lost my job. Guess what I chose.

That was a year ago and things have rocketed downhill ever since. I've been in and out of rehab programs—until now, nonresidential—I ruined my brother's wedding, though thankfully I have no memory of it, and I've sponged so much cash off of him I'd have to work for a decade to pay him back.

Rehab people always want to hear about Rock Bottom. Here it is: on my thirtieth birthday I showed up for dinner at David's strung-out and carting a gun, threatening to pull the trigger if David didn't give me $500. He had a roomful of people waiting in the dining room for my surprise party.

But that wasn't even the bottom. It was two more months before I ended up here, and David only managed that because I was too sick to fight him off. I sometimes wonder if I even have a bottom.

Don't ask what happened to the novel.

4. ADULTHOOD (30+)

The mind reels.

15

Saint Dymphna's Asylum

July, 1934

Dear Peter,

Six months have passed since I last wrote you. A longer stretch than I ever imagined I'd be here. I have missed an entire year of your life.

After my last letter I came down with pneumonia. Dr. Winthrop thinks it is a good sign—if my defenses are weakening enough to fall ill, then recovery is not far away. I think it is more likely due to freezing baths.

I slept through most of my illness, a deep, unrouseable sleep that the nuns are calling a coma, but I know was something else. Often people appear to be sleeping when they are not, or think they are dreaming when it is more similar to traveling than anything else.

Some people, that is. Since I was a child I have known I was one of them. Though for years now I've pretended otherwise.

Before you can see my dreams, I must explain who I am. Or was. I am a far different woman than I was a girl.

I grew up in Maine. Possibly not far from this hospital—though I don't know exactly where I am, I recognize the landscape. We lived poorly and simply away from civilization, in a one-room cabin my father built himself. My father had emigrated from Norway when he was fourteen; my mother was of the Abenaki tribe. They lived alone and secluded because she was not accepted in his world, and her world had no home—her people had been wandering for a century. My father used to tell me, on our infrequent trips to town, to always beware of the white man. I was seven or eight before I knew he was one of them. Still, I did not understand his warning—he was the kindest and least deceitful man alive and I couldn't imagine that men who looked like he did would be much different.

My birth name is Mesatawe, which means Morning Star. It was not changed to Mary until I entered your father's world.

My mother rarely spoke; she sang. Songs while she was working, stories to me at night. Even her instructions and reprimands were musical—delivered in a clear voice that could range from deep and serious to trilling and birdlike. She sang about her family, most of whom I never met, serenaded me with ancient stories. Even the most vicious stories sounded beautiful in my mother's voice. One was about the first inhabitants of the world, twins, one so impatient to be born he forced himself out his mother's side, killing her in the process. I remember asking her if I had been born in this way. She sang her laugh. Only boy-children are so impatient that they force themselves down the wrong path, she said. I didn't agree. Sometimes, even as a small child, I felt impatient enough to rip through anyone without considering the consequences. I just wasn't sure what it was I was impatient for.

In contrast, my father was a slow, serious speaker. He took all questions with the utmost gravity and was often oblivious to teasing, though it never stopped my mother. If you asked him how something worked, or the meaning of a word, you had to be prepared to settle in for the answer. My favorite time with him was while he was chopping wood—he would tell me about when he was a boy, his voice rising with excitement with each blow of the axe. He described a land of ice and sharp water, summer sunsets that ran into the next sunrise so that night dangled like an unattainable treat, and winters where the sun barely peeked above the horizon before it was swallowed up again.

At night I would dream about this place, walk hand in hand in an eternal sunset with a boy who resembled my father. It was my dreams that told me how much he missed his home—he never said so in his stories—but the boy in my sleep wandered around tearfully, saying good-bye to everything he saw in a language I did not speak but understood regardless.

I was not expressly forbidden to speak of my dreams, but I learned to keep them quiet. Mentioning them made my mother uncharacteristically curt. This was a disappointment to me, as I always remembered my night journeys, and to me it seemed as though I had half a life I wasn't allowed to acknowledge. As soon as I was old enough, I began to draw images from my dreams, on the paper meant for my lessons. My mother taught me to read and write and calculate sums, though my father loudly disapproved. She needs to be ready for the world, my mother would say, and my father would make a dismissive noise that sounded like our horse when he was feeling stubborn. This is the only world she will need, my father would say. And my mother would turn from him, so easily, though it was something she rarely did, and say: You are wrong.

My mother collected books. One wall of our cabin was devoted to them, stacked on shelves built by my father. My mother would read anything; she had books on history, philosophy, science, even a Bible. My father left the house in protest whenever she took the Bible from the shelf. She often asked me to read aloud from poetry or plays while she was cooking. My favorites were the novels. Every free moment I had I tucked myself into a corner with another world. My father thought so much reading was time ill spent, but as he couldn't stop my mother, he rarely tried to stop me. On every surface of our house, a book lay open, never waiting long for someone to return to it.

Everything changed in my eleventh year. Or perhaps that was when I began to notice I was different.

I was unhappy. For a child who grew up with much freedom and the knowledge that she was loved, this sorrow was a mystery. It began at night. Rather than my joyous traveling dreams I had nightmares from which I would awake screaming but could never remember. I was old enough now that I slept in my own bed, curtained off in the corner, but my night terrors became so fierce that my mother moved me back between her and my father. My father wanted to wake me whenever I screamed, but my mother believed this was dangerous, and chose to just hold me down until it passed. Her arms were covered in scratches and bruises, which she blamed on her chores, but I knew came from me because every morning I found skin and blood under my nails.

Both of my parents tried to remain cheerful, though it was clear that they were worried and losing sleep. Their attention, for the first time in my life, irritated me. I began to wander off by myself, deep into the woods, where I would remain for hours, neglecting my chores and forcing them to search for me at mealtimes. I told them I was reading, or exploring, because I could not tell them the truth. I was not sure what I was doing alone in those woods, besides nothing. I did not sleep, or meditate or draw, I merely sat, steeping in my new misery, until I thought I would die from it. Trying to distract myself from it only made it worse. It was as if a poison had entered my brain, and it needed my attention for food. This was how I began to think of it—a poison that lived inside me, dormant at times, flaring up in my dreams and more and more in my waking life. It infected all my senses—my eyes could not focus, everything I looked at wavered and lunged at me. Inanimate objects were bad enough, but if I looked at another person I would thrash my arms as if warding off attack. My hearing was amplified—small noises were explosions, my mother's singing so abhorrent to me that when I could not get away from it I complained cruelly until she was silent. I no longer enjoyed food—underneath it, no matter how salty or sweet, there was a metallic taste—the taste of the poison on my tongue. My body felt wrong. My mother told me that I was approaching womanhood, that aches and clumsiness and new odors were both natural and good. I knew she was wrong. My body had ceased to feel any pleasure. The cool air, the warm sun, the splash of water, the smell of fire, all of the things that had once been small gifts to my senses, were now repugnant. Reading and drawing were the worst. I no longer understood the structure of sentences; words seemed to dance just beyond my mind's reach. My fingers seemed to have lost their dexterity—my drawing was juvenile, lacking dimension. Everything that had once felt good now hurt me, and the details of the world exacerbated my pain, like a thumb pressed into a bruise.

This first illness went on for two seasons, and in the spring, just when I began to forget that I had ever been that other happy girl, it was gone. It faded gradually but my realization that it had left was instantaneous. My father said something that made me laugh, and it was the quality of that laughter, bubbling, mirthful and unforced, that told me I was back to myself. My father saw it too, but held himself back from comment. I think he knew, as I did, that things would never be the same. Though I slept quietly, felt joy, savored my mother's voice and the flavor of her cooking, experimented with a set of oil paints my father gave me, underneath it all I was still tender. Suspicious. I did not trust myself. I was not as strong as the poison.

It returned in disguise in August. There was no warning, and my symptoms had changed. One morning, while carrying the hot water for my mother's bath, I lost time and space. I was walking with the pot, and the next thing I knew I was on the floor, half a room away from where I'd started, soaking wet and pain burning down my arm. My mother told me I had tripped, knocking my head and spilling the water, which was hot enough to scald my arm and bring blisters. I couldn't remember tripping. When it happened again, and again, when I lost steps every day for a week, opening my eyes to my parents' crouching worry, they told me the truth. I was having fits. Eye-rolling, body-thrashing, tongue-biting fits. I emerged from them exhausted and spent, with blood in my mouth and a fierce pain in my head that any movement made unbearable. I spent much of the month lying in bed, a wet cloth over my eyes, listening to my parents whisper about me. When I wasn't bedridden, I might as well have been. Everything I did, even the simplest chore, seemed terrifying in its consequences. I could not use a knife or scissors because my fear of them, the terror that I would use them to draw blood, caused my hands to shake. I was afraid to let my parents out of my sight, certain death would befall them as soon as I could not watch for it. I woke not with nightmares, but with the sensation that I had stopped breathing, with a pressure right at the hollow of my neck that would not leave, that hovered just above choking me, and all that kept it from doing so was vigilance.

My parents did not know what to do. My mother bloated me with herbal remedies, my father tried reasoning with my fears, taking me along on his chores and pointing out how safe everything was. Nothing helped; I seemed to grow worse with every cure they thought up. They argued when they thought I was asleep.

"I want to bring her to town," my mother said once. "To a doctor."

"Don't you understand?" my father hissed. "Those men are ignorant and fearful. They will call her possessed and kill her with their remedies. Or they will tie her down, lock her up, and we will never see her again."

"We must do something," my mother said. "I'm afraid she will die otherwise."

"You know what she needs. Medawlinno," my father said. The word was in my mother's language, though I'd never heard it and did not know its meaning.

"I will not let them near my child," my mother said softly. The softer her voice, the less likely you could change her mind. "You have never seen what they do. I will not allow it."

They could never agree on anything except what they had already tried—watching me and waiting. Though somehow they remained cheerful with me, I heard the truth in their nighttime voices. They were even more afraid than I was of this poison, afraid there was no cure. I had already resigned myself to this and thus was less afraid.

It was my uncle who saved me. By the time I was thirteen, two years of poison had left me with little will, most of my waking thoughts involved fantasies of accidental death. Suicide did not occur to me merely because I did not know what it was.

My mother's brother arrived as he always had, unannounced, with many gifts and loud, defiant laughter that was out of place in our soft-spoken home. I had not seen him since I was seven, but I remembered the feeling he brought to a room—he seemed to both shrink and expand whatever space he occupied. He was a large man, six feet five with hands as big as my head. His boots alone, when they were not on his feet, looked more like pieces of furniture than items meant to clothe a man. Even my mother, who was taller than my father and solidly built, looked petite and pale next to her darker-skinned monster of a brother. Eventually I would grow to my mother's height, though at thirteen I did not spend time with children my age, so didn't yet realize that I towered over them.

My uncle was a traveler, he often boasted he had set his boots on every country in the world. His name in my mother's language was long and complicated, having something to do with wind, but because I called him Nzasis—Uncle—and my parents called him Smallest Brother, I can't remember it now. He always had stories, which, like my mother, he often sang, but his were rarely tactful. Either he was not used to children, or he did not consider editing for them, but in past visits his stories had often been interrupted by warnings from my parents about small ears. He ignored these requests and left me with many questions that my parents refused to answer, most of them about the private workings of the body that my uncle seemed to find a necessary element to every story. In addition, he often asked questions of my parents that left them blushing and annoyed. This visit, in the beginning, was no different from the rest.

"What is wrong with you, niece?" my uncle boomed at me after his first dinner. "You've hardly eaten, you're paler than your father, and the smell off you is too moldy to belong to a child."

My parents threw answers at him—she's been ill but is well

along in her recovery, the change to womanhood has left her quiet and sullen but it is only a stage. My mother began clearing the table, my father offered tobacco and the liquor he brewed in the woods that my uncle could never resist. Through all their stuttering and shuffling, my uncle looked at me, eyebrow cocked, his mouth pursed with disbelief. I tried to meet his gaze, thinking that this was what a normal girl would do, but it was difficult. My uncle was far too colorful and animated for my sensitive eyes. He said nothing more that night, but kept throwing scornful looks at me until my mother, to my relief, sent me to bed early.

But in the morning he was waiting for me. Ignoring my mother's protests, he insisted I accompany him on his dawn walk. We were gone for an hour, and it was an hour that changed my life. He asked me questions, almost as if he already knew the answers, about all of the maladies I had thought so secret and strange. He guessed things that I hadn't even told my parents— about the unbearable heat my body produced at night, about the way my brain prowled with dangerous thoughts. About the voices, not my own or of anyone I knew, that sometimes clamored in my head, and told me things that I didn't understand, but thought about nonetheless.

My uncle did not seem surprised or concerned by even the most shameful of my answers, but by the end of the interview he was angry. He crashed open our cabin door, startling my parents who were sitting at the table, with not even a cup of coffee between them, as if they were waiting for news so disturbing, even the smallest amount of nourishment would be a blasphemy.

"What is the matter with you?" he yelled at my mother in their language. She did not flinch but could not look at him either. "Is it this man you married? Has he poisoned your soul until you cannot remember even the simplest teachings of your people?" By now my father had risen, trying to protect my mother, but looking like a boy next to my towering uncle in his rage.

"It is not because of him," my mother said, her voice level with the eerie calm that she used in response to my own yelling. "The decision was my own."

"Then tell me why, when your daughter has the dreamer's gift, the power most cherished and feared among us, you choose to ignore it?"

"There is no place for dreamers in her world," my mother said. "The old ways are dead and following them is as dangerous as it is pointless. I will not allow my child to be burdened with such strangeness."

"It is not for you to allow," my uncle said. "You will kill her if you try to stifle it, or have you forgotten that? Her gift is more powerful than any of your desires, more powerful than her own. She is meant to be the leader of her community, and you have no right to keep her from it."

"There is no community for her to lead," my mother said. "You are a fool if you believe otherwise."

All this time I'd been standing in the open doorway, motionless despite the frigid wind blowing past me into the room. Though it was January, I could have sworn I smelled the thaw of spring in the air. I stepped forward, a hundred questions on my tongue, but before I could form them, I lost myself in a fit. When I woke, my limbs shuddering in the last of the convulsions, I was on the floor near the table, with that familiar fear at having lost the movement across a small but significant space. But what was not familiar, what was so alien to my usual emergence from these states—the sight of my parents' terrified faces feigning encouragement—was my uncle above me, one huge hand cradling my head, with a smile on his face that suggested I had done something extraordinary.

16

Paperwork

ABENAKI MENTAL HOSPITAL

IN-PATIENT SUMMARY

Patient: *Alba Elliot*
DOB: *2/15/78*
Today's Date: *6/15/2003*
Doctor: *Julia Miller, M.D.*

Current Diagnosis: *Bipolar with a significant anxiety variant.*

Current Medications: *Lithium 400mg T.I.D.; Klonopin 2mg Q.I.D. and as needed for anxiety; Neurontin 300mg T.I.D.*

Side Effects Reported: *dry mouth, thirst, vertigo, hand tremors, confusion, word recall, difficulty concentrating, psychomotor retardation, loss of libido, and a general blunted, dazed feeling.*

Summary: *Alba has been under my care since her admission in June 1993 at the age of fifteen. Initial diagnosis was mania complicated by psychotic state, with a familial history of manic-depression. (Alba's mother committed suicide when Alba was only four. To date, Alba has refused to discuss her mother, claiming she doesn't remember her.) Interview with father revealed that Alba had been pregnant, a fact she managed to conceal until she was almost full-term. Adoption was arranged for the infant—a boy—at birth, after Alba began to exhibit psychotic delusions and hallucinations. A month after the delivery, Alba set fire to her family home and was referred here by the emergency room at Mount Auburn Hospital in Cambridge. Alba was at first unable, then unwilling, to discuss either incident, but admitted experiencing symptoms of depression and mania from the age of twelve.*

Since 1993, Alba has been readmitted every year in either manic or depressive episodes. She has attempted suicide by vertical wrist slashing and drowning, and has engaged in self-destructive behavior (fast driving, unprotected sex, shoplifting, starvation and bulimia). Her admissions generally follow the discontinuance of her lithium, which she complains leaves her feeling "half-dead." We have tried a number of substitutes for lithium, including Depakote, Topamax, and Lamictal, but their results have been short-lived. Alba has also abandoned her meds for a variety of alternative medicines, including homeopathy, acupuncture, reiki, yoga, herbal remedies, dietary restrictions, fasting, hypnosis and hormone therapy. Nothing she has tried appears to have the long-term efficacy of lithium.

Despite the fact that Alba loses a significant portion of each year to mania and depression, she is a fairly successful children's writer. Her series of books are about a life-affirming orphan named Sam Waban (*Note:* Waban is the Abenaki word for dawn, surely she learned that here?) and follow, chronologically, the age of her son. Most of her writing comes out of creative spurts that accompany the hypomanic state preceding mania, during which she can do a year's work in six weeks, another excuse for her to abandon medication. She finds writing at a level mood difficult and slow. She has managed, with the help of her father, who, along with the family lawyer, acts as her agent, to keep the severity of her illness a secret from her publisher. She continues to live in her childhood home with her father; attempts at independence usually end in relapse. She has no close female friends and seems to spurn associations with women in general. Her relationships with men are short-lived and obsessive, and generally end with the onset of mania or depression.

Current Issues: *Alba's latest manic episode has been controlled by lithium, but since entering the hospital she has developed symptoms of panic disorder. Klonopin relieves the panic attacks but adds side effects that further impair her ability to write. Alba has a tendency to want quick fixes rather than commit herself to long-term medication and the ongoing work of psychotherapy. This is an issue we continue to address.*

About once a year, Alba talks about trying to find her son, though she never takes definitive steps to do so. Her guilt at "abandoning" (her word) him runs very deep and is, I believe, a factor in her depressions.

Recommendation: *I don't recommend release until the panic attacks subside and the Klonopin is lowered (the addictive qualities of Klonopin concern me especially). She was severely suicidal when admitted and has been known to relapse quickly if she is sent home prematurely. I propose further review in three weeks' time.*

17

Denial

ALBA.

Hi, Dad.

What could you possibly have been thinking?

I can't imagine what you mean.

Don't give me that crap, young lady.

If you're referring to my panic attack, it didn't require a lot of forethought.

I'm referring to your sneaking off at the state fair to neck with some junkie.

Neck, Dad?

Whatever you call it. Obviously it was more than you could handle.

Dad, have a seat. When you stand over me like that I feel like I'm in kindergarten.

Alba's father sits gingerly in the grimy lawn chair, careful of his suit. At her level he must see that she's paler than usual, or the circles under her eyes, because his expression softens. He has told her that during a panic attack she looks like she's in physical pain.

How do you feel? he says gently.

Stupid, she exhales.

Well, it was a pretty stupid thing to do.

I meant slow-witted because of the Klonopin, but thanks.

Alba, he says, shaking his head. You were doing so well. Why do you insist on pushing yourself beyond what you can handle?

Pardon me, Dad, but I didn't consider a little kissing beyond the pale. I do still have blood in my veins.

I've never tried to keep you from having a social life, Alba. But you pick the most inappropriate times, not to mention characters.

Alba sighs, rubbing her eyes so roughly, he reaches out to stop her.

I know, she says. Never mind him, he doesn't matter. It wasn't about him anyway.

What wasn't?

My panic attack. It was because of the boy.

There were children involved? Her father smiles. Now that she's begun to agree with him, he's relaxing into joke mode. She's not willing to follow just yet.

The boy at the fair, she insists. I could have sworn . . .

Alba, her father warns.

He'd be ten now, Daddy. It was his birthday last week.

Don't do this to yourself, he says. What she hears underneath is: *Don't do this to me.*

I want to see him.

Impossible.

I think it would help. It would be like therapy. I know you know where he is.

I don't actually, her father says. I've told you that. I have no reason to lie to you about it.

Sure you do, Alba thinks, but she turns her head. Sometimes, she can't bear to look at him. She's afraid she won't be able to stop herself from doing something sudden and violent to his poised, placating face.

Don't cry, darling, her father says.

She shakes his hand away, reaching for a cigarette.

It's the fucking Klonopin, she says. It makes me stupid *and* weepy. It's like a dose of PMS disguised in a sunny yellow tablet.

Her father chuckles, as she meant him to.

Maybe they should give it to me, he says. You might find me more empathetic. He winks.

That and simulated childbirth would satisfy me, Alba says, wiping away her tears.

Her father nudges her as if to say, Good one, kiddo. This is their routine, making light and trading sarcasms, and she follows it, even though sometimes when he makes her laugh, she hates him for it.

He spends the rest of the hour telling her about his night out with an alcoholic benefactor of the museum. Her father, while telling a story, is loud and animated, his face and hands dancing along toward the climax. The first word people use to describe him is *charming*. When Alba uses that word, it never sounds like a compliment.

When it's time for him to leave, she walks him inside. As he hugs her good-bye, she pushes it by whispering into his chest.

Sometimes, I miss him, she says. More than I miss Mom, even. Isn't that crazy?

Shhh, her father says. It is not the noise of comfort he pretends it to be. It is a hiss, a warning, and he hugs her tighter to take the edge off.

I'm thinking of going away again, Alba says.

Mmmm, Dr. Miller says. You are a bit twitchy. Feeling restless?

Could you stop fucking diagnosing me for a second and listen to what I'm saying? Alba barks. I think I should travel. It would be good for my writing. I can't go back to that house.

Alba, I am, as you know, all for you moving out of your father's house. But one thing at a time. Let's talk about the panic attack.

We exhausted that topic last time, Alba says. She slouches in her uncomfortable chair, knowing that it makes her look like a teenager, but too angry to care.

We talked about seeing the boy, Dr. Miller says. That's as far as we got.

That's as far as it goes, Alba says, mimicking Dr. Miller's inflection. Dr. Miller raises her eyebrows, but decides to ignore it.

What about Oscar?

I told you, it had nothing to do with Oscar. The kissing was great.

You told me you were upset that he seemed tempted by the drugs.

So?

Did you feel betrayed? Lied to?

Well, a little. But it wasn't why I panicked. It was thinking about my . . . you know, that boy.

I'm just trying to see how these things might be related, Dr. Miller says. Her face has that half-amused look it gets when she thinks Alba's being obtuse.

Okay, I give up, Alba says. Enlighten me.

What happened with your son involved lying and betrayal. So did, I might add, your mother's death.

Alba sits upright in her chair, crosses her legs, then recrosses them rapidly.

My father was trying to protect me.

I know that. But did he?

I just think that if I saw Sam, Alba says, saw what he looked like and that he was happy, I'd feel better, that's all. I'd be able to stop the medication. Go forward.

Do you want to know what I think?

Not really.

I think that your manic-depression is a biological problem that will not go away with a reunion. Separate from that, unless you are able to talk about the issues surrounding your son's birth, not to mention your relationship with your father and your own mother's leaving you, seeing Sam may make you feel worse, not better. I think it might be dangerous, frankly.

My mother didn't leave me, Alba sneers condescendingly. She died. There's a difference.

Yes, Dr. Miller says quietly. I know the difference, Alba. There's also a difference between a mother simply dying and taking her own life.

Shut up, Alba warns. What do you want from me?

I want you to think about what you can do, right now, without a pilgrimage, to feel better.

It started when he took Sam away. My illness. Are you saying that's a coincidence?

No. I'm saying I think it would have happened regardless. You were exhibiting symptoms before that.

Then what's the fucking point in talking about it? Why not just give me a lobotomy? Alba says. She can feel her face crumpling, she hopes Dr. Miller will stop before the tears start.

Alba, Dr. Miller says, gently now; she's seen the threat of tears. What about your father? How did he react when you told him about the fair?

He doesn't want to help me, Alba says.

Why do you think that is?

Oh, it's not that he doesn't *want* to, Alba says. He *thinks* he's helping me; he thinks he knows better, that's all. I'm sure I scared him— my panic attacks terrify him. Apparently, I look like I'm dying.

They scare you, too.

Alba's grunt is noncommittal.

You've never told your father how much you resent the way he went about the adoption?

No.

Why not?

Because it would hurt him. He didn't mean to hurt me, so hurting him on purpose wouldn't be fair.

Do you think it was fair the way he handled it? Dr. Miller is taking notes again. Alba wants to rip the pen out of her hands.

Why do you hate my father so much?

I don't hate your father, Alba. It's okay to be mad at him.

You do hate him, Alba says loudly. You want me to hate him, too. The tears are coming now. It doesn't help when Dr. Miller looks at her so sympathetically. Dr. Miller hands her the tissue box.

You've got to get me off this Klonopin, Alba says, swiping at her eyes. It makes me cry.

Do you want to try something else? Dr. Miller says. So far, Klonopin's worked the best with panic.

I want to be able to smoke in here, Alba says.

It won't kill you to cry a little, Alba.

Alba's face wrenches and she turns her head to the window.

My father, Alba mumbles behind the lotion-coated tissue, is all I have.

I know. Dr. Miller sighs. That's not fair either, is it?

18

Saint Dymphna's Asylum

January 3, 1935

Dear Peter,

Forgive me for neglecting our letters. It is rare that I
have the privacy to write anything of length, and,
truthfully, I imagined I would be home by now. It was
not to be. So I take up my pen again, though not
knowing if you'll ever read them makes me less
inclined to pour myself into these communications.

We have a new doctor; he moved into the
Physician's Cottage with his wife and two young
children just after Thanksgiving. I only see the children
from afar, but occasionally I hear their laughter echoing
in the hills where they go sledding, and it is heartening.
Dr. Madden is a jovial, energetic young man, and his wife

is very handsome. They have already instituted a number of changes that have made our lives a bit more pleasant. The pavilion plan, which Dr. Madden considers inconvenient and old-fashioned, has been abandoned. He moved us all to the main building; the dorms are cleaner and better heated than the cabins. We were allowed a Christmas tree with ornaments we crafted in Occupational Therapy. On Christmas Eve we watched a film in the cafeteria and now we have been promised a new picture every other Friday. I have hopes that once he is settled, this doctor will allow me to post my letters. Some of the women who have been here for longer than I have are not as elated by the change. "They are all like that," Mrs. Biddle told me. "Especially the young ones. Full of piss and vinegar in the beginning—determined to cure us all. It won't be long before your Dr. Madden loses heart and takes it out on the lot of us."

I pray these are bitter words that will not come to be wise ones.

With love,
Mother

January 25, 1935

Dear Peter,

Mrs. Madden has acquired a dozen pairs of ice skates from the local charities, and now we are allowed to take our exercise on the frozen lake. I was given only ten minutes on the blades, but they were a glorious ten minutes. It has been a long time since I felt the simple gladness that fresh, cold air and movement can bring.

It made me miss you and the girls all the more.

Mother

April 14, 1934

Dearest Peter,

I write you with a heavy heart. Uselessly as well, as it seems my letters are destined to remain at the backs of books no one bothers to peruse. I spoke to Dr. Madden about mailing privileges. Apparently I am free to send letters anywhere but the one place I would have them go. It is written in my chart that your father will refuse all correspondence from me. If I actually mail something he will return it unopened. Dr. Madden said that the nuns must have tried to spare my feelings by concealing this information under the guise of a hospital rule.

"I can't say my feelings were spared as much as my freedom," I replied before I could censor myself. Dr. Madden smiled but looked very sad. He has promised to solicit your father's sympathy. Dr. Madden is a kind man, but, as far as your father's concerned, I fear he is destined to be ineffectual.

Still your,
Mother

August, 1935

Dear Peter,

Something has occurred that I must relate, even if the telling of it is lost in oblivion, unread in the back of a guide to New England ferns.

I have told you of the fits I had as a girl. Eventually, with my uncle's help, I learned to enter these states at will. It has been many years since I have practiced what I learned that winter. Your father's family thought me odd enough as it was, my thrashing and drooling would certainly have added insult to injury. My uncle once told me that my gift was not one I could ever escape, but I have managed to keep it hidden until now.

It took hold of me with little warning in the dayroom. I'd just risen from the puzzle table to go to the lavatory. The next thing I knew I woke by the nurse's station, my head bruised and ringing from my convulsions against the linoleum. For lack of a proper gag, someone had shoved a broomstick between my teeth, which left a splinter in my palate. The nuns carried me off to Hydrotherapy, where they attempted to regulate what they thought was an overheated metabolism. I was tied down and wrapped in wet sheets, a hot water bottle at my feet, ice pack at my head, and left for the remainder of the morning.

I was called to Dr. Madden's office that afternoon. He seemed excited by the reports of my seizure and for a moment I thought about telling him the truth. Telling him where I'd journeyed in that lost space between the puzzles and the doorway. But his first words were discouraging.

"How long have you been an epileptic, Mary?" he said, pen poised eagerly for my response.

"I beg your pardon, sir?" I said.

"Are you not familiar with the term?"

"I've heard the word, Dr. Madden, but I fail to see its connection to me."

"You had a seizure this morning, Mary, with convulsions and prolonged unconsciousness characteristic of an epileptic fit. I find no mention of this in your chart. Has it happened to you before?"

"Not for a long time, no. But . . ."

"We must obtain a complete history," Dr. Madden said. "When it began, how often it occurred, related symptoms. Epilepsy is a serious neurological disorder and I'm afraid your therapy here could have been more successful had we known what we were dealing with. No matter, now that we've determined the illness we can make a plan for your recovery."

"I am not ill," I said. "I was unjustly institutionalized by my husband."

Dr. Madden looked concerned and wrote one long word on his pad.

"Are you of the belief that normal, healthy individuals have seizures, Mary?"

"Not normal, no."

"I know this must come as a shock to you. Please answer everything you can and perhaps we'll find a way to get you home to your children."

I sighed and gave myself over to the interview. Poor Dr. Madden, he means well. Perhaps if I can't make him understand, I can at least make him believe he has cured me.

I answered his questions as best I could without mentioning my uncle or my training. He seemed to have a remarkable understanding of the physical symptoms that accompany my spells. He asked if I ever experienced an "aura" prior to a seizure and at first I did not know what he meant.

"Do you smell something, something odd or out of place, just before you collapse?"

I must have gone pale, for he offered me a drink of water.

"How do you know about the signs?" I said. I have never discussed the calling since my uncle first explained it to me.

"It is common to have sensory hallucinations just at the onset of a seizure. Smell seems to be the most common, though there are those who have auditory or visual hallucinations."

"I smelled my son," I said. Dr. Madden looked up from his notes. He knew what I meant, you see, having a son of his own. He is familiar with the particular odor of boyhood. I imagine he goes home at night and holds his boy and learns about his day as I once did with you. I could tell when you'd been in the marsh, or gone to the pub looking for your father, or had a tussle with neighbor boys. It was imprinted on you, your day mingling with the odor that belongs particularly to you, that I had inhaled lovingly since you were a baby. I have remembered it often in this place, this jail that reeks of moldering souls beneath the guise of disinfectant. But there is a huge difference between remembering it and experiencing it, as I did before my journey they call a seizure. I cannot explain it away as hallucination.

My interview with Dr. Madden went on for nearly three hours. He finally excused me at the supper bell, promising we'd meet again soon.

"Have you anything to ask me, Mary?" he said. This is something we all admire in Dr. Madden. The nuns and previous physicians never encouraged our questions.

"I am curious about the history of this hospital's land," I said. "What was here before, I mean."

"There has been a hospital here for more than a hundred years. Before that it was wilderness, I suspect. I can find out for sure if you like."

I know the answer already. Something unspeakable happened here. I saw it in my dream.

"I'd appreciate that," was all I said.

September, 1935

Dear Peter,

I cannot tell the doctor where my fits take me, so I will tell you. Here are my dreams, my journeys, my seizures.

The landscape is this one. Despite the absence of modern dwellings, how could I fail to recognize the view I have watched through barred windows every day for the past two years? There are no doctors, no sculptured lawns, no searchlights left on in the moonlit hours. All that is here is a village like the ones my mother once described but I never saw. They were long gone by the time of my birth.

They are of the Abenaki tribe, like my mother and uncle. I recognize their language, though not as precisely as I might have once. I miss words, sometimes phrases, but I can follow the general tone and meaning of most conversations I eavesdrop upon. It is eavesdropping, for most of them do not know I am there.

The village is just as my mother described. A few teepees, but mostly low rectangular huts, their length depending on the size of a family, some so long they look more like tunnels than dwellings. The atmosphere is both lively and relaxed. Children run free as you and your sisters once did in our neighborhood, because there is always a mother or grandmother watching. Babies are wrapped tightly to their mothers—pressing skin to skin through chores and meals and conversations. The clothing is a strange mix of traditional and modern—some of the men wear trousers that end below the knee, others wear skins that barely cover their nakedness. There are a few women who seem to be wearing what were once elegant evening gowns—now worn from everyday use, corsets and petticoats missing so their bodies move freely beneath the fabric. Everyone is draped with jewelry, polished stone beads wink from their ears, wrists and necks, and it gives the impression of celebration, as though a normal day is special enough to wear one's best. There is an abundance of laughter here, and though everyone seems to work hard, few are averse to stopping for a nap in the sun, to admire a baby, or even to engage in a heated quarrel.

The oddest thing is that there are white women here. At first I thought they were of mixed origins like myself—products of affairs or marriages with the citizens of a nearby town. They dress the same as the Abenaki women—a florid combination of society clothes and animal skins, their faces darkened by the sun, their teeth worn down or missing altogether. They are, for the most part, alone. They live with families like spinster aunts, no children or men of their own. Their speech is a strange combination of English and Abenaki, but they seem to make themselves understood. I had heard stories as a child about white women living with the Abenaki, but so many in one village—I have counted over a dozen—seemed odd to me. I found out who they were when I watched a new one arrive.

Some children ran in from the road and announced the approach of a white man on horseback. He dismounted at the edge of the village, easing a woman down to stand beside him. The woman was thin and drawn in the face; pain had ravaged her, but it was clear that she was once beautiful. The man held her arm easily and led her past the villagers, some curious at the limp shuffling of this woman, others uninterested, as if this were a normal occurrence and not worthy of distraction.

An Abenaki man came out of a large teepee, steam evaporating in his wake, and nodded to the approaching couple. He was the village healer; I recognized him by the face markings once described by my uncle, and by the way he looked at this woman, as if he were peering through her skin and into her soul. The two men shook hands.

"My wife," the white man said. "She cannot carry a child. She has lost three to bleeding, and the last one almost killed her.

Since then, she will not eat or speak or tend to herself. The doctors can find no cure. Someone told me . . ." He faltered, looking around. He raised his voice, as if suddenly concerned that his English was not being understood. "I was told you could help where others have failed."

"She is welcome with us," the healer said. "We'll do what we can." His English was precise, polished, and it was this as much as his words that seemed to put the man at ease.

"I'll be able to come back for her?" he said. The healer smiled slightly, respectfully, as one might smile after a recent death.

"If you wish to," he said. The husband looked as though he couldn't decide whether or not to take offense at this.

"Of course I do," he said. The healer kept the kind and patient smile on his face. An Abenaki woman came over and began speaking gently to the wife, taking her from her husband and leading her toward a low hut. The husband watched her being led away, panic and submission taking turns in his face. He turned back to the healer.

"You are Christians, are you not?" he said.

"We are what you call a praying village, yes," the healer said.

"I could not leave her if I thought—"

The healer interrupted. "I understand. Her soul will be safe here."

The husband nodded, relief raising his shoulders a bit. He put his hand out. "I am grateful to you," he said, and the healer shook his hand. Though they were hiding it, you could see this was difficult for them both. Contrition between men who, under normal circumstances, would not acknowledge each other as equals.

"Travel will be difficult soon," the healer said. "You may return in the spring."

The husband, happy to have a plan, murmured in agreement. He left then, not looking back, his posture on the horse a little firmer now that he did not have to curl protectively about his wife.

I watched the Abenaki woman dress and bathe the wife, soothe her with oils, urge her to drink tonics, comb out her long, neglected hair, and put her to rest on a pallet in a clean, cheerful room in the longhouse. The healer came in and sat by the woman's side a while, watching her sleep. The Abenaki woman came to stand beside him.

"Will he return?" the woman asked, and the healer shook his head.

"No," he said. "He has another woman waiting for him."

"If you know these things, why do you bother with the manners?"

"It is better that she is away from him. It's simpler if I pretend to believe—it eases the guilt. Guilt makes men angry."

"If they want this land, they will take it," the woman said. "Whether we have their women or not. Their wives and daughters cannot save us."

The healer reached out and wrapped his arm around the woman's thighs.

"I know," he said. "But perhaps we can save a few of them."

The part of the dream that most frightens me is the part I understand the least. It comes to me in flashes, brief and unexplained images that are often the last thing I see before I awake, still convulsing on the hospital floor. The woman brought by her husband always ends up writhing in a pool of blood so large, I know it must come from more than one slaughtered body.

19

Recreation

I'VE HAD MY SHARE of dreadful situations. The kind
where you'd almost rather die than face the person
you've wronged. Where you don't know yet whether
they will hate you or forgive you, and, frankly, you'd
rather not find out. When my brother walked in on me
me shooting up in his bathroom, for instance; or when he
gave me the surprise party. I'd never been so small. That
is, not until I walked across that lawn to Alba—in that
moment, I was miniscule.

She was reading another old library book, turned to
handwritten pages in the back. I wondered if they were
her notes, but the handwriting looked old-fashioned. I
was standing behind her; she hadn't noticed me yet.

More bird-watching? I said, and my voice actually
shook. She slammed the book shut. I could see tiny

bumps rise on the back of her neck. That could mean a lot of things, I thought. Hatred, fear, attraction. I was hoping for the last, betting on the first. Despite her panic attacks, I didn't think of Alba as the fearful type.

I stepped around to face her and instantly my dread took a backseat. She looked awful. Circles the hue of bruises under her eyes, limp hair, a mouth that teetered on the verge of collapsing.

You're still here, she said. I told myself that I was imagining the hopeful tone in her voice. She wouldn't look me in the eyes; her gaze lined up with my belt. I balled my fists in my pockets to hide the erection her voice had initiated.

I think they're keeping me around for some sort of experiment, I said. Not even a smirk from Alba. But no dismissal either. Yet.

I sat down on the lawn. Are you all right? I said to Alba. Because you look—

Please don't tell me I look awful, Alba said. I've heard it seven times today.

Are you sick?

No, I've had a few panic attacks, that's all. And the meds for them are pretty life-sucking.

I'm not generally known for my ability to apologize. In fact, it's been at the top of the list of what my girlfriends called my shortcomings. I've been like this since I was little; it used to drive my mother crazy. She'd send me to my room until I was ready to apologize and eventually she'd have to let me out to keep me from starving. I don't know what my problem is with it exactly, except that apologizing seems like giving up. Not just to someone else, but on yourself. If you say you're sorry, then you feel even sorrier, and it's a never-ending downward spiral from there.

So I was pretty shocked when, not for the first time, I burst out with the forbidden words in the presence of Alba.

Alba, I'm really sorry . . . I started. She actually waved me away. If she had known how many people have wished for that sentence from me, she might have savored it a bit more.

It wasn't you, Alba said. I let the doubt show on my face. Really, she said, looking straight at me now. Don't imagine you have that much of an effect on me. Panic attacks precede you.

I don't, I said, fumbling. I'm just sorry for the situation, that's all. There was that word again. What was wrong with me? I should have been saving my infrequent apologies for people who actually wanted them.

So, Alba said. Did you buy the drugs? She was glaring at me—back to her old fierce self in an instant.

Of course, I said.

Do you regret it?

I paused. Actually, I do, I said.

Because you got caught?

No, I said. Well, that's part of it, obviously. I felt pretty stupid. But I'd regret it anyway, I think.

Why?

I don't know, I said, shrugging. I didn't want to tell her that ever since it happened, I'd regretted mostly that she'd seen me like that. Hungry for drugs. Never one of my better moments. And, since meeting Alba, I'd started to want those better moments—those I'd abandoned hope of long ago—back again.

Was I going to admit something like that to the ferocious eyes watching me? No way. Not even with the memory of how soft she'd become during our kiss.

She let me off the hook then.

It wasn't you, she said quietly, sincerely this time.

What? I asked, trying to catch her eyes. She glanced my way briefly, then away, flustered. I felt a little thrill at that—looking at me affected her.

My panic attack, she said. It wasn't because of you.

I thought I'd disgusted you, I said lightly, hiding my relief.

No, no, she said. She fished a cigarette out of her dwindling pack. I saw her shake the blue box and squint at it with concern— almost empty. As an addict, half her mind was now focused on obtaining another pack.

The opposite, actually, she said, after she'd lit up, sighing out smoke. You made me feel, she began, then, looking at me, she flushed and shrugged the rest away.

What? I whispered, leaning in as close as I dared in front of our baby-sitters.

Made me *feel*, she explained. And that's rare, lately. For a long time, actually. Feeling without danger, I mean. Without losing myself.

Well, I said, clearing my throat. If you want my professional opinion—when you find a therapy that works, stick with it.

And, for the first time that day, she smiled. I swear it almost stopped my heart. Because I knew—I could see it in her mouth— that she was going to let me kiss her again. Soon.

I never understood how my captors at Abenaki could lecture about maturity, then sponsor junior high school events like a dance on Friday night. My first thought was: *Will she be there?* Not far behind— before I even realized the irony—was: *How can I sneak beer in?*

I mentioned the event offhandedly on Thursday, and Alba laughed, then blushed. The etiquette was similar to junior high—

we arranged to see each other there, but asking her to be my date would have been too forward. Not to mention ridiculous. What was I supposed to do—pick up a corsage in the gift shop?

I agonized more than you would think possible over which of my four shirts to wear, even half-considered calling my brother and asking for something from his closet. I settled for a careful shave and the rare combing of my unruly hair. Detox seemed to be thinning my hairline.

Abenaki actually has a ballroom—I suppose it needs one considering most of its clientele. There was a decent band, and white-clothed tables crammed with fancy hors d'oeuvres. I noticed quite a few people dressed up, and felt further mortified by my jeans and sneakers. The canapés were an enjoyable distraction.

The people in the room were divided—not into boys and girls, but into similarly uncomfortable throngs of junkies and lunatics. A select few without inhibitions were dancing in the center. I looked for Alba and pretended not to see Max, who was gesturing for me to join her on the dance floor.

I spotted Alba in the opposite corner, talking to a handsome, twenty-something attendant with dreadlocks. I started over and saw her smile at him. Was she flirting? I smoothed the pill-riddled flannel of my shirtfront. Alba was wearing a miniskirt above clunky black motorcycle boots. Her legs looked long and luscious in black tights. I put my hands in my pockets—a gesture that was surely familiar to her by now.

Hey, she said as I approached, gracing me with a rare, uncynical smile. This is Larry, she added, gesturing to her companion.

Duty calls, he said before Alba could introduce me. There was some sort of altercation brewing at the punch table.

You look wonderful, I said when he'd left. I'm sure I was grinning like an idiot.

Thank you, she said sullenly. Not a compliment taker, my Alba.

We stood for a moment and watched the crowd. The band was playing swing, and I saw a tuxedoed Charles twirling Marta on the dance floor. She was surprisingly graceful. There were a few other patients I didn't know, and Max had found a greasy-faced young addict to gyrate with.

Do you want to dance? I said.

God, no, Alba said. Do you?

Not really, I said, feeling foolish. I think joining in gives you Privilege points, though.

I have a better idea, Alba said. I raised my eyebrows. Let's get out of here, she said, grinning.

Don't tell me there's a bar, I said.

Alba rolled her eyes and gestured for me to follow her. We walked by Larry, who was offering a sobbing patient a paper cup of punch. We'll be in the kitchen, Alba called out to him. He gave her a distracted thumbs-up.

She took my hand, which was enough of a thrill that I almost stumbled. She led me through swinging doors, where a number of recognizable cafeteria employees were arranging food on silver trays. One woman, in a chef's cap and apron, looked up and winked at Alba. Still gripping my hand, Alba marched us along the linoleum, turning twice in a maze of stainless steel counters and dangling cookware. We reached a back door where Alba quickly punched digits into the security pad.

Who are you, James Bond? I whispered.

Theresa used to be my dad's cook, Alba said. She closed the heavy door gently behind us. I hadn't been outside after dark in weeks—the smell of Maine woods at night assaulted my senses, stirring up not-so-sober memories.

Let's go for a walk, she said. We can't be gone long.

I hesitated, imagining getting caught and restricted to ward again, but one more look at Alba's little skirt was enough to get me moving.

Away from the hospital, the landscape was dark, feeble starlight shining from a moonless sky. We walked downhill, past the admissions cottage, through a grove of birch trees, crossing a small stream on slick, menacing rocks. Finally, we came upon a clearing with eight log cabins, four on each side, and a courtyard in between.

I've seen these from my window, I said. There was a fountain in the center of the courtyard, the water still and filmed over with green algae. Gravel paths overgrown with flowering weeds led diagonally outward. What is this place? I asked.

Patients used to live here, Alba said. Twenty-five women to each cabin, with private rooms for the watch nurses. There used to be more of them, and another courtyard, but they burned down in the forties. She paused, looking concerned.

What? I said.

Nothing, she replied. I just remembered something I read about, that's all. Want to go inside?

They're probably locked, I said. I was feeling nervous all of a sudden.

Not all of them, she said, taking my hand again. She pulled me toward the far cabin on the left.

This is the one they refurbished for the movie with Meryl Streep, she said. A horseshoe lock hung open on its hinge. Alba slid it out and pushed open the door, which looked like new wood, purposely antiqued.

Inside it was pitch-dark and it took my eyes a moment to adjust. The room was filled with single beds, a chest for belongings at each footboard. A long table with mismatched chairs stretched in front of a large stone fireplace. Here and there throughout the room were reinforcement pillars that appeared to be entire tree trunks, stripped of their bark and refinished. I imagined settling in front of the fireplace with a joint. If I could get drugs, this would be the perfect place to hide them.

Alba was watching me look around. My pulse began to beat hard and loud in my ears. She moved away, stretching my arm then letting my hand fall, and leaned against one of the tree trunks, inviting me. I swallowed hard, stepping toward her, stopping a safe distance away. I tried to concentrate on her face, tried to smile, but my cheeks felt paralyzed. I wanted a shot of tequila, maybe two. Alba looked straight at my mouth, more confident than I'd ever seen her. I hesitated, looking around, and when I looked back, her eyes were uncertain. What was I waiting for? I took another step toward her and paused.

Should I? I said, glancing at her mouth.

I'm practically begging you to, she smiled.

Her whole body seemed to release as I kissed her, relaxing into me with the same soft abandon as her mouth. It was the way she'd reacted at the fair, after initial awkward reluctance, and I remembered how it had thrilled me. Now, though, the same surrender was scaring me. I tried to relax, kissing her deeper. She dragged her hands down from my shoulders, pressing my shirtfront, then grabbed onto my hips and pulled me closer. I felt her soft belly and the hardness of her pubic bone against my halfhearted erection. This was exactly what I wanted, but all I could think about was what a liar I was. If she knew me, heard the thoughts that went through my mind, knew that I was never completely focused on her, the idea of drugs always lurking in the foreground, she would not want me like this.

I put my hands to her face, broke our openmouthed kiss, changing it to a few light kisses on her cheeks and mouth.

Hey, I said gently, but she heard the protest and stiffened.

What's wrong? she said.

Nothing, I said quickly, stepping back. I just . . . I fumbled.

Now she looked frightened.

After last time, I said, I thought we were going too fast.

Oh, she said flatly.

Hey, come on, I said, hating the sound of my voice. It's not as if I don't want to throw you down on one of these cots, I added.

Alba let out a cruel little laugh. Clearly she didn't believe me.

We should get back, she said, and walked swiftly out of the cabin. I followed, opening my mouth to say something else, then closing it again. It was too late now to pretend I was anything but a fool.

20

Saint Dymphna's Asylum

March, 1936

Dear Peter,

I hadn't intended to continue the story of my childhood in these letters. It was bringing up too many painful memories, and, for a while, explanation seemed pointless. But, given what is occurring now, I need to explain how it began.

My uncle undertook my education as a healer, although technically my mentor should have been another Medawlinno. At first it appeared as though my mother would not allow him. They fought about it for the three days I lay in bed recovering from my fit. Seizures often left me weak and slow-witted, as though I had a fever or had just arisen from a powerful dream.

Though it was by no means a pleasant feeling, it often seemed like one in comparison to the anxiety that gripped my neck with increasing severity before my episodes. The recovery was almost peaceful; I seemed to care about absolutely nothing while going through it. I was devoid of all emotion or ambition and it did not occur to me to be frightened by the relief this brought.

The fight between Mother and Uncle was not conducive to relaxation. There was a quality to their arguments that both fascinated and worried me. They seemed to have no boundaries, no limit to how low they would sink in insulting one another. My mother was never what you would consider a subservient woman, but when fighting with my father she seemed willing to concede certain issues for the sake of others. She fought cleverly with my father and me. So cleverly she often made us feel foolish. With my uncle she was not clever; she lost her wits. She threw things, screamed and sobbed, called him names I'd never learned in her language but I could tell were rude by my uncle's flushed face. His behavior was similarly childish—once I actually saw him pull her hair. This led to her attacking him with her fingernails, which my uncle quickly deflected by sitting on top of her, laughing as she thrashed and swore beneath him. They reminded me of boys I'd seen in town, mashing each other's faces into road dust.

"Why do they fight like children?" I had asked my father, during my uncle's last visit.

"Because they were children together, I suppose," my father said. He swung his axe with strength and grace, splitting the firewood as cleanly as if it were made of wax. We were avoiding the house, though we could still hear the breaking of crockery.

"But they're grown-ups now," I insisted.

My father smiled. "Families are strange, little one," he said.

"You'll understand when you're a woman, and your mother and I still drive you to temper tantrums over Christmas."

He flinched at another shattering noise. "That sounded like something valuable," he said, but he calmly resumed chopping wood.

The fight they had after my seizure was the worst I could remember. The context I could gather with my fuzzy, bedridden mind was this: my uncle thought I was gifted. Not sick, not disturbed, but magically, traditionally gifted. In a line of reasoning I could not follow, my illness made me qualified to cure others. My mother, oddly enough, didn't disagree with his diagnosis. But she refused to encourage it.

"She could die from the training," my mother said to him. "How can you ask me to allow it?"

"She will die without the training," my uncle said. "Quickly or slowly, but certainly in misery. If we were at home you would never consider denying her calling. It is this life you have chosen—no connections, no loyalties—that has left you so foolish and self-centered."

"Who are you to criticize my life? You who travel with no consideration beyond your member and where you'll park it next?"

I wanted to ask who this member was, but they fell into a wrestling match. In strength, my mother was no equal to my massive uncle, but she was more willing to hurt him than he was her—he would hold her down, pinch her occasionally—but he never hit or bit or scratched as she did.

Periodically, in between their battles, my uncle would interview me. How long had I been ill, how did it start, did I dream much and where did I go in my dreams? Had I ever had the urge to hurt myself with cutting or burning? This last answer was a secret I had kept even from my parents: the fact that I had been slicing carefully and precisely with a paring knife, leaving a history of my illness in a horizontal pattern on my thigh. My mother looked as if she might slap me when I revealed this—but my uncle was encouraged.

For three days they screamed the same slanderous things, while my father hid outside with his chores or sat quietly at the kitchen table mending the latest object my mother had smashed in anger. They might have continued on this way for weeks, had my father not finally decided to interrupt them. This was a shock to us all; my father never interfered in their arguments, whether because he thought he would be ineffectual or because he feared their wrath turned on him, I'm not sure. But in the middle of a screaming dialogue about my "destiny," he broke through with one quiet but fiercely spoken sentence.

"No one has asked the little one," he said. This silenced them both. He paused to make sure they were listening, and looked at me.

"She is thirteen years old. Neither of you has asked her what she wants her life to be."

My uncle looked embarrassed, my mother annoyed. They both turned to face me. "Mesatawe?" my father prompted and for a moment I could not imagine what my answer would be. It seemed to me that no matter what I decided, my life would never be as it once was. I'd been secretly hoping I could go backward all this time.

"I don't want to be ill anymore," I said finally.

"If you work hard at the training, you will conquer the illness," my uncle said. "You will turn it into something else."

"But you will be an outcast," my mother said. "There are few left who will respect you—most of the world will think you dangerous or unworthy."

I thought about this while they watched me.

"Mother," I said at last, "who would think me worthy as I am now?" She knew I was right. I could tell by her silence.

"All right," she said quietly, and I wanted to take it back when I saw the weariness in her broad shoulders. She looked at my uncle with resentful resignation. "She's my child," she said, and my uncle nodded. Then she left me there, with two exhausted men, neither of whom looked particularly victorious.

When my mother determined I was well enough—when I'd become restless and was again brushing imagined pressure away from the hollow of my neck—my uncle took me into the woods.

We hiked for the entire day toward the mountains, the snow so deep in places that we needed snowshoes. Before dusk, long after I had decided I could not walk another step, my uncle stopped by a waterfall. The drops splashing outward froze to ice chips in mid-air that exploded with sharp noises against the rocks.

I sat down by the stream, removing my gloves to cup water in my hands and drink. It was so cold my fingers ached, and I dried them quickly and covered them again to avoid frostbite. My uncle gestured me toward the cliffside, and I was right upon it before I saw the sliver of a cave entrance. I had to turn sideways and duck to get inside; my uncle had to crawl.

The cave was larger and warmer than I would have expected. There was a center space with a high ceiling and a shallow dip in the rock floor, and four small openings that led to cozy chambers. I could see my uncle had been here before; a round hearth of stones had been constructed under an opening in the ceiling that did not look big enough to serve as a chimney. I recognized blankets and warm clothing from our cabin, heaped against the wall, alongside a store of vegetables and grain, a kerosene lamp, a shovel, various utensils including a large knife, and what looked like our first-aid kit. There were sleeping pallets already made up of skins and wool in two of the rear chambers, and I looked at them with longing.

"First you must eat," my uncle said, beginning a fire with the kindling that was stacked neatly beside a store of wood and an inexplicable collection of smooth stones. "Then you may sleep. Do both with enthusiasm, for tomorrow you begin your fast; you will not eat or rest for seven days."

Already, I wanted to go home.

My uncle went outside for a while and came back with two rabbits. He roasted them in the fire along with potatoes. I ate little because I was not hungry; my stomach was heavy with the thought of what was before me. After supper, my uncle lit his pipe and took a drink from the crock supplied by my father. He offered me a small cup, which I swallowed, coughing at the flame in my throat. Once in me, the drink was soothing, like a hand stroking my tension from the inside. I took a second sip.

My uncle sang some of the silly songs I had enjoyed as a child—I believe he was trying to put me at ease. When my eyelids were heavy with smoke and exhaustion, I asked if I could go to bed.

"Hear me a moment," he said as I started to unfold my legs and rise. My nerves snapped awake at his tone.

"Tradition demands that you do this alone," he said, relighting his pipe. "My compromise to your mother was that I would stay with you. I will be here as a guide, but you must do it alone nonetheless. Do you understand?"

"I think so."

"You have a gift, but it is useless by itself. It is your will that can bring you magic; if you have no courage or conviction, if you do not work, you will be nothing. From now on, I do not want to hear from you: 'I can't.' When I ask you to do something impossible, you must say: 'I will try.' "

"Yes, Uncle," I said. Though, in truth, the forbidden words were already insistent in my head.

When I woke the next morning, I knew it was early before I opened my eyes. I was often the first one up at home, as I am here. There is a time, just before dawn, that is both the most peaceful and the most invigorating time of the day. Before anything happens, when everything you hope for is still cradled in possibility.

I was surprised and disappointed to see my uncle already up. I remembered what this day was beginning, and was instantly tired enough to go back to sleep. But my uncle noticed me watching him and gestured for my help.

He was gathering water from the stream with a bucket and pouring it into the shallow pool of stone in the center of the cave. I put on my boots and jacket and took up the second bucket, and we worked until he determined the water was deep enough.

My uncle stoked the fire and gestured for me to wait. I sat by the pool's edge and thought about butter melting into warm bread. He added wood until the fire was hotter than would be needed for cooking. I took off my coat, then my cardigan. I began to wonder what harm there was in breakfast before a week-long fast. Perhaps, when my uncle left again, I could filch an apple or some of my mother's wheat bread. When the fire was roaring, my uncle began to drop large smooth stones into the blue center of the flames. In time the stones glowed red, and he removed them with a shovel and dropped them hissing into the pool at my feet. Steam rose rapidly in columns from every stone, then mingled

thickly until my face began to sweat. My breathing became
shallow because the air was too wet to draw deep into my lungs.
When the cave was suitably unbearable, my uncle sat down
opposite me. With no introduction, he closed his eyes and began
to chant. I couldn't catch all the words—his singing was so fast it
sounded desperate—but what I could understand made little
sense. He seemed to be praying, but to various elements—gods,
people, animals, the dawn—until I began to think he would
address the entire world piece by piece and it would take the
whole seven days. But then he began to sing about me, asking for
guidance, calling me a magician, saying that I would be the
leader, the one to restore communities torn asunder by the illness
of the world. I wanted him to stop singing, speak English, explain
exactly what it was he expected me to do.

He had mentioned my destiny as a leader before. This
seemed improbable, as I was not even very adept at conversing
with strangers. His praise made me want to go home and crawl
into my bed and stay there for the next fifty years.

My uncle got up to heat more stones and transfer them to the
pool. That was when something odd happened. As I watched him
through the haze as he swung the shovel from fire to pool back to
fire again, he changed. He seemed to shrink to about half his size.
At first I thought it was a trick of the steam. But then I saw that he
was younger, his face gentle and almost girlish, his clothing
different and too large for him, and he was not transferring stones
with his shovel, but dirt. And he was crying, tears running one
after the other along two slick paths down his cheeks.

The image was gone as suddenly as it had appeared, and he
was my uncle again, and I felt nauseous and a bit frightened. I
wondered if he was casting some spell on my mind. I'd never
seen such things while awake before.

I'm not sure how long the singing and steam went on, but by the time it was finished, I was weak and thirsty and on the verge of tears. My uncle stopped stoking the fire and let the air clear, then brought me a mug of stream water, urging me to drink it slowly. The sweat had left my clothing damp and I began to grow chilled and not a little bit resentful. If I'm miserable now, I thought, how will I feel in a week?

"Discouraged already?" my uncle said, and only then did I realize how loudly I must have sighed.

"How can I promise to try if you won't tell me what I'm trying at?" I snapped. My uncle smiled.

"That's more like it," he said, and he left the cave. He was gone so long I considered napping just to spite him, but I was too hungry and furious to sleep.

"What did you see?" my uncle said when he returned. We were sitting facing one another across the fire.

"What?" I said. I was hardly listening, doubt was so loud in my mind.

"During the steam." My uncle was impatient. "What vision did you have?"

"I had no vision," I said. I watched his eyebrows furrow then drop. I could have lied my way out of it. I could have pretended to be nothing but a sickly girl with bad dreams. That was my chance to go home a failure and never have to try at anything again.

But at the time I was not yet a proficient liar. I was still too curious to see what the truth would reveal. Also, I was vain. I had very quickly latched on to this idea that I was special, and I wasn't ready to let it go.

"You were altered," I said, and the eagerness in my uncle's

expression was my reward. "You were a boy, and you were shoveling dirt. Burying something."

"Yes," my uncle sighed. "Yes. I was your age, just thirteen, and I was burying my father." I waited for the rest. He tossed wood on the fire, though it was still too warm in the cave. He watched the volcano of sparks as if it would tell the rest of the story.

"Your grandfather was a great man," he said finally. "He was a leader, a medicine man who was known throughout the Eastern Tribes. By all rights, he should have been your teacher. Even the white man brought their sick to my father. But he could not cure everything. He died in the epidemic that slaughtered three-quarters of our village. It was brought in by a white woman he had agreed to help. It is said there was a time, hundreds of years ago, that such diseases did not exist in this land. They were brought here by the Europeans, like guns. They were too quick, too unfamiliar, their source unreachable, and our medicine men could not cure them. It killed my mother as well, and three of my siblings. Only your mother and I were left.

"I wanted to train to follow in my father's path. But I had no signs of the gift, and there was no one to teach me if I had. Your mother and I were moved to a reservation up north by the border, a charity village run by Jesuits. They were kind enough, some even spoke our language, but we were expected to leave behind our traditions and adopt theirs. Your mother was more willing to do this than I—at least, she made up new traditions for herself that rejected all she had been taught. I left soon after she married your father. I have not had a home since.

"You had this vision of me for a reason. Your gift allows you access to the source of people's pain. When someone is ill, a healer determines whether the illness is a reaction to the physical world, in which case he prescribes herbs and medicines, or a deeper contagion lodged in the spirit. Soul-sickness is said to occur when a part of a person's soul breaks away and becomes lost in the spirit world. It is the healer's job to find what is lost, if he can, and return it to its owner, healing the fissure of the spirit and making the ill person whole again."

He paused, waiting for my reaction. All of this sounded suspiciously like the sort of talk my mother refused to have in her house. Dogma, she called it. Religious delusion.

"Do you understand?" my uncle said.

"Yes," I said automatically, then started out of my thoughts. "No. How am I supposed to find people's souls?"

"You already have the gift to do so. You must learn to make it an ability."

"But how, Uncle? I don't understand."

"Yes you do," he said. "You'll find them in your dreams. When your soul leaves your body and travels in the spirit world."

"I thought the soul left the body only in death," I said.

"Yes," my uncle said. "But then it does not return. You must learn to journey into death and come back again."

"And you know that I can do such a thing?" I said.

"I *believe* you can," he said. "The knowing is up to you."

My uncle left me alone for an hour. There was a part of me, the part that still belonged to my parents, that thought my uncle was mad. I'd been raised to believe only in what I could see, touch and taste. Religion, my parents thought, was an ignorant escape from the reality of the world. Focus on an afterlife made you neglect the only life you had. My mother liked stories of magic—

her own and those of my father's world—but she didn't believe in them. Or so I had thought.

Why, then, had they let me come here? If they did not believe in life after death, why had they allowed me to be trained to travel in the spirit world? Was this some sort of test on their part, to see if I had the intelligence to reject my uncle? Or did they know, as it seemed so with the droop of their shoulders when I was leaving, that my uncle was right? That a world they had kept so vigilantly at bay was now claiming me for its own?

There was a story my mother had sung to me as a child. It was about Glooskap, the maker of the world, who had left it behind in frustration. Sometimes, Indians of special powers could see the path he'd left for them to follow. It was blazoned on the trees, a mark in the old way to tell travelers they were nearing a village. On the quest for Glooskap, the marks disappeared as soon as they were passed. The traveler had no way of backtracking or even making sure he was still headed in the right direction. He had to wait in hope for the next sign.

It was with the memory of this fable that I understood what was before me. There was no one I could depend upon to help me decide. I had to do it myself. I had to know, as my uncle had said, that I could travel where others couldn't. I had to believe in this magic, even if, in the end, I turned out to be wrong.

21

Impulse Control

ALBA READS THE REST of the letters—all the way through to the last one dated August 1942—during one sleepless night in her room. She'd been saving them before—one book's worth for every trip to the library—because they were something to look forward to. The days are long at Abenaki, and even the thought of beginning her new book tightens her throat, so she needs distractions to suck up the time. The two things she looks forward to lately are the letters and her meetings with Oscar. Though most encounters with Oscar don't turn out the way she would like them to.

When she brought Oscar to the cabins, she remembered Dr. Stockwell's book about the history of Abenaki. She turns her room upside down looking for the volume. She flips to the section of case studies she'd merely skimmed before and finds it: ten pages devoted to Mary X, committed to the hospital from 1933 to 1942.

Once she reads this, she can't parcel out the letters anymore. She doesn't even care that the night staff will tell Dr. Miller that she didn't sleep—usually indicative of the onset of mania. She is not manic, she just needs to know what happened. Even before she finishes, she has an idea. An idea that, if she shared it with Dr. Miller or her father, would certainly result in a new dose of pills.

In the morning she photocopies all of Mary's letters in the library, as well as Dr. Stockwell's case notes. She makes three sets—one for herself, one for Oscar, the last one to save for later. She arranges them carefully, making sure the corners don't crease, in her knapsack. The satisfied feeling she has is similar to printing out the first full draft of a book. Even better, she thinks; I didn't have to write it. She has to hurry to be on the lawn by eleven.

Oscar is already waiting for her when she gets there. She hasn't seen him since the dance; Dr. Miller ordered her ward-bound for three days after noticing how jittery she was. Seeing him there, leaning against their tree, his hands busy picking at leaves on low branches, sends a jolt straight down her torso and back up again. When he spots her and smiles, she tries to keep her grin from growing as large as it wants to. She concentrates on walking, lurching forward on legs that prickle as if they've been asleep.

Hi, Oscar says as she approaches, and he starts toward her, lifting his arms as if in preparation for an embrace, but then he stops short, remembering the ever-watchful attendants. He smiles sheepishly, digging his hands in his pockets. Alba glances over in time to see the handoff—Larry muttering into his walkie-talkie that she has arrived from the library. She salutes him. He waves back, giving her his usual thumbs-up sign that would accompany, if he were within whispering distance, a *Looking good, girl.*

Alba is suddenly embarrassed by her appearance. She's wearing a skirt again and a little bit of makeup. She hopes Oscar doesn't notice. Or rather, she hopes he notices, but in a vague way that doesn't include an understanding that she has primped for him.

They settle themselves into the lawn chairs, both of which the attendants now know to leave there. Oscar makes a joke about their audience; she laughs, barely listening. She is reeling—so hypersensitive to his presence that every expression, every shift of limbs, seems to carry a clear message. She is still confused about his behavior. On Friday night she felt rejected, but now he is glancing at her mouth as if he wants to kiss her, as if he is remembering kissing her, and, like her, he can hardly stand it until they are alone. When he waves at a group of drug addicts making their way down to the lake, she thinks: *He's humiliated to be seen with me. He's sitting there trying to think of a way to let me down easy.* Then he plucks a violet from the lawn and balances it on her kneecap, and she realizes again that the mutuality of their attraction is undeniable. She is getting a headache from the rapid-fire changing of her mind.

Are you going to the movie tonight? Oscar asks.

I think so, she says.

We're in the eighth grade again, Oscar says.

She smiles vaguely. She knows what he means, but only second-hand. Nothing like this ever happened to her in the eighth grade. Her history with men is short and, for the most part, uncomfortable to look back upon. She prefers to pretend that most of it never happened; though she's had boyfriends she is likely to say she's never had a real one. Like her mood swings, she can't look back on her relationships without regret, so she is always starting over.

Alba, listen, Oscar says. She is careening between the thrill of his voice speaking her name and the thudding dread evoked by his tone.

Yes? she drawls, trying to sound unconcerned. She resists the urge to brush at her throat. She doesn't want to have to cut their meeting short for a trip to the nurse's station for more Klonopin.

About the other night, Oscar says.

Or maybe, she thinks, leaving for the nurses' station is a good idea.

I'm sorry, he says.

Don't worry about it, Alba says. She pulls at the collar of her shirt.

It's not that I don't think about it, he says, massaging his shoulder. He does this, she's noticed, when he's nervous. I just meant we should slow things down, he says. Get to know each other better.

Men always want to be friends with Alba once they realize that crazy is not as glamorous as they had imagined.

Sure, she says coldly. We could bridge the communication gap between junkies and lunatics. Start a pen pal club.

Hey, Oscar says. She won't look at him. *Hey!* He reaches over and takes her hand, pressing it. She is reminded of how soft his palms were on her face. She looks up and his eyes are so focused on her she can barely hold his gaze.

Don't do that, he says. I'm just trying not to fuck it up.

She has never known anyone, besides maybe Dr. Miller who doesn't count, who speaks with such candor. She imagines that this is what happens to people when they fall in love; they become addicted to a certain quality—a frank, open gaze, earnest confessions—and later, when they are alone again, they spend all their time trying to find it in someone else.

I brought you something, she says.

I hope it's the key to a motel room, Oscar smiles.

She is about to laugh when she sees her father walking toward them.

Hello, sweetheart, her father says. He's holding flowers. He must have heard about her panic attacks—she had two more over the weekend that she hasn't told Oscar about.

Oscar has already dropped her hand and is standing up to introduce himself. They shake hands, her father looking bothered at having to shift the flowers, and she wants to close her eyes. She doesn't want to see them side by side like this—her father pompous and overprotective in his three-thousand-dollar suit, and Oscar threadbare and pale, trying to look unimpressed. She rarely brings men home to meet her father—she can't bear the comparison. When put together, neither one of them—her father or the man—quite measures up.

Jameson, her father is saying. That's Scottish?

Irish. Like the whiskey, Oscar says. Alba's father chuckles horribly.

Dad, Alba sighs, what are you doing here? She knows she should stand up next to Oscar, take the brunt of her father's gaze, but she thinks her legs might buckle if she moves them. They're feeling sleepy again. It occurs to her that this is due to her medication rather than a side effect of lust.

I'm going to London tomorrow, remember? her father says, sighing. As if he's not surprised that she couldn't hold that small fact in her fragile brain.

I'll be gone through the weekend, he adds. Then he squints. Are you wearing makeup?

Now is the time, she thinks, for Oscar to go away.

I'll leave you two alone, Oscar says. See you later, he adds to Alba and she tries to smile apologetically.

Good luck, her father says as Oscar walks away. *Good luck?* she thinks.

Her father sits down and watches with his usual disdain as she lights a cigarette. He has always blamed this habit on her mother, who smoked incessantly, even while pregnant.

Alba, he sighs, looking at the violet balanced on her bare knee. Is this something I need to worry about?

Only if you have nothing better to do, Alba says.

The theater at Abenaki—a commercial-sized wide screen with stadium seating—was donated by a movie star who rehabilitated from a coke habit in the late eighties. Most of the movies shown are harmless romantic comedies, both new releases and classics. No dark themes, suicide, murder, or mid-life crises are allowed. Alba has a theory that such cheery, unrealistic movies make the patients even more depressed—too many of them and you start thinking the lanky, stunning, widely smiling actresses are normal, and that you will never, no matter what drugs you take or refuse, be mistaken for one of them.

Alba finds Oscar alone in the back row, a box of peanut M&M's already empty in his armrest cup holder. The previews have started, and the colors from the screen play off his face; he is brilliantly lit one instant, angled with dark blue shadows the next.

After Alba's father left, she had watched through the glass doors as he approached Oscar in the lounge. He'd put his hand on Oscar's shoulder and said something. Now she asks Oscar what it was.

What do you think? Oscar says.

Stay away from my daughter? Alba says.

Something like that, Oscar grins.

I'm sorry.

Why? You didn't say it.

Shhh! someone hisses from a few rows down. The movie's starting.

It's *Bridget Jones's Diary*, a movie Alba has seen before. They settle in to watch for a while. Alba begins to imagine that Oscar looks a bit like Colin Firth.

There's way too much drinking in this movie, Oscar says after a while.

I'm surprised it made it past the censors, Alba whispers.

Shhh! they hear again.

Do you want to go someplace else? Alba says.

Another escape route?

Not exactly. Follow me.

They thread their way down the row and walk up the aisle to the swinging doors. Outside, four attendants are laughing, but stop as soon as Alba pushes through the door. This means, she knows, that they were talking about a patient.

We're going to smoke, Alba says.

Stay where we can see you, one of them mutters, waving them along. He already checked her knapsack on the way in.

Alba leads Oscar across the lobby and outside to a small patio that has four sand-filled ashtrays and two benches pockmarked with cigarette burns. There are also two empty barrel planters filled with butts; the gardeners have given up hope that anything will grow in the blue-tinged air.

They sit on the bench so their backs are facing the window, and Alba lights a cigarette.

I'm leaving tomorrow, Alba says. She's a little thrilled at the disappointment that blooms across his face.

Already? he says. I didn't think they'd want you to go so soon after what happened.

They don't want me to go, I'm just going.

Breaking out? Oscar mocks.

It's not as hard as you think, Alba says. He's just beginning to realize that she's serious.

They'll call your father, he says.

My father will be on a plane to London tomorrow night, Alba

says. It will take him a couple of days to cancel everything and get back. That's all I need.

For what? Oscar says. Where are you going?

I'm going to find someone, she says. To deliver letters.

Ever hear of the post office? he says.

Alba explains the library books as quickly as she can. She gives Oscar one of the photocopies; he skims through the first few pages with a skeptical look on his face.

You want to give these to her son? he asks.

She nods. She hopes he will believe her; she's not ready to tell him why she's really going. For a moment he just stares at her. He is smiling, but with concern.

Are you crazy? he says finally.

Actually, yes, Alba says, smiling back at him. Even now, he is looking at her mouth like he wants to devour it.

Thank you, she says, for finally noticing.

22

Saint Dymphna's Asylum

August, 1936

Dear Peter,

I have been neglecting the present. Despite various humiliating "therapies," and daily appointments with Dr. Madden, I have continued to have the fits. What the doctor and nuns think is a sickness is actually making me stronger. It is making me real again. I pretended to be someone else for so long, I had begun to wonder if I'd ever truly existed.

A new inmate arrived about a month ago—a woman named Josephine Brennan. Unlike most of the new admissions—women who seem angry, confused or frightened, but still in possession of themselves— Josephine was far gone. She was plagued by various twitches, could not bear to be touched by anyone, though the nuns manhandled her anyway, and, once settled, emitted a constant, high-toned wail. This cry of hers was powerful and unsettling—it sounded so much like the secret sorrow of every woman here that we were all affected by it. There were a number of setbacks: Mira reverted to losing her temper at the puzzles, Mrs. Winnow was criticizing people to tears, Gabby began pulling at her hair again, ruining the portion of her scalp that had grown back so nicely. The women began to resent Josephine; she was reminding them that their hearts were broken.

Josephine is young; I know from the staff she just turned twenty-three, but she has the face of a middle-aged woman. Her arms are bandaged from wrist to elbow; I saw why when a nurse changed the dressing. She'd cut herself—deep, straight, brave lines, now raised into lumps of gathered skin and stitches. I have seen a lot of wrist scars since coming here, and Josephine's are the serious ones—wounds meant to kill rather than maim or serve as a distracting pain. Her scars are so determined looking, it makes me think her keening comes from the sorrow that she did not succeed.

There was a time when I knew I was meant to cure someone the first moment I laid eyes on them. It was as if I could see inside them, like an X ray of bones, and recognize the gash in their soul. This time took longer. One morning while we were all squirming to her keening in the dayroom, I had one of my seizures. And I dreamt about Josephine.

She was in love. Newly married, living in a small but cheerful apartment; she filled her days with brisk walking of her thin red dog, much reading, and joyful housekeeping. Each afternoon she bathed, washed her long auburn hair, and put on a clean dress, which she covered with an apron while she prepared the evening meal. By five o'clock, she was flushed with kitchen heat and checking out the front bay window every few minutes. By five-fifteen, her husband was usually in sight—a tall, thin man with large ears and a smile that made him handsome. He would hurry down the street, practically trotting, his tie loosened, cowlick jutting out from his hairline, a look of expectation making the other lumbering husbands feel cheated. He'd take the stairs three at a time; Josephine would remove her apron and run to open the door, and they'd crash into each other's arms. There would be a few moments of sighing and laughter, a battle between the choices of hugging still and tight, or kissing while pressed into the doorjamb. Occasionally the husband's arm would escape long enough to greet the dog dancing in joy beside them. Then their breathing would deepen, the door would be closed and locked, and dinner, still warming in the oven, would be forgotten until after eight, when they would eat in their dressing gowns, savoring food more seasoned with each other than any of Josephine's careful marinades.

When winter came and she was pregnant, they added new rituals. Her husband would kiss her first—a long, slow, focused kiss, then he would lean down and press his mouth to her rounded belly. She would cup her hands to warm his ears, blotched purple from the cold and a hat that didn't fit properly. They would have dinner, chatting and laughing quickly, then go to bed early and make slow love that often left one or both of them in tears. Josephine, who was too happy to sleep well, would practice her knitting into the night, pausing her needles periodically to touch the cheek of her husband snoring softly beside her.

Then it was spring again, Josephine was large and uncomfortable, and they were both nervous, stopping everything at each twinge of her belly. Her contractions began one morning during breakfast, and they took a taxi to the hospital, smiling through their fear. Josephine's mind blurred with a pain that had no release, and eventually she was put to sleep, too exhausted to question her husband's worried whispering with the doctor.

When she woke up and looked at her husband's eyes, dry and full of panic, she knew their baby was dead.

"Where is it?" she said, pushing him away as he tried to take her hand. "Where's my baby?"

The baby, a boy, had been born with the cord wrapped twice around his neck. They couldn't save him.

"I want to see him," she said, but they wouldn't allow it. It was not advisable, the doctor told her husband, to let the mother hold a stillborn baby. If she never saw it, the grieving would be faster, easier, the next pregnancy less fearful.

Every day in the hospital, Josephine asked for her baby boy. Her husband was torn between his wife's need and the trust he had in doctors. He had seen the choked baby himself and the image haunted him. He was having nightmares about finding Josephine just as blue and battered, that same look of effort frozen into her dead face. He could not bear the thought of her seeing it too.

They postponed the funeral until Josephine was well enough to attend. At the wake, in front of fifty embarrassed men and empathetic women, Josephine tried to pry open the doll-sized casket that housed her child. The lid was sealed already, the undertaker also of the opinion that no one should see such a small death, and Josephine scratched at the seam until her fingers bled. It took her husband and his three brothers to pull her away and hold her down, thrashing and screaming, on the soft, somber rug of the funeral home's floor.

Her husband took leave from his job to tend to her. She barely ate, slept fitfully all night and most of the day, often getting up to search for the mislaid baby. When her husband managed to convince her she'd been dreaming, it was like the baby's death all over again, and she screamed until the doctor came with a shot to make her sleep. After a few weeks, when she still looked awful but seemed calmer—she was back to housekeeping and walking the dog who had not left her side, keeping guard by the bed—her husband went back to work. He came home the first evening to the dog whimpering and cowering by the bathroom door, and found his wife unconscious in what looked like, given the dimensions of the puddle, every last drop of her own blood. The emergency room doctor convinced Josephine's husband to commit her for a rest in a hospital named after an Irish saint. He was too frightened by how close she'd come to leaving him to ask if there were any other options. When he went in to say good-bye, her eyes were cold and unrecognizable—the wife he knew was gone and a frightening husk of a woman was left in her place.

When I awoke from this dream, I was on the floor, a gag wedged between my teeth, the nuns leaning bruises into my arms. They rushed me off to the hydro room for an ice bath that was so painful I mercifully passed out for the majority of it. By the time I was brought back upstairs it was lights-out, and the whole dormitory had settled into fitful sleep. When I was sure that the nurses had left, I wriggled out from under the sheets they'd tied to my cot and padded barefoot across the cold tile to Josephine's bed.

She was awake, her gaze wide-eyed and darting around to the ceiling shadows, a wail droning softly in her throat.

"Josephine," I whispered, and when she didn't look at me, I raised my voice and shook her. "Josephine!"

She looked at me reluctantly.

"I can help you," I said, and she closed her eyes with weary impatience. "Josephine," I said angrily. I was not overly fond of this girl. To tell you the truth, Peter, her bliss before the tragedy had made me envious and her keening had gotten to me as well—I'd started to hear you and the girls crying inside it. But whether I liked her or not was irrelevant. The dream had told me what I must do.

"I can help you, Josephine," I said again. "I can bring you to your baby."

She opened her eyes again and focused on mine.

Arrangements needed to be made. A dreaming cure is not something that can be done quietly, and in dayrooms and dormitories there is no space for secrets. I needed a plan and assistance to carry it out.

I spoke first to Isabelle. From a prominent Massachusetts family, Isabelle has been at Saint Dymphna's for seven years. She was committed after a long history of promiscuous behavior culminated in a scandal at her sister's wedding. She is not a beautiful woman—years here have made her old before her time—but she is still sensuous and bold enough to keep the nurses aggravated. She alters the dowdy clothing she is given with rips and tucks that expose cleavage and thigh. She wears bright, garish makeup whenever she can; though the nuns confiscate it she always acquires lipstick or rouge from new admissions or the Mother's Day packages that others are too worn out to enjoy. The sisters are hardened enough to be cruel when necessary, but Isabelle's blatant sexuality—her language in the dayroom could make a comatose patient blush—often makes them nervous, especially the novices. Because of this she enjoys a certain freedom—the nuns leave her to herself most of the time to avoid the embarrassing questions she is liable to ask about their female cycles.

Most importantly, she has a relationship with the night guard. From midnight to five A.M., there are no nuns on the ward, only a boyish-looking middle-aged man named Thomas. The rumor is that Thomas studied for the priesthood but was never ordained due to an incident, the details of which are much debated. He is in love, or at least in lust, with Isabelle. Their nightly trysts can sometimes be overheard in the dormitory, where passionate exclamations and heavy breathing sound blasphemously out of place. Thomas is not the sharpest knife in the drawer, which proves how harmless the staff thinks we are in our medicated sleep. As he holds all the keys, I needed Isabelle's wiles to get outside the building.

Once I'd convinced her I had no intention of escape (she won't do anything that might get her lover fired), Isabelle arranged to have us let out onto the grounds after midnight. I needed someone to accompany us, to be in charge in case something went wrong when I was in the trance state. I chose Sandra, a small, wiry woman who chain-smoked and did daily calisthenics, because she seemed the most pragmatic. Sandra was committed after one of the many times her husband beat her and she fought back, this time with a cast-iron pan that crushed his skull. She was not interested in escaping—she thought jail would not be as comfortable as the hospital.

On a Friday night, when the heat of the day had barely broken and the women lay atop cot sheets sticky with perspiration, Thomas let Josephine, Sandra and me out the service entrance. "Be back before dawn," he said. He looked at me suspiciously. Isabelle was there, and she reassured him by pressing her breasts to his chest, grinding her hips as they kissed.

The night air was still and thick, the sky clouded over with the promise of a storm. It had been so long since I was allowed outdoors after dark, the odor of night left me stumbling with homesickness.

I led my charges across the lawn. We passed the barn, the lowing of cows the only alarm that we were loose. We took the path that ran parallel to the vegetable gardens past our old pavilion cabins, deserted now, and into the woods. When I felt we were far enough away not to be overheard at the hospital, we stopped in a small clearing circled by tall pine trees. I propped Josephine against one of the trunks and Sandra and I gathered wood for a fire. When the flames were high and strong, I laid out the blankets I'd brought from the dorm and had Josephine lie down on one while I covered her with another. After a moment of hesitation—Sandra had asked no questions but was watching me with curious attention—I removed my clothes. This was something I'd discovered early on in my healing education—I entered the dream state more easily when I was naked. In my first practices with my uncle, I would rip at my clothes while entering a trance, as if the material were keeping my soul hostage. At first this embarrassed me, but once I experienced how deeply I could delve into others, my own nudity seemed insignificant. Sandra raised her eyebrows at the sight of me naked and goose-pimpled, revealed in full by the glow of the fire, but she said nothing.

I knelt on the other blanket next to Josephine and began to chant, placing my hands on key spots along her body, searching for her entry point. Every person has a part of her body that is weaker than the others, the place that lets in pain and disease, and lets out pieces of a broken soul. I can often determine where this is by asking about physical symptoms. Frequent headaches, for instance, or chronic stomach pain. But Josephine had yet to speak a word since she'd arrived, so I had to search for her opening. I brushed my hands along her warm body until I felt a cold, hollow sensation emanating from her neck. I had found it. I had often seen Josephine's hands flutter at her throat as mine once did—my opening is in the same place.

I lay down next to her, one hand lightly beneath her chin, and I closed my eyes and let go. Though I had yet to initiate my own trances in the hospital—the involuntary seizures are a less powerful and less controlled form—it was surprisingly easy to fall back into.

I entered Josephine's dreams. The landscape was an amalgam of the places of her life—an enormous house with angled corridors, curved staircases and graceful rooms of wealth and taste—the houses of her memory pasted together into one large maze. There were people in every room, clustered in somber groups as though at a funeral reception. They spoke in low tones, turning their heads as I passed but saying nothing. I ignored them. Some could have pointed me in the right direction, but in my experience, most people I met at the entrance to the dream world were souls trapped between life and death, too bitter to help rescue another. I searched on my own.

I had to find the right staircase. There were dozens in the house but only one would lead down to the world of the dead. I'd already determined that what I was looking for was not caught in the in-between. I turned down halls, opened doors and descended stairs, finding myself in a schoolyard, a beach house, a pediatrician's office where a humorless doctor was holding young Josephine's arm still for a shot.

I kept moving on to the next staircase, descending level by level through the years of her life. Finally, I opened a door and saw the familiar stone steps, leading down an impossible distance, lighted by an invisible source. There was no banister, only what felt like limitless darkness on either side. The only sound was my bare feet slapping the worn stone. My breath, which had become labored with my swift search, was gone. I did not need to breathe in this place.

A woman was waiting for me at the bottom of the stairs. The baby was in her arms, still a newborn, tightly swaddled in a blue cotton blanket.

"They told me you were coming," the woman said. It was Josephine's mother.

"How are they?" I said, but she flashed me a look of disapproval—she knew I was not allowed to ask. She handed me the bundle quickly, with the confidence of a woman who has carried newborns all her life. I took him with the same confidence; you never forget how to hold a baby, even though you think you have just before each of your new ones is born.

"Hurry now," Josephine's mother said. "I'll wait here for you." I took one last fruitless glance beyond her, then turned back the way I'd come. I retraced my journey up stairways and along corridors, avoiding the entreaties of those I passed. Now that they saw my charge, they wanted to join me.

When I returned to the woods, the smell of night was dense after visiting that odorless world. I saw Sandra, leaning against a tree, smoking and tossing her butts in the fire, watching us sleep. My body lay still beside Josephine's; we could have been dead if not for the almost imperceptible rise and fall of our chests beneath the blankets. Josephine's spirit was sitting to the left of our prone bodies, translucent in the light of the fire. When she saw me a cry escaped from deep in her throat—a wail that was nothing like the keening I had heard for weeks. This cry had an end, a definition, a tenor of hope.

I placed the baby in her arms.

"Well, hello," she cooed in the way of mothers, recognizing the child they have felt only as a presence inside them. "Hello, my little one." The baby opened his eyes and looked at her with a clear, steady gaze. Josephine unbuttoned her nightdress and offered up a swollen nipple. The baby latched on greedily, and I heard the familiar slurps and cooing that once delighted me when you were a newborn.

"I'm sorry it took me so long," she whispered. I wandered off to give them time alone.

When the night underwent that subtle change—silence giving way to rustling—that indicates the approach of dawn, I went back to the fire that Sandra had kept blazing. Josephine was singing softly to her boy, rocking back and forth, a smile transforming her haggard face. She tried to pretend she didn't see me even when I stood right in front of her.

"I need to take him back now," I said. Her arms tightened.

"Please," she said, looking up at me. "Take me with him."

"I can't," I said. "You will go there soon enough." She began to cry, not the tearless wailing of before, but wet, wracking sobs.

"Your mother is with him," I said. She nodded. She kissed his forehead passionately and then, though she could not offer him up, she allowed me to lift him from her arms.

When I returned, Josephine's mother was waiting at the top of the stone stairs.

"We are grateful to you," she said, taking the baby back. Then she paused, pondering my eyes.

"I will tell your family you asked for them," she said.

"Thank you," I whispered. And I wound my way back up to the world.

When I awoke, cold and stiff from the root-laced ground, I could tell that we hadn't much time. I dressed hastily, waking Josephine with my voice. She emerged with difficulty from sleep, looking around in confusion.

"Where am I?" she said. Sandra arched her eyebrows, impressed at the emergence of Josephine's voice. I didn't have time to explain to either of them.

"We must get back," I said. Josephine stood up, unsteady on slippered feet.

"I had a dream," she said meekly, as if she wasn't sure we would listen to her.

"Yes," I said. "I know."

We reached the service entrance just as the first birds began to sing. Thomas ushered us inside with panic.

"Look sharp," he whispered. "The sisters are at the front door." We scrambled for the dorm. As I tied the cot covers around me, I heard the tread of the nuns' heavy-soled shoes, and the manly voice of Mother Superior.

"Quiet night, Thomas?"

"Slept like the dead, they did, Mother."

I closed my eyes, though I was too invigorated to sleep. I opened them moments later to find Josephine crouching over my cot.

"Get back to bed," I said. "They'll be doing morning checks soon." Josephine reached out as if to touch me, then withdrew her hand.

"Was it real?" she said.

I pointed to the front of her nightgown. It was soaked through with two large circles. She clutched her breasts as if they were the baby who had just fed from them.

"Why?" she said. "Why would you do that for me?"

"Because I am able to," I said. I turned away from her. I didn't want her to see the sudden flush of resentment blooming across my face. I had given her the thing I most wanted for myself.

I felt her hand shyly graze my shoulder. Then she went back to her own bed, as if she knew I could bear no more.

Josephine went home yesterday. Her stay was short for our ward; she has a husband who wants her back.

This morning, Sandra came up to me as I was pretending to sort the pieces of a puzzle depicting Maine blueberries.

"Who's next?" was all she said.

23

AWOL

ANYONE WHO KNOWS ME would have already guessed that I went with her. Some would think it stupid, others noble—it could have been either really, or even both. The fact is, I didn't take the time to impose intention on my actions. I just went. Selfish or altruistic; I couldn't bear to let her go alone.

And, anyone who thought it never crossed my mind that, once outside, I might get a chance to sneak a hit or at least a martini, doesn't know me very well. It crisscrossed my mind in a frenzy; there were moments when it was my sole reason for going.

I'd prefer to be relating the tale of a dangerous, black-and—white cinematic prison escape, complete with searchlights and bloodhounds and foul sewage tunnels, but I'm afraid the whole thing was fairly uninspiring. I did stuff my bedcovers with clothing and wait until the evening shift was in the conference room giving report to the night shift, when it was easy enough to sneak by the student nurse left on desk duty. After that I easy entered codes into the security keypads next to each door. (I had gotten the numbers from Max, who had seduced them out of her janitor.) I was both gleeful and appalled at how painless it was. I could have walked out weeks ago, I thought. My brother's money wasn't going far where security was concerned.

Of course, as Alba would rub in later, that was the point. I was self-committed; it was not the hospital's job to keep me there, just to help me if I chose to stay. Dennis would have said the only person I was deceiving was myself. This was such a depressing thought that I immediately brushed it away.

Alba was leaning casually against our tree, wearing her overalls under a burgundy leather jacket, and I was overwhelmingly tempted to press her into the bark and kiss her until it buckled her knees. Since our adventure would be seriously stilted if Alba had a panic attack on hospital grounds, I contained myself. As a result, I must have sounded less than enthusiastic when I greeted her, because she frowned at me.

You don't have to come, she said.

I want to, I said.

You don't look like you want to.

There's nothing more frustrating than having reined-in lust mistaken for indifference.

I want to, I said, and I reached out and slid one finger under the strap of her overalls. I pulled slightly for emphasis. I do.

For an instant I thought I'd gone too far—I felt rather than heard her breath catch, and she looked as though she were contemplating stepping closer to me. But I let go, and she swayed a little, got her balance and smiled.

Let's go then, she said.

We had to walk for what seemed like all night, but it was really just a few hours. Alba led me through the woods toward the river, which we crossed by way of a shoddy-looking but fairly stable beaver dam.

You've done this before, I said at one point. She shrugged.

Once.

Will they look for us?

Probably not, she said. They'll call your brother and my father. My father would call the police, if he were here. But even if your brother reports it, the police can't do anything.

Why not?

You're an adult, Oscar. You're responsible for yourself.

So are you.

Not exactly.

What does that mean?

Nothing, she snapped. It's complicated, and I'd rather not talk about it.

It suddenly occurred to me that I could get in trouble, not for leaving, but for leaving with Alba. If her father called the police on her, what was he likely to do to me? I refrained from asking. I thought I'd save further questioning for when she was in a better mood.

We got to town at about three A.M., and thumbed along the main road for about twenty minutes before the first car that passed picked us up. It was a road-sign-yellow Land Rover—a couple of rich college boys on their way home from Montreal. They were clearly more interested in Alba; they plied her with questions and pretty much ignored me. Alba was charming, which surprised me. I'd assumed that my role on the trip would be one of interpreter, protector in case one of Alba's panic attacks rendered her unable to speak. But here she was, laughing and flirting, while I stared dumbly at my own reflection in the window.

Mind if I smoke? Alba said after fifteen minutes. I'm sure they would have let her build a fire in there if she'd wanted to. The guy in the passenger seat—Chip or Chaz or something equally dim— turned around to light her cigarette with a monogrammed miniature blowtorch. He then reached into the glove compartment and took out a joint, lighting up with the same crisp blue flame. He exhaled, blowing excess paper and ashes away from the smoldering tip, then took another drag and held it. I could feel his anticipation deep in my own lungs; in about ten seconds, the smoke would be stroking his brain.

He turned around and offered the joint to Alba, wordlessly, as he was still holding his breath, his eyes bulging. Alba shook her head. I could feel her stiffen and he reluctantly offered it to me. My fingers clutched at the plush seat fabric, grabbing on for dear life.

No, thanks, I said, trying not to breathe through my nose, avoiding the delicious, cloying smell I knew was already filling the car. Maybe later, I gasped. I rolled down my window.

The kid shrugged and handed the joint to the driver. They passed it between them for an interminable three minutes, while I practiced breathing exercises, the ones I had ridiculed just days before when they were demonstrated by Mitch.

Breathe in deep, blow it all out. Breathe until the urge goes away.

The urge wasn't going away: breathing was making it worse— it was too much like inhaling. What calmed me down was repeating to myself: Maybe later, maybe later. *Maybe later, when we get to Portland and Alba isn't looking, I'll have another chance.*

Listen, Alba said, after her boys had dropped us off in Portland. Do you have any money?

Money? No. Well, ten bucks.

Shit, Alba said. I only have twenty.

Are you joking? I said. She looked disdainful, which was just enough to set me off.

How were you expecting to fund this adventure on twenty dollars? I snapped. I was already on edge from the car ride—they'd smoked another joint while Alba was napping, but I had turned it down, certain she'd wake up just as I put it to my mouth. Plus, it was embarrassing to admit that my bankcard, along with my cell phone, was still in the possession of the nurses at Abenaki. The fact that I hadn't thought of it either made me no less frustrated with Alba.

My wallet is in Cambridge, she said. I forgot we'd need enough for the bus. I guess we'll just have to hitch the rest of the way.

No, I said. No more hitching. With my luck, I thought, the next driver would be freebasing cocaine.

What do you suggest then? Alba said. She was annoyed at me now, which really pissed me off. And I was hungry, so ravenous I could have bitten anyone who got in my way.

My sister-in-law works in town, I said. Let's get something to eat and I'll go see her at eight.

We had breakfast in the one open place we could find—an all-night diner near the docks. The only other customers were lobstermen who murmured in low voices to the waitress, occasionally laughing until they started to cough. Their accents—deep Maine drawls—combined with some of their expressions, reminded me of my grandfather.

I had the Hungry Man's Special #5, so much food there was barely room on the Formica table for Alba's bagel; she kept glancing at my greasy plates with unveiled horror. I ignored her and shoveled it all in, relieved when the lobstermen left and I didn't have to chew so ferociously to block them out. I never understood how David could want to live here, surrounded by that drawl, when he had tried just as hard as I had to get rid of his accent, because even our own voices were too much of a reminder.

At a little after eight, Alba and I trudged uphill from the docks, slipping occasionally on the freshly hosed cobblestone streets. David had bought Bethany a bookstore in the Old Port shortly after he became a billionaire. I saw her through the window, sipping coffee and counting the contents of the register drawer. The door was locked. I knocked on it, preparing my countenance for groveling.

Bethany glanced at her watch and then up, expecting an overly eager customer. When she saw me she didn't look surprised. Her full mouth hardened into a line and she closed the money drawer.

She unbolted the door and swung it open, clanging the little bell that was supposed to jingle a welcome.

Oscar, she said dully. You'd better be on a field trip.

Hey, Bethie, I said, trying to smile. I wasn't sure which would make me seem more pathetic; humor or severity.

Can we come in for a sec?

Bethany took a moment to consider this, then stepped back and let us in.

We should have hitched, I thought. I'd forgotten how painful it was to have her look at me like that. It was the same way David looked at me—like he didn't trust me for a second, but he still wanted to, and would do just about anything to let me prove him wrong.

Bethany, this is Alba, I said, once we were securely inside, the crisp smell of newly printed pages calming me slightly. David should have bought *me* a bookstore.

Hello, Alba said, employing her charming, sane smile.

There was a painful pause while Bethany sized Alba up.

Hello, Beth said reluctantly.

I'll just look around, Alba said to me. I nodded, though I didn't want to face this alone. Alba wandered off to the children's section, where a small table and chairs were set up with art supplies. Bethany led me to an opposite corner.

I'm not giving you a cent, Oscar, she said.

Nice to see you too, sis.

I'm serious.

We were standing under the Self-Help sign. There was a whole shelf dedicated to twelve-step programs. I stepped sideways into Cooking.

Look, it's not what you think, I said. I'm helping Alba get home. We just need enough for the bus to Boston.

Going to a party?

No, Beth. It's not about that. I don't have time to explain.

You never do.

Sixty bucks, Bethany, that's all. Give me a break.

Bethany glared at me, furious now. For a small woman—tiny really, she can't weigh more than a hundred pounds—she can look pretty daunting.

Give *you* a break? she hissed. Do you know how much money David has shelled out for that place? She glanced over at Alba, who surely heard us, but was pretending to be absorbed in a Dr. Seuss book.

He'd give you everything he has, Bethany said. If he thought it would help, we'd be out on the street. But you don't give a shit, you never have.

Spare me the lecture, I said. I know how much David resents me.

Resents you? Bethany yelled. He worships you, you stupid fuck. He always has. Ever since you were boys and you saved his life. Oh, yes, he told me; it's the only thing that keeps me from hating you myself.

He's exaggerating, I said.

David never exaggerates, Bethany said. I didn't respond to that. She was right.

We both looked over at Alba. She'd finished reading and was trying to cut off her hospital wristband with kiddy scissors. They were right-handed scissors in her left hand and she looked like a kindergartner learning how to use them—she was even sticking her tongue out in concentration.

Bethany sighed. Is she a drug addict? she said.

No, no, I said. She's just crazy. I knew Alba would smile at that.

Tell me again why you're doing this? Bethany said.

I'm trying to help her.

Why? Bethany's blue eyes were almost navy with anger. She was as gorgeous as ever. No wonder she chose David.

I don't know, I floundered. I glanced at Alba—she was still wrestling with the scissors—and lowered my voice. Because she needs help, I said. I think she needs *my* help.

Bethany softened a bit then, looking surprised. Nothing makes me more uncomfortable than people sizing up my motives. I always feel like a fraud.

All right, Oscar, she sighed. She walked behind the counter and got her purse. She counted out three twenty-dollar bills and handed them to me.

You realize I'll probably end up divorced over this, she said.

Thanks, Beth, I said sheepishly, shoving the money out of sight. The phone rang, and Bethany turned to answer it. I walked over to Alba.

Want me to do yours? Alba said, snapping the scissors open and shut in midair. I let her snip my tag away. She put it in her knapsack and handed me hers. A souvenir, she said. *Elliot, Alba, 2/14/1978,* it read.

You were born on Valentine's Day, I said.

Yes. Alba sighed dramatically.

Bethany was muttering something into the phone. I hoped it wasn't David.

Look, Alba said, gesturing to a dump—a cardboard stand that publishers produce to display certain books. There were multiple copies of two young adult titles, with beautifully illustrated, old-fashioned covers.

My books, Alba said.

You're kidding, I said. She shook her head. I picked one up, flipping it over to read the summary on the back cover. There were gushing quotes from J. K. Rowling, Madeleine L'Engle and Katherine Paterson. I heard Bethany hang up the phone.

We've got to get going, I said.

Fine, Bethany said. She looked pale.

She wrote these books, I said, gesturing to Alba.

Bethany looked alarmed. *You're* Alba Elliot? she said finally.

Mmmm, Alba said, actually blushing.

Your books sell very well here, Bethany said. They sell well everywhere, from what I hear. She was looking at Alba with a little less condemnation now.

Thank you, Alba said, smiling vaguely.

Let's go, I said. I could see that Alba was uncomfortable.

We walked toward the door. As I opened it, jingling the welcome bell, Bethany called out.

Uncle Oscar, she said. I turned around. Come home soon, okay?

Oh, right, I said guiltily. I forgot to ask you how you're feeling.

Pretty nauseated at the moment, she said. And she waved us on.

24

Saint Dymphna's Asylum

Dear Peter,

Another year has passed, four more seasons without a
glimpse of you or the girls. Christmas was a disaster.
Mrs. Madden tried to make it nice for us: a huge tree,
caroling, Secret Santa gifts between the nuns and
patients. At first, everyone was enthusiastic, but then
the Yuletide joy began to backfire. The patients
quarreled over the decorating of the tree, the choice of
carols, the shapes of sugar cookies. By Christmas Eve
they were barely speaking to one another. Poor Mrs.
Madden, she couldn't figure where she'd gone wrong.
She doesn't realize that so much attention to
Christmas makes us miss it all the more.

Dr. Madden is encouraged by my progress; since I have not had a seizure since the fall, he thinks I am getting well. He is planning on presenting my case for review to the board when next they meet, which is not until April. He thinks I have an excellent chance of release, especially since I've shown no "sexual aberration"—a matter of great concern to a board made up of priests, nuns, and Catholic doctors. I have begun to let myself imagine it again— coming home to you. At this point I would even be happy to see your father.

The snow is heavy and unrelenting this year and it is sending my mind back to that winter with my uncle. Among the many things I learned that season was the healer's call. My uncle told me that healers have the power to be heard over any distance—by one person or by many. He made me practice this in the woods. He would go off on a hike while I stayed in the cave; I was supposed to ask him a question that I did not know the answer to. I couldn't do it at first; besides being exhausted and weak with hunger, I was concentrating on sending my mind's voice after him and that never worked. Not until he explained that it was another voice I should use, the one of my trances, my soul's voice, did I succeed in communicating. My uncle heard me from two miles off, and I heard his response—not a sound in my ears but a movement inside me, a foreign ripple in a place so private and untouched it felt like an invasion at first. Eventually, this became my favorite part of the training. After a few days I was able to contact my mother, and felt rather than saw her drop a pail of well water in shock. Up until then, my gift had made me feel strange and removed. This traveling of voices comforted me. I thought that it would mean that I would never truly be alone. It would be spring again before I found out I was wrong.

My first journeys to the Land of the Dead were messy ones. Part of the reason I was denied food and rest, my uncle said, was to break down my body's defenses and send me into fits. It was these fits, which had once so abhorred and frightened me, that were my greatest gift. They were my entrance into the world of souls.

In the cave I was having three to five seizures a day, more than I'd ever had before in succession. If you'd asked me I would have insisted I couldn't live through so many. Each time I awoke, still shuddering with the last convulsions, embarrassed by the tears I'd made in my clothes, my uncle asked me to share my visions. At first, I insisted it was the same as always: utter blackness and lost time. I had never seen anything during a fit. But as they happened more frequently, and he plied me with questions, I began to remember things I had never realized were there. Faces, some familiar, most not, looming up at me out of the darkness. With each face—and that's all they were at first, merely free-floating heads—came a corresponding physical sensation. Sometimes it was a pain, sharp and so quick it left me nauseous, or a steady, escalating ache, the sort that you try to rub away because motion disperses it into bearable. Other times I wouldn't be able to breathe, or I would be partly or completely paralyzed. Sometimes the faces spoke to me, though most of what they said was nonsense; their words were out of context, without subjects or objects, as though I had arrived mid-sentence. I couldn't seem to get anyone to back up or start over; just as one voice began to make sense to me, the face would be pulled away, so quickly that a vague outline of its image was left for an instant on top of new, unfamiliar features, like a shadow too lazy to follow its owner.

When I emerged from the fits I sobbed in frustration.

"There are too many of them," I said to my uncle.

"Focus," my uncle said. "Choose one and ignore the others. You're no good to all of them at once, you have to save people one at a time."

"The Land of the Dead is a miserable place," I said. Even without a religious upbringing, I had cradled a vague idea, formed mostly from novels, that death was a peaceful journey toward completion—a place where all your questions and half-formed connections were answered and explained. I didn't like this vision of a world comprised of bewildered, screaming souls.

"What makes you think they're dead?" Uncle said.

"I thought that's where I was supposed to be going," I said.

"You will go to the Land of the Dead to look for what people have lost. Right now you are still mingling with the half-dead, the ill, whose souls have been broken despite the fact that their bodies still rise every morning."

In the end I chose a woman from the nearby village, mostly because I recognized her face. Her name was Una McIntyre; for as long as I could remember, she had waited on us at her father's store. Mr. McIntyre handled the orders for grain, tools and lumber; Una presided over a counter backed with floor-to-ceiling shelves that held bolts of cloth. Though once a pretty young woman, and even more handsome in her forties due to her rigorous attention to cleanliness and attractive clothing, Una had never married. It was generally thought that she was a little slow; though proficient at her work, she rarely managed conversation beyond "how many yards" and "this pink would suit you." Even those words were whispered, as if she were uneasy at the sound of her own voice.

In my dream state, Una's image was as quiet as her real self. She did not pound me with pleas and questions, and I believe this was why I returned to her face. There was also the look in her eyes—now that I saw it I realized it had always been there. Her eyes held pure fear, her pupils dilated so wide there was only the faintest rim of blue surrounding them. They brought to mind something my mother once said to my father after a visit to McIntyre's. "I'm afraid to imagine what happened to that girl."

Taking my uncle's advice, I began to follow her in my dreams. Each time she took me deeper into her life, through the rooms of her childhood where her mother still lived, and the spaces of her adult life that revolved around tending to her gruff, ungrateful father. There were doorways she could not open to staircases she could not descend, and my uncle told me these were the important ones—the entrances to death where I would find the source of her pain. For a while, I was unable to open them as well. My own fear left my wrists too weak to turn the taut knobs.

It was on my fifth fit with Una that I found her soul. In a poorly lit barn, warm and heavy with the clean smells of hay and dung, Una, milking the cows on the morning after her mother died, was violently raped by her uncle. She was thirteen.

I watched the whole thing, and felt it as though it were happening to me. The pain was unbearable, like a knife had severed the soft place between her legs and was twisted and thrust, its movement only encouraged by the slick warmth of her blood. I didn't fully understand what I was witnessing—what I was feeling—at least not with my mind. I knew about sex only vaguely—that it involved rhythmic rocking under bedcovers, that it was the way babies were made, that it was an expression of love. I had no knowledge before that moment that the act had any relationship to violence.

When he was done with her—he finished with a last great thrust and shuddering groan—Una's uncle slipped down to lie on his side, one leg still hooked over her damp, blood-stained thighs. He put his arms around her shoulders and kissed her hair, her cheeks, her neck—big, grateful, exaggerated smacks that made me flinch.

"If you tell anyone, I'll do it again," he whispered. "Only next time, I'll kill you when I'm through."

He got up, tucked himself into his trousers, wiped his hands on his seat, and headed for the door.

"Hurry up with the milk, love," he called back. "You've made me hungry."

That was the moment where Una's soul cleaved in two. The ravaged, bloody girl sobbed as she straightened her clothing and picked hay from her hair. But walking away from her was the girl who had been there just an hour earlier. She trod across the hay with a fervent, childish step, oblivious to her twin now retching in the sawdust. I knew without my uncle's prompting what I was meant to do. I turned my back on the violated Una and took the hand of the bright-eyed little girl.

"Where are we going?" the girl said to me.

"Home," I said.

And I led her up to what was left of her, forty-three and fearful, a woman who spent her days measuring and cutting cloth, the smell of hay and blood between her legs still fresh, so much so that she had to bite her lip until her eyes watered rather than speak to the kind neighbors who asked after her.

I still remember that late winter as the happiest time of my life. My uncle stayed on, working as a logger in the early mornings, teaching me in the afternoons. Once I'd recovered from sleep deprivation and hunger, my parents saw that I was well again. My seizures were gone—I now entered the trance state voluntarily. There were no more fights between my mother and my uncle; she began to show him a grudging affection. I was living in an ideal world—I was still the child who read whenever she wanted, did her chores alongside her parents in happy contentment. But I also had an adult's purpose: I was healing people. There were only a few up to this point; my uncle concentrated more on my perfecting the rituals and learning the medicines and herbs, but the promise was there. Until now I had always assumed I would grow up to live an ordinary life like my parents—one of routines and hobbies and love but lacking any genius or driving ambition. This had both comforted and disappointed me. I was thrilled to discover I had been wrong. My ego was swelling so that my father began to joke about setting an extra space for it at the table.

Then, one day in April, the first day that I noticed the sun was not the bleak, silver light of winter, but warm and golden on my skin, my mother came home from town with a headache. She was dead by bedtime.

My father, who had been to town with her, and spoke of an outbreak of influenza, died the next afternoon. By then, my uncle had fallen ill, but he lasted four days. I nursed him on my own cot, my parents' bed already crowded with their stiffening bodies, the cleaning and dressing halted halfway through. Every surface of the house was littered with herbs and tonics; I had tried every one in my collection on my parents, who seemed to deteriorate faster with each cure. I tried them on my uncle at first, but he stopped me.

"Don't waste them," he said. "This is an illness you cannot cure."

So I wiped his brow, bathed his hot, sweating body which, unlike my father's, was devoid of hair aside from his privates. I washed and replaced the clothes that he coughed into; first they came away yellow, then a greenish-brown, and finally the bright red of blood. On the third day, as his fever raged, he spoke to people I could not see, but on the fourth day he seemed to improve. His eyes were clear and steady, his sweating had abated, he even ate some soup. His face, though, looked as hollow as the souls I saw in my trances. I did not know yet, as it hadn't happened with my parents, of the deceptive false recovery that often occurs just before death. But my uncle did.

"I don't know what will happen to you now, little one," he said. I wanted to scream, but I held his hand gently instead. "Try to find our people. It is only among them that your gift can flourish."

"Yes, Uncle," I said. It occurred to me that I had never met another of the Abenaki tribe. I'd never even seen a stranger who looked as though they had native blood. I wondered where they all were, but did not ask. I was too embarrassed to admit that I'd never noticed this before.

"I am proud of you," he said in my mother's language. "And indebted to you. This winter with you—it is the first truly worthy thing I have ever done."

"I will find you again," I said. I'd been too frightened by the onslaught of illness to remember—I could visit them all in the Land of the Dead.

My uncle's expression frightened me. It was the same sort of sad look that I remembered my parents having, whenever they had to tell me some truth about the world that contradicted my childish hope.

"You won't find me," he said. "Or your parents. It is only strangers you can heal and visit, little one."

"But that makes no sense," I whined. "What use is my gift if I

cannot visit my own family or heal my own broken soul when
they leave me? That is unfair."

"There are reasons," my uncle said. "But they will be no
comfort. And this will not break you, Mesatawe. It will hurt, it
will scar, but you will leave here whole."

He's wrong, I thought, starting to cry. I can feel myself
shattering already.

He left within the hour, left me thirteen years old and
orphaned, in a cabin with three corpses and a gift that suddenly
seemed the most useless thing in the world.

They found me ten days later, a dirty, hungry, raving girl still
tending to her dead. From the comments and faces of the four
men I knew that the smell was strong. Honestly, though, I never
noticed it. I barely took note of the swarming flies in my fever-
driven determination.

They assumed I had not buried them because I, too, was ill—
even healthy, how would a girl, even one as big as she, manage
that? they said. I had never considered burial. I thought with my
family's bodies around I could still find a way to their souls.

One of the men lifted me from my father's chair where I had
been sitting vigil, blankets still swaddling my shoulders, and
carried me out to his carriage. He signaled the driver to go on,
leaving the others behind to deal with the bodies.

"How did you think of it, sir?" the driver said. "I didn't even
know anyone lived out this far."

"I had a dream," the man muttered, and I opened my eyes to
look at him. He was dressed in a suit, a silk scarf at his neck. I
remember thinking that he must be very rich.

"How's that?" the driver said, and the man looked away

from me. His jaw was clamped tight but I noticed a small trembling in his lower lip.

"It just came to mind, that's all," he said loudly.

"Lucky for the girl, I guess," the driver said. I was too sleepy to protest that I was far from lucky. There were fur wraps in the carriage, and I fell asleep and dreamed of my mother laughing.

Eventually, after I'd grown stronger in the rich man's house, I was sent to Boston. I never saw him again—he had the maids tend to me until the day a doctor declared me well. I heard one of the house girls say that she was surprised—it was unlike the master to take in a stranger, let alone an orphaned and flu-ridden Indian. I left without a good-bye from him, though I knew he was in an anteroom off the foyer, smoking and listening to me go. I have often wondered what my life would have been like had I stayed in that house. At the time, I was too numb to consider that I might have some influence over my future.

The last person I saw before I was put in a car bound for the train station was Una McIntyre. She came up to me on the street and handed me a brown sack of licorice. She opened her mouth to say something, then changed her mind and simply smiled at me.

That smile broke my heart more than any of it, I think. She was a stranger, not someone I loved, yet I had saved her and now she was the only person on earth who looked at me with sympathy. I hated her for it, if you want the truth. Actually, it wasn't the sympathy that bothered me as much as the hope in her expression—hope I no longer had. It took all my composure to thank her and climb into the car, beginning my journey into the loneliest years of my life.

I would think about Una often over the next few years, especially when your father, and before him, your grandfather, forced himself on me. In the barn I had helped her because I was supposed to, but I also blamed her. I thought she hadn't fought hard enough; I believed that a scream or a well-placed kick would have saved her years of misery. As it turns out, fighting only makes it worse. Una must have known this already.

25

Aftercare Planning

ALBA IS STANDING in her father's bathroom, a massive, painfully neat space tiled in 1930s octagonal porcelain. It is here that her father keeps her medications, not behind the mirror but under the sink in a lock box. He doles them out to her weekly, various pills and capsules organized in an oblong plastic case with seven hinged openings, the days of the week marked in initials and Braille. He keeps the pharmacist's printouts on side effects in a business envelope, filed alphabetically.

Alba has always known that he stows the extra key under his shaving mug. There are pills in here that she hasn't taken in years; the expiration and refill dates have long since passed. Perhaps her father saves them for reference, his own version of a drug history. There are so many different bottles; if a burglar broke into this box he would think Alba was elderly or terminally ill.

She fills up an almost empty, warning-stickered CVS bottle with a variety of pills—a week's worth of lithium, some Risperdal, Neurontin and Klonopin which, unwisely, looks like yellow Smarties candy. She's not planning on swallowing any of these pills—this is an emergency stash. Since she left the hospital, her blood has begun to purify itself, and she feels wonderful. Clearheaded, energetic, appreciative of details. It's like being able to taste and smell again after a long, suffocating cold. Though from experience she knows this happiness could lead to mania, she is reluctant to let go of it. She should be safe enough for a few days at least. And, if things go as she plans, she will be safe forever. In a bit of twisted superstition, she believes if she brings her pills along, she may never need them again.

On her way downstairs to her father's study, she checks on Oscar. She had left him in the kitchen—a gleaming, modern expanse with a dark green marble island and professional appliances—working his way through a slab of Brie and a package of crackers. She finds him in the living room, slavering over her father's well-stocked bar. The package of Stoned Wheat Thins hangs forgotten from between his fingers.

Hey, she says, intending to startle him. It works; he drops the crackers, then picks them up sheepishly.

Nice house, he says, sweeping his arm around to indicate the antiques, the rugs, the mahogany bookcases, the piano.

I suppose, Alba says. The house is her father's showpiece—not necessarily meant to impress but to blend in with his impressive world. For some reason, Oscar's admiration of it embarrasses her.

This must be what they call Old Money, Oscar says.

That depends who *they* are, Alba says, imitating Oscar's condescending tone. Anyway, it's not my house, it's my father's.

Where do you live? Oscar says.

Alba sighs. Upstairs, she mumbles. Oscar smiles smugly, drumming his fingers on the bar.

What she doesn't understand is that, during inappropriate moments, when he is his most infuriating, she wants to kiss him. She resists the urge by trying to avoid eye contact. Not because she thinks he would grimace or push her away—because even if he didn't, she would feel awful, dishonest, even easy.

Oscar's mind is clearly not on the same page—he is practically caressing the bar with sidelong glances. His temptation is making her nervous—she felt it in the Land Rover when those boys were smoking pot—it was as if his whole body were growling with need.

Can you drive? she says. Oscar looks confused.

That's a matter of opinion, he says. Technically, yes.

She tosses him the keys to her father's car. He fumbles to catch them, but manages to keep hold of the crackers.

I just need to grab one more thing, Alba says. The car's in the garage.

Alba goes into her father's study. This was her favorite room as a child; it is dark and always warm, crowded with heavy oak furniture, an oversized leather couch, and piles of books stacked alongside already crammed ceiling-high bookshelves. It is always a mess—the overwhelming odor of the place is dust, with a sweet remnant of tobacco even though her father quit smoking fifteen years before. As a girl, Alba felt privileged that she was allowed in here. Her favorite spot was the crawl space beneath the massive desk, where she would strain her eyes reading while her father talked on the phone. She wrote her first story under this desk, which her father edited with red pencil and then typed up for her after she'd made the corrections. He gave her a plastic report cover for it, which gave her a sense of importance similar to the feeling she had years later when she saw her first story in print.

Alba rarely comes in here these days. She has her own writing room in the attic, just as dark and dusty, with prints and quotes lining the walls and her books in various languages stacked in piles on the carpet. Her office makes her nervous most of the time; she has to force herself to go in there. She is always afraid she will sit at the cherry table she uses for a desk and find her brain as dusty as the surface. Entering her father's study makes her sad, in a different, older sort of way.

She moves quickly toward the corner where, underneath the faded oriental, there is a safe hidden in the floor. She twirls in the combination, her birthday—it angers her sometimes how trusting her father can be, especially when he's being untrustworthy himself. She paws through the mess of bonds, birth certificates, and her mother's jewelry. There is one folder she knows by sight, because she's looked at it many times over the years. She has always been afraid to open it, but now she takes it, tucking it into her knapsack. The tabbed label bends as she shoves it down—the title in her father's neat block letters reads simply: ORPHANAGE.

When Alba walks outside, Oscar is coasting around the circular driveway in her father's silver Jaguar. He stops alongside her and opens the passenger door with a flourish.

Nice car, he says, his hand vibrating on the leather stick shift.

It's—Alba starts.

I know, Oscar winks. It's your father's. I fear this may all end with car theft added to my already spotty life record.

I promise not to press charges, Alba says, climbing in beside him.

Oscar gives her a wide grin, and her stomach clenches; she

keeps her head down and concentrates on her seat belt to hide the blush she feels creeping up her neck.

Where to, my lady? Oscar says.

Quincy. Take the Southeast Expressway.

What's in Quincy? Oscar says, sliding the car into gear.

If you'd read the letters I gave you, you'd know, Alba says.

Yes, well, Oscar says, checking for traffic before he squeals out onto the tree-lined street. I've been so busy playing the fugitive I've fallen behind on my homework.

Alba sighs. Do you take *anything* seriously? she says.

Do you take anything *lightly*? Oscar rebuts. When she doesn't answer he drops his grin. A couple of things, he says, negotiating a left-hand turn. But that's a recent development.

Eighty-five Squantum Street is a narrow, white clapboard house with attic gables and a modern wood deck attached to its side. The street is also lean, with cracked sidewalks that children on Rollerblades are treating like a challenge. Laundry is hung out to dry in many of the yards, on metal contraptions that twirl with the wind, looking like radars. This is the sort of neighborhood she wanted as a child—yards overlapping, neighbors chatting over fences, mothers calling their children's names from porches. Alba's neighborhood in Cambridge is deathly quiet; her neighbors slip in and out of their burglar-alarmed doors without her seeing them.

Alba jogs up the red brick steps and presses the doorbell.

A woman opens the door, leaving the screen closed so she has to squint to see them clearly.

Can I help you? she says suspiciously. She is wearing the bright, crazily patterned scrubs favored by the nurses at Abenaki. Hers depict kittens cavorting with balls of yarn.

Hello, Alba says. We're looking for Peter Doherty.

If you're selling something, no one here is interested, the woman says.

Alba, annoyed at the reprimand, opens her mouth to snap back, but Oscar takes her arm.

Do I look like a salesman? he says, and the woman's shoulders relax; he has charmed her with his smile.

Mrs. Doherty? the woman calls back into the house. Some people here looking for Peter.

The muffled voice from another room must be an assent, because the nurse opens the screen door for them. She leads them down a hallway made claustrophobic by too many framed photographs and garish, vine-patterned wallpaper. Alba, confused by the "Mrs. Doherty," momentarily imagines that it is Mary they are going to meet. She has to remind herself that if she were alive today, the Mary of the letters would be more than a hundred years old.

The woman in the lace-heavy living room *is* old—she has wispy hair dyed a neutral beige and a slack, pale face set off oddly by magenta lipstick. The nurse introduces her as Grace Doherty, and Oscar reaches out his hand to the woman, who, fragile and diminutive within the plump wings of her chair, hasn't risen to greet them.

I'm Oscar Jameson, ma'am, and this is Alba Elliot.

Mrs. Doherty lifts her hand in the air and leaves it hovering for Oscar to clasp. She smiles and speaks to the empty air beside him.

What can I do for you young folks?

Alba realizes the woman is blind. For some reason this makes her nervous. As if the woman will be able to hear something in Alba's voice, like the manic desperation she is trying to conceal from Oscar.

We're looking for a man named Peter Doherty, Alba says. I have some old letters we believe belong to him.

Please, have a seat, Mrs. Doherty says, gesturing in the general direction of the couch. Alba follows Oscar around the coffee table and they sit down gingerly on the pastel floral cushions. Mrs. Doherty asks if they'd like tea, and they accept. Mrs. Doherty sends the nurse, who is clearly annoyed, to boil the water. When she leaves, Mrs. Doherty leans toward Oscar.

I don't like that one very much, she whispers. She's very *hard*. The night girl is better company.

Do you live here alone? Oscar asks.

I do, yes, she says. My children and grandchildren are all nearby, and they keep me busy enough. They all want me to live with them, but I think a woman should have her own home. Don't you?

I suppose, Oscar says. As long as you're not lonely.

I lived in one crowded house after another for seventy-five years, Mrs. Doherty says. I enjoy the quiet.

After a few minutes of uncomfortable silence, the nurse thunks down a tray with a teapot, china cups and saucers, sugar, milk and a plate of shortbread cookies.

Please serve yourselves, Mrs. Doherty says. I'm not as deft with a teapot as I once was.

Oscar pours tea for everyone, handing a cup and saucer gently to Mrs. Doherty. Alba is surprised at him—his manners, his comfortable chatting with this old woman. She hadn't imagined Oscar would be so charming with strangers.

Mrs. Doherty raises her teacup to her mouth. Her nails are perfectly manicured, the same bright magenta as her lipstick. She is wearing a powdery pink jogging suit and a matching silk scarf. She must have been a fashionable woman, Alba thinks, if she still cares about coordinating even though she can no longer see.

An awkward silence is growing. Oscar keeps looking at Alba, waiting for her to speak. Mrs. Doherty seems perfectly at ease sipping her tea.

I'm sorry, Alba says finally. Have we come to the right place? Do you know Peter Doherty?

I should say so, Mrs. Doherty says, setting her cup carefully in its saucer. He was my husband.

Was? Alba croaks. Is he dead? She feels Oscar flinch at her lack of tact.

Oh no, dear, Mrs. Doherty smiles. No, Peter is still alive. He's still my husband; I never did divorce him. We're Catholic, you know. But he hasn't lived here in fifty years.

It's the sort of statement, especially coming from someone of an older generation, that makes one feel uncomfortable pressing for details; further inquiry might prove embarrassing.

You said you had letters for Peter, Mrs. Doherty says, breaking the silence. May I ask whom they are from?

They're from Mary Doherty, Alba says. His mother.

Mrs. Doherty's face, glued in a pleasant expression until this point, seems to fall.

His mother, she says. That's . . . remarkable. Peter never heard from her all the years she was gone.

She wasn't allowed to mail them, Alba says. She wrote to him in the backs of books in the hospital library. I found them because I . . . well, I work there.

Mrs. Doherty doesn't buy that last bit for a second, Alba can tell, but she pretends to.

How very sad, she says. It might have made a difference, had Peter seen those letters. Then again, it might not have.

I don't mean to pry, Alba says, but do you know where he is now?

Oh, it's not prying, dear. I don't believe in keeping family secrets. I'm not a gossip, mind you, but keeping the past locked away just makes it more shameful and dangerous. That's my opinion.

I suppose I should tell you all of it, she sighs. I believe we'll need more tea.

I was born on this street in 1925, so I've known Peter all my life. Knew his mother too, though she was a quiet woman who kept to herself. By the time I was six and playing with Peter's sisters in their yard, I could see how much she doted on them, and I was never afraid of her like some of the other children were. She was quite beautiful, with the same dark hair and blue eyes as Peter, and though there were rumors that she had mixed blood, that her mother had been an Indian woman, at the time I paid little attention to them. Later, I knew it was important, but not in the shameful way others thought. All people can be narrow-minded, I suppose, but this neighborhood was particularly so back then. It was mostly Irish immigrants like my parents. The Irish had it so rough that you'd have thought they'd be kinder to others, but it was just the opposite. Discrimination tends to breed discrimination, my father told me at the time, though I didn't understand why that was. I still don't.

Anyhow, as saintly as Peter's mother was, her husband was the exact opposite. The sort of man who makes you believe in evil. No one was fooled by him, though most pretended to be because his father, who was just as evil, had been an important man in town. My father didn't allow me to play there after five o'clock, as he didn't want me anywhere near Mr. Doherty.

Nevertheless, I saw him hit her once, Peter's father. Back-handed his wife right in front of the children. It was quite obvious by the way he did it, and the vigilance, not surprise, I saw in Peter, that it was a common occurrence. Poor woman. She always seemed to be pregnant, which, though not unusual in those days, was still difficult enough without being beaten regularly as well. Sometimes I helped her daughters with their chores, because I felt so sorry for them all. Mrs. Doherty always thanked me, but never spoke to me beyond that. She was proud. You'd never know how miserable she was if you looked at the tilt of her head.

It was a huge scandal when she left. Her husband had her carted off in the middle of the night by the sheriff, declared her insane. The neighbors were no help to her, mind you. A lot of people were out of work then, and tension was high, and her oddities grated on them a bit more, I think. The fires were the last straw.

Fires? Alba interrupts.

I'm afraid so, dear. Fires she set herself. Sometimes in the yard, or in the woods that used to border Squantum Street. In the middle of the night, wearing her nightgown, she'd sit there and chant until her husband dragged her home by the hair. She'd say strange things over the fires, things the neighbors would report the next day, things about people in town that were true, but supposedly secret. Who was having an affair, whose child was illegitimate, whose father had been inappropriate with his daughter—that sort of thing. Things no one likes to hear out loud, though they certainly enjoy whispering about.

The strangest thing was, they said that she never remembered it in the morning. As though she'd been sleepwalking. She wasn't well, that was clear enough. Her eyes were glazed and unfocused, she muttered to herself, the house was a disaster, and Peter was taking care of more things than any ten-year-old should be expected to. Still, it was cruel the way her husband handled things. Tearing her away from children who worshiped her with no warning whatsoever. And though he promised she'd be back, it was clear he was lying, when within weeks, he began courting a woman who worked in his office. There had been rumors about an affair even before he sent his wife away. Years later, he divorced Mary and married the other one. By the time that happened, Peter and I were in love.

He'd always been an odd boy—sensitive, dreamy, a loner. After his mother left he grew even more withdrawn. He scowled most of the time, barely spoke, not even the polite responses expected of children in those days. People started saying he was too like his mother, not all there, and that it would cause him grief later.

I saw a different side of him. Playing with his sisters gave me glimpses of how careful and loving he was with them; if any of them was hurt or frightened, it was Peter they went to, not their father. I suppose I romanticized him a bit. He was so unlike other boys, who could be cruel and serious and . . . slippery somehow. They seemed to have no substance to them. Peter, by the age of twelve, was already more like a man than a boy. And, though he didn't notice me until years later, I never had eyes for anyone else.

By the time he was seventeen most people were afraid of Peter. He was intensely moody, seemed to be angry all the time, and with his long black hair and ragged clothes and his tendency to mutter to himself, he seemed almost possessed. He had strange scars on his arms—straight, deliberate lines that cut through his tan and increased, row by row, every few months. Though he was very smart, he quit school as soon as he was allowed to and took a job at the local quarry. This embarrassed his father—the Dohertys had a tradition in the law—but at six foot three Peter towered over him and could no longer be beaten into submission. He disappeared sometimes; once his sisters were older and able to take care of themselves, he would leave for days at a time, and return looking worse than usual. No one knew where he went, but there were rumors of drinking binges and houses of ill-repute in the city. Later he told me he usually went camping alone in the woods, but he never corrected the gossip. He simply didn't care what anyone thought of him.

Though I was considered one of the prettier girls in the neighborhood, it was not easy to get Peter to notice me. When he finally did, it happened in an instant, as though he'd been looking at me for years and one day he saw me for the first time.

It was the night of the sophomore spring social. I got ready here with his sister Maggie. When we came downstairs in our gowns, Peter and his father, both reading separate sections of the paper, looked up. Mr. Doherty merely glanced, his expression disapproving, and went back to reading. But Peter stared. He asked who our dates were; I told him I didn't have one. Not that no one had asked, just no one I wanted to.

He ended up changing into a suit and taking me of course. Everyone thought I was mad to show up with him, though I caught some of the girls admiring him. We didn't dance, or mingle with the other kids. We sat at a corner table and stared at one another. I can't remember which of us started talking. We talked until the dance was over, we talked half the night on my parents' porch swing. I'd never heard Peter utter more than three or four words at a time. I flattered myself, thinking I had unlocked something in him. I learned later that it was just one of his moods, these rambling confessions, and it hardly mattered who was listening.

He told me some strange things. Frightening, really. That he heard his mother speaking to him, not only in his dreams, but during the day when he was wide awake. He knew things about her no mother would tell her son. He thought he could read people's minds. He'd tried to kill himself on four separate occasions but something always went wrong. He heard voices addressing him in the wind.

You're probably wondering how I could still want him after that. He was clearly mad, although at the time it seemed more romantic than dangerous. It was him reading my mind that did it. He knew about my brother, you see.

When I was eight years old, my mother had her fifth child—a boy who came out wrong. Deformed, obviously brain damaged. At the time my mother, in her grief, thought it was her fault—that she was being punished. My father gave the baby away to a home, told everyone, even my younger siblings, that it had died. I was the oldest and helped my mother during her recovery. For the first few weeks she woke every night, screaming about her guilt over abandoning him. After a couple of months she never spoke of him again and neither did I.

But I thought of him and Peter knew it. Even knew his name—Kevin—the name I'd given him when the priest was called in to baptize him. My father hadn't wanted to name him at all.

When Peter mentioned it, I was angry at first. I thought my family was the victim of gossip. Who told you such a thing? was what I said.

Peter looked embarrassed. No one, he said. I know things about people. I dream them. My mother did it too.

It gives someone a special power over you when they know your secrets. Not just know them, but understand them. It was like he had opened up my soul and peered inside, and that somehow those stormy but kind eyes were still inside of me. And so I married him. At the time I couldn't imagine marrying anyone else.

But first his father married that woman from his office. Mr. Doherty was granted a divorce by the courts and, after a weekend away, came home with a new wife and little explanation. Peter was a mess over it. There were a few loud confrontations, then Peter disappeared for three weeks. While he was gone, his father, along with his new wife, died in a boating accident. There was no foul play suspected—they'd been sailing and come upon a sudden storm—but years later, when I saw what Peter's moods could do, I thought that his anger might have killed them. Even if he never laid a hand on that boat, his mind may have conjured up the waves. I know that sounds fantastic, but Peter was different. He made you believe in such things.

Once Mr. Doherty was gone, my parents consented to my early marriage—mostly because I threatened to run away with him if they didn't—and I moved in here with Peter and his sisters. It wasn't long before Peter went off to Europe to fight in the war. I lived in a houseful of women that year; even our first child, born while Peter was away, was a girl. Sometimes I think of it as the best year of my life—though at the time I missed him terribly. But my fantasy of what our life would be when he returned sustained me.

He was dishonorably discharged. Something about a mental breakdown that I was never given details of. Whatever happened, it was around the time his mother died in the asylum. Though I was the one they contacted, Peter already knew when he got home.

He tried; I'll say that for him. Tried to have a normal life with me, though a part of him was never there—ransomed, was how I thought of it, to his demons. We had five more children, he worked in the quarry, his sisters married and built homes of their own nearby. Peter cured many of the children's illnesses with herbs he'd learned about from his mother. Sadly, this was when he was best with them; when they were ill. Peter himself would be well enough for a few months but eventually he would stop sleeping, babble about visions, frighten the children, and then he would take off— for days, sometimes weeks, and return filthy, smelling of drink. He didn't lose his job because the foreman of the quarry at the time was my cousin. I took him back again and again because I still loved him, you see. My love for him never cooled. Eventually, though, I could see the children were frightened of him. Ultimately, he lost his job; my cousin had limits to his patience. The final straw was when he hit our eldest son so hard he lost consciousness. I put my foot down. I loved my children more, you could say. I chose them over him. Most mothers will, if they have the chance.

He went to Maine, got a job running a lighthouse. A life solitary enough that his quirks went unnoticed. I visited him occasionally that first year, but I stopped because it was too hard. He sent us money every month, sometimes a letter that made me want to ask him back, but I never did. He stopped writing years ago. The children tried to reconnect with him, once they were grown and starting families of their own, but by then he didn't remember them. Or said he didn't.

He's been in a home for about fifteen years now. The state sent him there after he tried to burn down the new computer-operated lighthouse. It's a home for mentally ill seniors. They say he's a schizophrenic, has been since his childhood. That's what they said about his mother too. I wouldn't have believed it once, but they know more about these things now, doctors do. They've got a pill for everything. I often wonder if our lives would have been different if they'd had such pills when we were married.

Pills can't fix everything, Alba says, startling Mrs. Doherty, who seems to have forgotten her audience.

No, I suppose not, dear, Mrs. Doherty says, smiling in Alba's general direction. But they say he's content now. Peaceful. That's something he never had in all the years I knew him.

Where is the nursing home? Alba says.

It's in Maine, Mrs. Doherty says. A town called St. Francis.

Really? Oscar says, clearing his throat. He looks shaken by the news.

Yes, do you know it?

I grew up there, Oscar mumbles. He must be in the Angel of Mercy.

That's it, Mrs. Doherty says. I'm sure they'll let you see him, but I don't know if you'll be able to give him the letters. They might worry about upsetting him.

Mrs. Doherty, Alba says, her voice loud and quavering slightly. Do you think they were crazy? Your husband and his mother? Or do you think they were gifted?

I've asked myself that for sixty-five years, Mrs. Doherty sighs. I don't think my answer is the one you're looking for.

What is it? Alba whispers.

Both, Mrs. Doherty says. I think they were both.

26

Saint Dymphna's Asylum

April 29, 1938

Dear Peter,

Dr. Madden has left us. Terrible things have happened
since I last wrote, but, for me, I fear the worst is yet to
come. Without Dr. Madden, I don't know how I will
ever make it home.

His son is dead. I tried to stop it from happening,
but somehow it now looks to Dr. Madden like I was
responsible.

I have continued my nighttime healing. Sandra has
been an invaluable assistant, taking care of the details—
the fire, the negotiations with Thomas, the patient
waiting list—so all my concentration can go into the

trance. Three women have been released after sessions with me, four more have improved greatly and have begun to take an active interest in life on the ward. The nuns are a bit confused and, it's quite obvious, annoyed by the changes. More women are talking back to them, asking the identity of pills they formerly took blindly, fighting tooth and nail on their way to hydrotherapy. They have had to hire a male attendant—a man named Joe who tends to fondle the patients under the guise of holding them down.

My nights have been busy; even when I'm not healing I'm having vivid dreams that help me choose my next patient. Faces come to me with a frequency that hasn't occurred since I was thirteen, and I have lost the skill of singling one out and ignoring the rest. Often I wake up with the pain of three or four women converging in my body and I cannot distinguish what symptoms belong to each. I have started keeping charts—my dream notes plus interviews—in order to keep the women straight. I'm recording them in the library books like your letters; I keep a few volumes with me in the dormitory rather than leave them hidden on the shelves.

It was during one of my dreams, as I was trying to focus on Muriel Parsons, who'd been locked in a cockroach-infested broom closet as a girl, that I saw Dr. Madden's son. His sister, who started school this year, often wanders off with her friends when she's supposed to be watching him. He spends this time alone by the lake, immersed in a project of bravery he believes will make him a more attractive companion. He practices a high-wire act on a low-hanging tree branch that reaches out over the water. The image of him teetering along the rough bark came back to me so many times that I woke up without a cure in mind for Muriel. It bothered me, the way it would if I found out you or the girls were practicing such bad judgment, so I decided to say something to Dr. Madden.

"Do your children know how to swim?" I asked him the next afternoon, at the end of our session, where the talk often turns chatty, as if we've just finished lunch.

"They do," he said. "My oldest better than her brother. I intend to give him lessons on the lake when it gets warm enough."

"Tell him to be careful," I said. Dr. Madden looked perplexed, then suspicious.

"I have," he said. I was about to interject with more specifics, but the nun interrupted us with his next patient.

The boy went missing the next day. They searched the grounds thoroughly, but it wasn't until a tearful confession from his sister that the lake was dredged and his body found. The rumor was that Mrs. Madden howled for so long that the nuns were summoned to bring a needle from the ward.

In his grief, Dr. Madden might have forgotten our conversation, had Joe not found, while he was retying my bed straps and ogling my breasts, the library book with my notes under the mattress. Dr. Madden read the sentences dated two days before:

M's son climbing tree over lake. Could easily lose balance and drown—no one would hear a thing.

Dr. Madden summoned me to his office that night.

He looked awful. Normally an impeccable man, he was unshaven and rumpled and clearly ripe with drink. The pain in his eyes was almost masked by fury.

"Dr. Madden," I said. "I'm so sorry—" but he cut me off, slapping his palm down on his desk and upsetting the files there.

"What are you?" he said coldly.

Sir? I said carefully. The room was very warm suddenly, and small.

"Are you some sort of witch?" He was slurring. "Did you use a savage's spell to kill my son?"

Dr. Madden, it was clear, was fast approaching insanity in his grief. As I have often seen with madness, he was guessing at a larger truth, though his facts were confused.

"I am a healer," I said calmly. "I have done no harm. I tried to warn you."

"Silence!" he barked. Spittle flew from his mouth and I felt it on my cheek. "I chose not to believe your husband when he told me you were dangerous to your own children. I believe him now. You are not a Christian. You are something else—something evil."

He would not listen to anything I tried to say. He had Joe take me away, ordered the nuns to put me in isolation for a week. By the time I got out, the doctor and what was left of his family were gone.

Though I doubt Dr. Madden shared his theories with anyone—to admit such a thing would be unscientific—his replacement, who is due in a few weeks, will surely read on my chart that I am a danger to others, and that Dr. Madden no longer recommends my release.

May, 1938

Dear Peter,

I feel a sense of urgency that requires me to hasten my story along. The nuns have taken away my job in the library, though

Sandra says they haven't discovered my letters. She is bringing me books so that I can continue writing to you. I still have to tell you of how I came to marry, and regret marrying, your father.

After my parents died, I was taken to Boston and placed in a Catholic girl's orphanage that was overcrowded in the midst of the flu epidemic. Every Sunday we donned the better of our two donated dresses and took our places in the back rows of the church. Before dismissing Mass, the priest would call attention to us "orphaned souls" and urge families—mostly Irish immigrants with children of their own—to take in as many as they could afford. I was the oldest of the girls and the only Indian, and was not surprised when eyes flitted guiltily away from me week after week.

Then, one Sunday in July, I was introduced to Mr. Doherty, who was visiting his sister in Boston.

His eyes jumped along the heads of the other girls and stopped on mine.

"I'll be needing a girl to help with the house now that my dear wife has gone," he said to the priest. The priest, relieved to be rid of me, most likely didn't notice Mr. Doherty's hungry glance at my breasts and hips.

"She looks strong enough," Mr. Doherty said. His pointy tongue darted out to check on his mustache. "I can give her a home and a Catholic education, which is more than a lot of her kind get."

"You're a good man," the priest said, barely listening, looking away to another girl who had just bitten her new guardian's wrist. "I'm sure she'll be grateful to you. Please excuse me. God be with you, Mary."

This is what the Catholics had named me, you see, when

they first wrinkled their eyes at my odd name. Mary was the name they gave every girl whose name was unpronounceable, forgotten, or simply lost in the trauma of their parents' deaths.

Mr. Doherty lived in Quincy, but before leaving he had his sister take me shopping. She bought me three dresses, one for Sundays, two pairs of boots, stockings and an apron. The saleswoman grumbled at my large measurements and let down the hems. Miss Doherty was a jumpy, insensitive spinster who barely spoke except to direct me. In the presence of her brother she was silent and tense, the set of her shoulders so much like Una's that I considered trying to dream her, but decided against it. I could not rouse any enthusiasm to help someone who so obviously resented me.

When my dresses were ready, and my waist-long braids had been chopped to a thick, fashionable bob, we left for Quincy. On the drive down, Mr. Doherty asked blunt, unsympathetic questions about my background. He was encouraged to hear that my father was white. I was lucky, he said, that I'd inherited the blue eyes.

"We won't be telling anyone in town about your blood," he said. "When they ask, you're a distant cousin on my wife's side. Her family was dark-haired, Black Irish they call it. Quincy folk might understand an Indian maid, but they wouldn't take well to you being part of the family. The priest made me adopt you so that's what you are. I expect you to be grateful and obedient and not bring any savage nonsense into my Christian home."

I could only nod. I didn't want to risk my voice because rising behind it was a sob I did not want him to hear.

"Are you able to read and write?" he asked. I nodded again. "That's fine," he said, seeming satisfied with himself.

It was late that evening that I first saw the house on Squantum Street—the house you know as home, but which never felt so to me. And it wasn't until the morning that I met Mr. Doherty's son, Michael, who was eighteen and whom you still, I assume, believe to be your father.

I remember I found him handsome in the beginning. Handsome in that small, wiry, wound-up way Irish men can be. There is something in them—a vigilance mixed with melancholy—that can come across as attractive. If it does not get swallowed up in the face of hatred.

Michael had finished high school and was still living at home, reading the law as an apprentice in his uncle's practice. Though he was scowling when he first met me, I still had hopes that Michael would be my ally. It was clear that he despised his father, though he also feared him. I could see that his mother's death had left Michael the more bereft of the two. There was a photograph of her in the sitting room, a dimpled, dark-haired woman with a long, graceful neck. When Michael smiled, which was rarely, he looked like her. I made a point of smiling at him when his father wasn't watching, and cooking the foods I noticed were his favorites. I knew he looked at my body and I let him. He was my only chance in that house, you see. He was still a boy, with the promise of becoming a good man. His father was the evil one.

I was not surprised when Mr. Doherty started coming to my bedroom door at night; I had locked it in expectation of such a thing. Not that the spiny key kept him away for long. For a while, he limited himself to quick gropes in the pantry or the yard. One day he came home early and found me in the attic. He ordered me to kneel down, and when I refused he hit me so hard on the side of my head I saw double. He held on to my throat and promised that if I did not keep my teeth out of the way he would break my neck. Later I found blood on my scalp and finger bruises like small plums just below my collar.

A routine began after that. He didn't want me daily; it happened about twice a month, and when it did he never seemed to enjoy it. Just before the act his mouth would curl in the same disgusted way it did if I neglected a chore. He would be angry with me afterward, call me foul names and often hit me whether I fought him or not. He preferred to take me from behind in an unnatural way that left me bleeding and ill. He said it was to keep me from conceiving a child, but I was sure he was doing it so that he wouldn't have to look at me. Whatever the reason, because of it I remained a virgin until I was seventeen, though with the soiled feeling that had developed in every inch of my body, I wouldn't have thought any of me had remained pure.

Mr. Doherty never sent me to school as he'd promised, but left me long lists of chores every day until I'd memorized them and he no longer had to instruct me. I'd never realized how much work was involved running a modern household. You would think the conveniences would be timesaving but they were outweighed by extra needs. I rarely sat at the table with them; I'd pick at my dinner in the kitchen while fetching them seconds or preparing the next course.

What Mr. Doherty didn't know, the small secret that sustained me, was that I did not spend every hour slaving for him. After I'd cleared up breakfast, when he and Michael were at work, I would close myself in their library and read. Many of the books with pristine spines were ones I had already read, but it didn't matter. For a few hours each morning I reentered the worlds of my childhood. Those books were the fuel that kept me going while I scrubbed and cooked and endured the visits from my adoptive father.

After these visits, I had vivid, horrible dreams where women and men I had never seen before begged for my help. I turned away from all of them. They no longer affected me; my body was too wracked with its own pain to respond to the invasion of theirs.

By my seventeenth birthday, I had reached my full height, which is just under six feet. A growth spurt, combined with the tension that made it difficult for me to chew food without gagging, caused me to lose so much weight I was surprised to overhear someone in town referring to me as "that skinny Doherty girl." My large frame had always made me look heavy, though I'd never cared much. The lengthening of my body made me stunning. At least, that's what Peter told me. If it weren't for him, I would never have believed I held any claim to beauty.

I met Peter at the Giorgetti Farm, when Mr. Doherty went there to buy a new horse. Mr. Doherty liked to ride, and went north every fall to hunt fox in New Hampshire, but last season his horse had broken a leg and had to be shot. It was September, and he needed a mount for his imminent trip. He brought me along so I could help with the horse, but also so he could take advantage of me in his car on the side of the road. Michael was bedridden with a head cold.

At my first glimpse of Peter, breaking a colt in the dusty ring behind the stable, I thought I was seeing the soul of my uncle. Broad shoulders that tapered down to a boyishly thin waist, hair like a black braided rope, so heavy on his back it barely moved. His face was shadowed by a Western hat, but I could see his arms, long, hairless and dark, with a deep red glow that made one think of a sunburn layered over a tan. I truly thought I was having a vision—who but my uncle wore such massive boots—until Mr. Giorgetti whistled.

"Boy!" he called, and the man reined the colt to a stop, and dismounted while another man held on to the bridle. When he sauntered over to us and tipped back the brim of his hat, and I saw his thin face and full mouth, my uncle vanished. What stood before me was just a boy, not much older than I was, with dark, bottomless eyes and a kind of beauty I had forgotten. He was an Indian, the first I had seen since the death of my family, and I had to stop myself from stepping closer to him before I even heard him speak.

"Yes, sir?" he said. He didn't look down, but held his head high, which in anyone else would have been normal, but in front of white men it seemed confrontational, cocky.

"Peter, Mr. Doherty's interested in a hunting mount. Round up the geldings and that beauty you broke over the summer and lead them round the ring."

Peter nodded, then glanced at Mr. Doherty, sizing him up, and scowled as if he found him lacking. Luckily, Mr. Doherty wasn't paying him any mind—he was merely a servant. Peter caught me staring at him, and I lowered my eyes. I don't know if it was the way he looked or the way he looked at me, but it made me feel naked. Naked in a thrilling way that had no relationship to the past four years of semiclothed incidents with my adoptive father. That was the first time in years, when Peter first glanced at me, that sex occupied a space in my mind separate from shame and violence.

It wasn't until Mr. Doherty decided on a horse and went

inside to bargain the price with Mr. Giorgetti, that I actually got to speak to Peter. I leaned against the fence as he walked over to me, and though my mind was galloping, I couldn't have moved from that spot if I'd wanted to. I didn't want to.

"What's your name?" he asked. His voice, for such a tall boy, was markedly soft. He spoke so quietly that later I often thought I hadn't understood him, until he leaned forward and I realized I'd heard every syllable. There was a delay between his speech and my understanding, as though what he said seeped into me slowly, like the voices of my dreams.

"Mary Doherty," I said. My throat was dusty; I stifled a cough.

He frowned in a halfhearted, teasing way. "What's your real name?" he said.

"I don't know what you mean," I said stiffly. The horse he was holding by its halter snorted and shook its head as though it were laughing at me.

"The name you had before that fat bastard began claiming to be your father." His language surprised me; not that I hadn't heard worse, but he seemed awfully bold for a hired hand.

"What makes you think he's not my father?" I said. It was clear to both of us that I was playing a game, but I wasn't willing to give it up just yet. Though he was attractive, I also found him presumptuous.

"I'd sooner believe you if you told me I was your father," he said, and he laughed, a clear, beautiful laugh I was immediately afraid of anyone overhearing. I wanted to keep it safe and to myself.

"If you insist then," he said when I hadn't answered, "call me Peter. I'll give you my real name after you've given me yours."

It was less than a week before he sought me out. I was in town buying fish for Friday's dinner and felt his eyes on me before I saw him. He didn't approach but hung back, shadowing me as I hurried to finish my errands. I took a long route home, past the docks and along the sandy strip that separated the sea from marshland that stretched from town center to our neighborhood and beyond.

When we were safe from prying eyes, we sat by the water. It was high tide and the beach was deserted; clam diggers had gone home for their lunch. For a long time we were quiet without awkwardness. I hadn't felt so safe in the presence of another person since my parents had died. My body, absent its usual tension, felt loose and light, as if a gust of wind could blow it away.

"What is your name?" he said finally, in my mother's language, and I was crying as I answered him. I had come to believe I would never hear the words of my home again.

I am Awasosis, he said, which in our language means Little Bear. It was a good name for him. Despite his size and strength and occasional hard language, Awasosis was a gentle man who tended toward mischief and who, in moments of tenderness, looked at me with a wonder that made him seem very young.

He met me whenever he could get away, always at the market, and he carried my parcels as we walked along the marsh. One Saturday he came to the house and convinced Mr. Doherty to hire him a few hours a week to care for and exercise the horse. While Mr. Doherty was at work and Michael at school, Peter, as I called him in all but the most intimate of moments, would come into the kitchen and make me laugh as I prepared dinner. He was a great actor, and could do imitations of Mr. Doherty, Michael, and the nosy, shrill neighbor women on my block. By joking about my world, he made me feel, for the first time, that I lived in a place separate from my sorrow, that my soul was free even while my body was not.

We became lovers at my insistence. Peter was reluctant—he wanted to marry me first—but I feared we did not have that much time. When we made love, I refused to let go when it was over, squeezing my legs to hold him, savoring the throbs his body released deep inside me. Sometimes he laughed, joking that I could not get enough of him, other times he merely held me as I cried.

At night I dreamed his death over and over again; I felt his heart stop, watched his eyes film over, cold and blind.

He refused to believe me.

"People dream what they fear," he said. "What we fear doesn't always come to pass." He was saving his pennies for the day we would run away. He wanted to go out west, to a reservation where his brother raised horses.

When Mr. Doherty asked him to help with the Thanksgiving hunt, I told Peter not to go.

"If I don't go he will fire me and I won't be able to see you," Peter said.

"I think he suspects something," I said.

"I'll be careful," he promised.

The story that returned from the woods was that the Indian boy had gotten himself accidentally shot. Mr. Doherty told Michael about it as I served them Sunday dinner. I had to return to the kitchen, where I was quietly ill in the trash pail, to finish preparing dessert.

We went to Boston for Christmas, and Mr. Doherty's sister, after an evening of watching me, asked him what he planned to do about my being pregnant.

He beat me, hoping I would miscarry, and when I didn't, he had a long, violent confrontation with Michael when we arrived home. They came into the kitchen where I was trying to cook dinner one-handed, as my right arm was badly sprained.

"You'll be married this Saturday," Mr. Doherty said. Michael, standing beside him, would not look at me. I saw blood staining the moist underside of his lips. "You'll live on here," Mr. Doherty said. "This house will be yours someday."

I said nothing. I couldn't argue—I had no choices left. But I didn't want to agree to it, not out loud. Later, at the altar, I made a noncommittal noise, which the priest chose to take as an assent.

I still had hopes for Michael then. Though I'm sure he knew about his father's advances on me, and had done nothing about it through the years, he had shown me small kindnesses, and often looked at me as though we shared the secret of his father's violence. I thought if I took good care of him, and urged him to move away from the influence of his father, that Michael could grow to love me.

On the night of our wedding we were given the guesthouse— a small ivy-covered building in the back of the yard with a woodstove and a canopied bed I had always coveted—as our honeymoon suite. I kissed Michael first, passionately, pretending he was Peter. Michael was rough with me. He tore at my clothing, took me not on the bed but on the hard, gritty floor by the doorway.

At the moment of our union, I saw his soul. Quick flashes that would return over the years whenever he pushed his way inside me, always with the same rough disgust. I saw him as a child, saw his father violate him in the same ways he had me, leaving Michael bleeding from his backside and choking on the taste in his mouth. I saw the hatred that had grown like deadly nightshade, until his soul was so full of it there was no room for any love to take root. And when I opened my eyes and looked at him, I saw that all his hopes of escape were now thwarted, and I realized what a fool I had been.

I had married a man who despised me.

27

Schizotypal Personality Disorder

ALBA, I'D STARTED THINKING, was the "gifted" one. She had me in some sort of trance. I'd gone AWOL on the last chance my brother had given me, set out on a wild-goose chase to deliver letters between dead and elderly schizophrenics, and now I was on 95 North, headed toward the town I'd sworn never to set foot in again. The worst part was, I used to do this kind of crazy shit all the time. But at least then I was stoned.

Mrs. Doherty had a crystal bar set in her dining room—the decanter half full of what looked like quality scotch. I was still salivating over the thought of it. If Alba had used the bathroom or something, I might have had a chance at a couple of shots to pull myself together.

Alba had been mute since we left Quincy, gazing blankly at the highway and clutching her backpack as if she were carrying drugs rather than a bunch of useless letters. I'd tried to get her to talk but so far she was only responding with monosyllables. You'd think she'd be more grateful with me driving her all over New England.

We crossed back onto the Maine Turnpike, passing the sign that reads WELCOME TO MAINE: THE WAY LIFE SHOULD BE. I've always hated that sign.

Are you hungry? I said to Alba, as we approached another McDonald's arrow.

No, she mumbled.

Do you mind if we stop? I didn't have any lunch.

Go ahead. She sounded annoyed. I was losing my patience pretty fast. I should have bought a joint off those Land Rover boys. At least now I'd have something to calm me down.

She waited in the car. The line inside McDonald's was depressing. Tired, grimy families fidgeting over the familiar smell of fries. Little kids so fat they looked like teenagers. I considered the McSalad for about thirty seconds. I didn't want to end up one of those flabby former addicts. Weight has never been a problem for me, but they say it all starts to change after thirty. By the time I got to the register I was salivating too much to think about a diet. I ordered two Big Macs and a Super Size fries.

On my way out to the car I found Alba sitting on a bench by some ornamental bushes. She was smoking and gazing ahead, as if cars creeping in and out of parking spaces were a breathtaking sight. I sat down beside her and offered her some fries. She shook her head, taking a deep drag on her cigarette as if it had some nutritional value. I opened my first burger.

How long to St. Francis? Alba asked. I had to finish chewing before answering her.

About four hours north of Portland, I said, wiping at my chin with a paper napkin. We'll be too late to see him tonight.

Is there somewhere we can stay? Alba said. The thought of her stretched out on a hotel bed momentarily stunned me.

It's not exactly a tourist spot, I said. But there'll be a motel or something on the highway.

Alba nodded and was quiet while I finished my burger.

You don't want to go there, do you? she said finally.

What makes you say that? I said. Burger grease was congealing in my stomach. Suddenly, I didn't want the other one.

Alba shrugged. Just a feeling, she said.

It's not my favorite place in the world.

How long since you left? she said. I paused, pretending I needed to count.

Thirteen years.

Are your parents still there?

No. They're dead. I wanted to get back in the car. I crumpled up my wrappers, shoving them in the brown bag with the rejected burger.

What did your sister-in-law mean when she said you saved your brother's life?

That stunned me. I rewound back to the bookstore. What else had Bethany said?

She exaggerates, I said. My grandfather used to pick on David and I'd get in the way that's all.

He hit you?

Sometimes, I shrugged. Mostly I just distracted him into drinking more and playing chess.

An image flashed in the space between us: my own bloody face in the bathroom mirror.

Chess? she said suspiciously. That's how you saved his life?

The night of our high school graduation was a bit of a scene, I said. Our grandfather was really drunk, angry at David, and he had his rifle out. I got it away from him, that's all. We left that night and never went back.

Jesus, Alba said. Are we going to run into him?

He died the next year. Left us the house. We sold it and used the money after our scholarships ran out.

Alba was quiet for a minute, watching me. In Scotland, I was thinking, they sold beer at McDonald's.

I didn't think you were the hero, she said.

I'm not a hero.

The hero, Alba insisted. Haven't you heard that one in rehab? In alcoholic families, kids take on roles. The Hero's usually the oldest. Then the Rebel, the Lost One, and the Clown.

Rubbish, I said. No rehab on the road, I added, trying to smile at her.

She kissed me. She came at me fast, and I reached up to hold her face. Her tongue tasted of smoke, mine of Special Sauce. The combination reminded me of high school. Except back then I was always stoned, floating somewhere above it all, and now every cell of my body was ringing with the movement of her mouth. This was a new kind of desire. I didn't just want to have sex with her. I wanted to lie down and lower myself, body and soul, inside her. I knew it would feel better than any drug I'd ever paid for.

This thought startled me enough that I broke our kiss. I held her face against my neck, listening to her try to control her breath.

We'd better get back on the road, I whispered, and she stiffened.

Yes, she said, standing up, instantly composed.

I wanted to say I was sorry. To tell her to stop, because she was already embedded in me in a way that could only be dangerous. Wanted to say: I gave up being the Hero a long time ago. Now I was the Rebel, and the Clown, and the Lost One. And that she couldn't depend on any one of them.

What I said instead was this: Do you need the bathroom before we go?

My most successful role, as always, was the Idiot.

We neared the St. Francis exit at around midnight. I pulled into a Motel 6 where a teenager desperately in need of Clearasil rented us a room. He actually winked at me.

The rest of the night was a disaster. It was obvious that Alba was expecting something—she spent half an hour in the bathroom getting ready for bed. When she was finished, I hid in there a while myself, willing my erection away. On the one hand there was this promise—I could go in there and make love to her and it would be the best of my life. It would change me, I could tell that already from the way we kissed. But once it was over the trouble would start. I'd be the same loser still craving a fix and, I had to admit it, she'd still be crazy. We'd expect more of each other, and neither of us would be able to deliver. It was safer to keep it a fantasy. That way, all the possibilities I had felt every time we'd kissed would remain alive; the image of myself as a good man—a man in love—would sustain me.

Of course, if you stripped the psychoanalysis away, the scenario was much simpler: I was a coward. I had a beautiful woman waiting in bed and I was too afraid to join her.

When I finally emerged from the bathroom, Alba was tucked into the nearest of the two queen-sized beds, wearing a tiny tank top that pulled against her breasts. She had the letters out again, but

I could see she wasn't really reading them. She was holding her breath, trying not to look at me.

I got in the other bed. Facing away from her, I faked an exhausted good-night, and lay there feeling lower than I've ever felt—and that's saying a lot. I could almost hear her expectation leaking away. If I had a drink, I thought, just a couple of stiff night-caps, I'd be brave enough to grab her and see where it led. Or at least numb enough not to care. As it was, sobriety seemed awfully harsh, like trying to sleep when you can't turn out the lights.

In the morning, Alba was up and dressed by the time I peeled open my eyes. From her dazed, jumpy look I guessed she hadn't slept much. She didn't look particularly friendly either.

I'm not at my best in the mornings. Before rehab, I always needed a kick to get me going; since Abenaki, my waking hours had been fraught with edgy confrontations. Morning and dusk were the times I was most angry at the notion of quitting drugs for good. The times I was convinced it was impossible.

So, by the time I'd showered and shaved, Alba had paid the bill, and we were back in the car, headed to my hometown, the tension fairly thick. I tried to make her laugh, giving a mock tour of down-town. The bowling alley, the A & P, the animal shelter where we'd once gotten a dog my grandfather ended up shooting. Alba was not amused.

That road leads to Waban Cove, where I sampled my first ille-gal substance, I said.

Where you started trying to kill yourself, you mean, Alba said.

I had no urge to cheer her up after that. As I pulled into the Angel of Mercy parking lot, neither of us said a word. There were plenty of them lining up in my head however.

The desk nurse seemed surprised when we asked for Peter Doherty. Alba told her we were friends of the family. The nurse gave us a room number and complicated hallway directions, and Alba set out, her boots squeaking with determination on the linoleum. I shuffled behind, wondering why I hadn't just stayed in the car when she wasn't acknowledging that I was there at all.

The door to 323 was ajar, Peter's name, engraved in plastic, permanently affixed to the doorjamb. Alba knocked softly and edged it open.

Mr. Doherty? she said. It was dark inside, heavy curtains pulled across the windows on the far wall. It took my eyes a moment to adjust after the fluorescent light of the hallway. The room was standard—a twin-sized bed covered with an inoffensive unisex quilt, scarred wood furniture that was formal, removed, the sort of furniture that never takes on the personality of its owner. Innocuous scenes of the ocean and woodlands were framed and hung on the walls alongside laminated sheets of institutional guidelines. An elderly man was sitting in an adjustable purple leatherette chair by the window.

Mr. Doherty? Alba said again. His head jerked up, revealing absurdly thick glasses that made his eyes look like large, wet stones.

It's not time for my medicine yet, he said, in a half-defiant, half-resigned tone that made me think he repeated this protest several times a day.

Mr. Doherty, my name is Alba Elliot. I spoke with your wife yesterday.

Peter looked from Alba to me and back again, as if trying to detect some conspiracy.

Are you with the Coast Guard? he said. I followed Alba closer to him and saw that he had ropes in his lap, his fingers paused in the tying of a nautical knot.

No, sir, Alba said, looking to me for an instant. We're from Abenaki—I mean, Saint Dymphna's. I have some letters from your mother.

You're Abenaki? Peter said. My mother was Abenaki.

That's why I'm here, Alba said, sounding desperate now. Because of your mother. She wrote to you.

Alba opened her pack and took out a folder of photocopies, holding it forward for Peter to take. He waved toward a shelf against the wall, which held rubber plants and more rope, indicating that she should put it down. Alba seemed disappointed but laid it carefully on the top shelf nonetheless.

Don't you want to see them? she said.

Mother will be by later, he said simply. She'll read them to me. My eyesight's not so good these days.

There was an uncomfortable silence—for us, at least; Peter seemed unfazed—then we were saved by a nurse.

Aren't you a lucky fella, having visitors today, she said, sweeping efficiently into the room, in that way of nurses who seem to think they're never an intrusion. She went directly to the window and yanked open the drapes. The sunlight flooded in, blinding us all.

I thought we agreed on some fresh air this morning, she said. She turned the window outward with a stiff metal crank.

This is my daughter, Mary, Peter said to Alba and me. She's getting married in June. His face wrenched suddenly, as if he were in pain, then smoothed itself again—an involuntary twitch.

The nurse wheeled over a blood pressure gauge, winding the cuff round Peter's flaccid upper arm. She chuckled as she pumped the ball.

Isn't it June already? she said. I'd better get busy, then. She paused, listening with her stethoscope and eyeing the gauge. Looks good, she said, ripping the Velcro undone and rolling the machine away. She picked up a chart from the end of his bed and jotted the numbers down.

Are you going to tell me your friends' names? she said.

I've never seen them before in my life, Peter grumbled, rubbing his arm. The inside of his elbow was mottled with needle bruises.

What did you come here for? he said, looking at Alba. He seemed suddenly depressed, resentful.

I . . . Alba whispered, taken aback. I guess I thought you could help me. She was blushing.

For an instant, Peter caught her eyes. He looked, for the first time, completely lucid, as if he were about to say something profound, and I caught a glimpse of what a powerfully handsome man he must have been.

The nurse interrupted them.

Have you read their fortunes yet? she called out loudly from where she was gathering an untouched breakfast tray.

Mr. D. reads all our futures in those knots of his, she explained to me, because Alba was still looking hopefully at Peter, who was staring at the ropes in his lap.

Does he? I said, for lack of anything more helpful.

Oh, yes, he's got a gift. Go on, Mr. D. Tell this young couple how happy they'll be. She left then, winking at us, bouncing away on her cushioned white shoes.

Peter looked downtrodden now, a scolded boy. Pick a rope if you like, he murmured, and I nudged Alba to cooperate. She took an old, gray piece of cotton line from the shelf and held it out to him.

Sit down, Peter said, waving it away. She sat by the window in the other chair, still holding the rope.

Slowly, he demonstrated how she should tie a simple knot. He corrected her a few times, under not over, in a gentle, patient voice. Once she was done, he took the finished rope from her and studied it closely. His hands had a slight tremor.

Your talent could save you, he said, but you haven't let it yet. His face twitched again, a spasm that lasted longer this time, and I glanced away, embarrassed for him.

Huh, he said, when he'd regained control, turning the rope over. He's been quite a disappointment, hasn't he?

Alba didn't respond, or ask whom he meant. I didn't believe in this sort of thing, but I couldn't help wondering if he was referring to me.

Leaving someone behind doesn't mean you can't love them, Peter said. Let yourself go forward.

I didn't leave him, Alba said. My father took him away.

I was talking about your father, silly girl, Peter said.

Alba stood up quickly, her chair scraping the floor.

I'm sorry, she said. I shouldn't have bothered you. She moved toward the door, and, feeling rude, I followed her.

No bother, Peter said. I just have to get the place cleaned up. My mother will be coming home soon.

When we left he was whistling—a strong, youthful, unbroken whistle—and Alba was fighting back tears. I was sure they'd have tempting pharmaceuticals at the nurses' station, but Alba was in a hurry and I couldn't begin to imagine how I would snatch them without getting caught.

28

Saint Dymphna's Aslyum

September, 1938

Dear Peter,

So much has changed in the last few weeks, I hardly
know where I am anymore. Ever since I lost hope for
my own life, I have defined myself as your mother. But
if I haven't seen you in five years, am I still that
woman? Or am I merely a raving lunatic who believes
she has the power to heal souls?

After the tragedy of Dr. Madden's son, there was
an official inquiry launched on the hospital. Men with
clipboards followed the nuns on their daily rounds,
taking notes with cryptic, suspicious expressions.
Some of the patients tried to plead their sanity to the
Clipboards—as is often the case when a novice nun

begins on the ward—but it was clear from the confused and slightly disgusted reactions that these men would not be saving them. After that, everyone held their tongues and started behaving with perfect decorum. We suspected that the nuns were being evaluated and, though we didn't like them, a strange loyalty arose. Just because they were our captors did not mean we were willing to trade them for new ones.

I was interviewed intensely regarding Billy Madden's death, but as it was clear from the day logs that I had not left the ward at any time that he was missing, there was really nothing they could accuse me of. Everyone is watching me now, though, very closely, both patients and nuns, and it is making me less enthusiastic about nighttime healing. I overheard a Clipboard saying that I could be transferred to the State Hospital if I proved too much for the nuns to handle. As Mother Superior doesn't like to admit defeat, she insisted I was not a problem, but I now have a new fear. I have heard that in the State Hospital women are kept locked in windowless rooms, their meals delivered through slots in the metal cell doors. They are only let out once a week for exercise. They certainly aren't allowed access to pen and paper (imagine what damage I could do with a pen!), so if I went there, I would lose you forever.

Later . . .

Well, the Clipboards' review must have been derogatory, because the nuns are leaving. The Church has decided to relinquish control of the hospital, and it has been sold into private ownership, to a doctor who is rumored to be forward-thinking and successful. I have my doubts.

January, 1939

Dear Peter,

For two weeks we were moved to one of the abandoned buildings while they refurbished the ward. When we returned, the odor of paint made our eyes water. The place is so changed it is almost unrecognizable. The formerly gray walls are now gleaming white, the nurses' station has doubled in size and is walled off in glass—it looks like the cockpit of an airplane. We have new cots with leather straps permanently fashioned on the metal rungs. There are large, sparkling locks on every door—before, the doors were propped open and we were allowed to wander freely from room to room, now we need to beg our wanderings of the nurses whose belts jangle with dozens of keys.

The nurses are the biggest change. The quiet stealth of nuns in billows of black fabric is gone. In their place is starched white; various hair shades frizz out from beneath bun caps, and stocking-encased legs—young and shapely to vein-lined—move with brazen nakedness across the linoleum. Where there was once a monastic silence, we now hear giggling, voices raised in humor or argument, the occasional whoop of hilarity. Out among us, the nurses are severe and businesslike; from behind the glass dome, which is not as soundproof as they think, the sounds of life erupt blasphemously from their lungs. It makes us miss the nuns; their somber manner at least had the guise of reverence, and we could convince ourselves that there was a quality of respect for our predicament. These nurses merely serve to remind us that we are outcasts—that life still laughs and ridicules itself everywhere but inside these walls.

There are now at least a dozen male attendants—large, beery men who look uncomfortable in their spotless white uniforms, which coordinate so well with the nurses they look like dance partners. Thomas has gone the way of the nuns; at night our dorm is locked and the ward is guarded by three of the larger men. So far, they all seem impervious to, even alarmed by, Isabelle's advances.

Dr. Stockwell is the new owner and chief physician for St. Dymphna's (now renamed the Stockwell Institute for Women, but no one calls it that). In addition to him, there are a number of so-called residents—boys younger than I, who are still in the process of learning the symptoms and plagues of female mental illness. I must confess, we have a bit of fun with them. They are jumpy and eager to please and seem to think it likely that any one of us is capable of biting them, even those not prone to biting. The nurses have little patience with them—they don't have time to answer so many inane questions—so the residents often hide away in a locked supply closet that has been cleaned out and renamed the Doctor's Lounge.

Sandra insists that we find a way to resume my healing sessions—perhaps on the ward, as it seems our nighttime escapes are now impossible. There are a number of women who believe I am their only hope. What I want to tell them, but I haven't the energy to articulate it, is that I suspect, under Dr. Stockwell's clinical eye, we all have less of a chance of being released than we ever did before. Whether we are well or not.

29

Paperwork

HISTORY OF A MENTAL RESERVATION

NATHAN STOCKWELL, M.D., PH.D.

CASE STUDY

Patient: *Mary X*

Date: *October 10, 1938*

Diagnosis: *Dementia Praecox (Schizophrenia)*

History: *Patient was committed to hospital (then Saint Dymphna's Asylum) by her husband in the spring of 1933, after exhibiting psychotic, delusional and violent behavior. Initial diagnosis focused on "female maladies" no longer considered valid causes of insanity. Later, patient suffered seizures and was rediagnosed with epilepsy. Ward observations over the years indicate confusion, hallucination, self-*

mutilation (hair pulling), sleepwalking and violent protests to medica-
tion. Hydrotherapy has proven unsuccessful beyond its short-term effects.

Summary: *Between confiscated writings and my sessions with Mary, it*
is clear that she is suffering from a number of delusions and hallucina-
tions, the most dangerous of which is the belief that she is some sort of
spiritual healer. She refers to herself as a Medawlinno, *and her commit-*
ment papers indicate that she comes from Indian origin. There are a
number of studies on the primitive beliefs of this culture (see attached
article). Shamans are often chosen for their aberrant, psychotic behavior
in early adolescence (i.e., introversion, self-mutilation, sleep depriva-
tion, hallucinatory visions). Most likely, Mary has had symptoms of
schizophrenia since pubescence, and was made to believe her illness was
some sort of gift. She has been practicing her "healing" on other
patients, and for now will be confined to a solitary ward to prevent fur-
ther abuse of her peers.

Treatment Prescribed: *Prolonged Narcosis*

Results: *The "sleep cure"—continuous administration of sedatives for*
weeklong periods—has proven useful in other patients to break the cycle
of autism and disturbance. So far, after three separate sessions, Mary
seems subdued and more cooperative. She has been talking in her sleep; I
instructed the nurses to record everything she said, and now have more
than ten pages of alarming dialogue. It is clear that she suffered incestu-
ous abuse at the hands of her uncle; she described a vivid scene in a barn
where he forced himself on her while she was milking cows. When I ques-
tioned her about this, her denial was vigilant; she claims her uncle was
her mentor. The man must have used this guise as a means to control her.
It will be a long process breaking down Mary's deep-seated denial; at
first she stopped her protests in mid-sentence and often seemed to be on

the verge of tears. Later, she became violent and had to be sedated again. I recommend continuing the prolonged narcosis until she no longer appears to be benefiting from it.

THE STOCKWELL INSTITUTE FOR WOMEN

CASE STUDY

Patient: *Mary X*

Date: *September 30, 1939*

Diagnosis: *Dementia Praecox (Schizophrenia)*

Treatment Prescribed: *Insulin Shock*

Patient administered insulin by IV push daily, increasing amounts until day 4 caused hypoglycemic shock. Imposed seizures are believed to produce the same calming effects as natural seizures in epileptics. Insulin coma prescribed daily for three months.

Results: *Mary is markedly sedate and absent of former mood swings. While still lethargic, her initial resentment has given way to acceptance. In our sessions she has admitted that she is ill and wants to recover. She has recalled her adolescent symptoms for me and I have explained how they correspond to the onset of schizophrenia. She has requested permission to communicate with her children, but I told her I do not think she is ready for that. We need to observe her to see if the therapy produces long-term effects.*

November 2, 1939: *Mary's last seizure resulted in the fracturing of her jawbone, so insulin has been discontinued until she recovers.*

30

Hypomanic Episode

WHEN ALBA FIRST began losing her mind, before she gathered the vocabulary of Abenaki to describe her symptoms, she repeated a three-word explanation at every interview they gave her: Something is wrong.

Something is wrong now, again, has been wrong since the night before, and it is getting too persistent to pretend otherwise. It's not just in her head, as various people have suggested to her—*it's all in your head, Alba, it's not real, calm down*—it is all over her body. Her legs feel rubbery, like they might give way. Her throat is closing, breathing is becoming difficult because all her energy is going to swallowing, constantly checking to see how much room is left. She is sweating—she can feel damp ovals spreading beneath her arms all the way down to her waist. She is grateful for the black cotton shirt that camouflages wetness and fears that Oscar will choose this time to put his arms around her, only to draw back, disgusted.

Of course, her head is wrong too. She hasn't yet reached the full-blown panic-attack point, where she can't move or look at anything because the pain—and that's what it is, slicing mental pain—has overtaken her. But she's having trouble focusing on anything for very long; inanimate objects lunge at her. Mr. Doherty's rope looked as if it were slithering on its own through her fingers. When Oscar speaks, she has trouble listening, for the darkness she sees in his mouth terrifies her. And she's no longer sure whether what she hears is coming from the world or the various voices that shout and whisper in her brain.

For instance, she has no idea if Mr. Doherty said what she heard him say about her father. She wants to ask Oscar, but no matter what the answer is, she'll look like a lunatic. She is befuddled by the cheap sideshow trick of fortune-telling. Disappointed by Peter's obvious confusion and his twitches which, she knows from the hospital, are those of a medicated schizophrenic. She wanted to believe that Mary's son had some gift, but now she feels like she often does after people try to cure her with crystals or soul massage or homeopathic remedies—tiny sweet spheres of broken-down elements that are said to share her oddly ambivalent personality traits. She believes that there are miracles beyond her understanding, but cannot understand why they never perform for her.

What she should really do is take some medicine, five food groups of pills to combat the various symptoms, but she doesn't want to. Never mind that they will tire her out, numb her to the point that she will only want to go back to her hospital bed; it would also be, she feels, like giving up. She knows, she's given up a dozen times before. It never gets her anywhere but back to Abenaki or her bedroom at her father's house, nodding in agreement to his newest plans for her future.

At the very least she should have taken something to sleep last night. It's going on three days now since she's been able to shut her eyes for longer than ten minutes. But last night she had been holding on to the hope that Oscar would change his mind; that one of them would get up the nerve to crawl into the other's bed; that she would finally be able to press all this longing she has for him against his body rather than letting it disintegrate into the air. If she'd taken Klonopin to sleep, her longing would have evaporated.

It appears that Oscar doesn't want her anyway. He seemed to once, but he must have been pretending, or else he's changed his mind. All she can hope for now is that he doesn't leave her before she finishes what she set out to do. She doesn't trust herself to drive.

What now? Oscar says when they're back in the car. Is it really this hot or is it only she who can't wait for him to turn the ignition so she can flick on the AC?

The only option she has left is to find him herself. She should have done it years ago.

Do you know where St. Anthony's Orphanage is? she says. Oscar looks confused.

It's part of a convent, he says. About twenty miles out on Route 2. My grandfather used to threaten to send us there.

Let's go.

Why? Oscar laughs. Are you becoming a nun now?

Just go, Alba says, too loudly. Did she shriek? Oscar's startled expression seems to indicate that she did.

Please, she says softly. He looks doubtful, opens his mouth to say something, to argue with her.

It's not as if you have anywhere to go, she says. He looks like he's just been slapped.

Hey, he says, his voice low. This shit may work on your boyfriends . . .

Alba laughs, a quick, ugly snort.

But I'm getting pretty tired of it. I may not have anywhere to go, but if you keep this up, I'll have no reason to stay either.

Part of her wants to push it, keep at it until he leaves, prove something. But she can't seem to remember what it is she's trying to prove.

You're right, she says. I'm sorry. The heat is throbbing in her face.

Oscar starts the car, his jaw tight, and Alba turns the AC on high.

A convent, Alba thinks, is far too quiet, too reverent, to contain a madwoman. Even her footsteps sound blasphemous. Her few inquiries so far have been met with alarmed but sympathetic looks, and now, as they wait in an office for someone in charge, Oscar is jumpy, looking as if he's prepared to tackle her if she does something dangerous. She wants to tell him that she is acutely aware of it all— that her voice is too loud, her expression too desperate, her hands shaking even more than they do with medication. She has never been one of those people who can go crazy without realizing it.

The Mother Superior comes in, looking nothing like the robed bride of God Alba expected, but more like a spinster schoolteacher, bifocals hanging from her neck on a gold chain, denting the starched ruffles on her blouse. She is holding a manila file, and for an instant Alba thinks it will be easy—she will be given the information and sent on her way, years of secrecy will fall away with a name and address scrawled on institutional paper.

But then the nun begins to explain, in a gentle, authoritative voice, the policies of the orphanage. Adoption is either open or closed at the time the child is given up; once the decision to be closed is made it takes a number of petitions and inquiries to open it back up again. The adoption of Alba's son, ten years ago, was closed. Mother Superior is not obliged to give Alba any more information than that.

Then I want to petition, Alba says. How do I petition?

I'm afraid you can't.

Didn't you just say she could? Oscar argues. He's only helping, Alba thinks, to shut her up.

Miss Elliot, the nun sighs. According to our records, you were not the child's legal guardian when he was placed in our hands.

But I'm his mother, Alba says weakly. I named him Sam.

I believe you were ill at the time? the nun asks, referring to the papers in front of her. Alba doesn't answer, but she knows it is written somewhere that she was committed.

You were also a minor, the nun continues. Your father was the boy's legal guardian because you were deemed unfit. He made all the arrangements with us. I'm afraid he's the only one who can petition. Except your son, when he is eighteen years old. The nun paused. I can tell you that the name on his original birth certificate was Samuel Elliot, but it has been changed.

This is all a mistake, Alba says. I never told my father he could do that. If you just tell me where my son is, I'll be able to explain everything.

I'm sorry, the nun says gently.

Alba, many times, has thought of herself as hitting bottom. She has sat in moments, heavy with the knowledge that they were the worst moments of her life. Only now does she realize that it will keep happening, over and over again, that she will never hit bottom, because the bottom is always moving. That the longer her life goes on, the further she will have to fall. Bottom would be a relief. It is the space she plummets through that makes her insane.

She doesn't argue, or scream, or fall apart. This seems to worry Oscar; he keeps looking at her, waiting for something to happen.

She is just as surprised as he is. Simply walking out into the summer afternoon without protest, Oscar's hand on her elbow, seems like a miracle. Only it's not the one she has been looking for.

In the car she starts to shake; it's so bad Oscar has to latch her seat belt for her. He drives like it's an emergency, back in the direction they've come, though she hasn't told him where to go. Her knees are bouncing; her teeth chatter if she doesn't clench her jaw to the point of pain.

Do you have any medicine with you? Oscar asks.

Why? Alba stutters. You want some?

You need to calm down, Oscar says. He sounds almost guilty. She was just trying to be ironic; it hadn't occurred to her until now that he might be tempted by her pills.

Alba, Oscar says, and his voice is gentler than it's been all day. You have to tell me what's going on.

Why? she says. Words are so difficult to form through the tremor in her jaw; she's afraid the wrong ones will emerge. That *Leave me alone* will come out *I love you,* or vice versa.

Oscar seems stumped for a moment. So far all I've done is be your chauffeur, he says. Maybe if you let me in I can help you.

No one can help me, Alba says.

Don't say that, Oscar says. Why would you say that?

It's funny how quickly he becomes just like everyone else. Yesterday he would have agreed with her, shrugged cynically and looked away. When faced with the absence of hope everyone was the same: they all became fixated on the bright side of things.

Pull over, Alba says.

Why? Oscar looks alarmed.

I'm going to throw up.

· · ·

I was going to have an abortion, Alba says.

They're back in the Motel 6 by St. Francis, in a different room that is identical to the first one. After an hour of retching by the side of the road, after Oscar practically carried her back to the car, suggesting that she might have gotten food poisoning, and Alba said that would only be likely if she'd eaten anything, then asked him to pull over again, Oscar decided to find her a place to lie down.

That was my first instinct, Alba says, sitting up in one of the beds, holding on to her knees to keep down the shaking. Oscar looks uncomfortable.

What? she says. You said I should tell you, so I'm telling you. Did you change your mind?

No, no, Oscar says. Go on.

I went to the clinic, I took a cab there. I was nauseous all the time but I don't remember ever throwing up. I must have looked awful because the cab driver offered to wait for me. He gave me his cell phone number for when I was ready to go home. He was so nice—he wasn't hitting on me or anything, just concerned—I couldn't stand it. I started thinking about how he must have kids he was really wonderful with and a wife he never ridiculed, that they probably didn't have much money but all knew they loved each other and I got even more nauseous and thought: I'm having a boy. I just knew, without a doubt, that there was a boy inside me and if I went into that clinic I would never see him. My mother killed herself when I was four, have I told you that?

Oscar shook his head.

She did. Anyway, I started thinking in that cab—wouldn't an abortion be sort of the same thing? I'd be abandoning him. He would never know it, but I would. Well, I knew I was fucked even thinking that way, and then I started to cry and I couldn't stop and eventually the cab driver just brought me home. I spent the next few days reading pro-choice pamphlets trying to get my courage up, but in the end, though I agreed with all the literature, I just couldn't do it. I even called the cab driver once, but it was really late and the woman who answered sounded like she'd been asleep, so I hung up.

I didn't tell anyone, not my father or my friends. I told my boyfriend I didn't want to have sex anymore and that got rid of him. I quit smoking, took prenatal vitamins, and wore baggy clothes.

I'd been sick for a while. Or getting sick anyway. My mother was manic-depressive, and after she committed suicide—I began to worry that I would turn out like her. So when I was twelve or thirteen and I started feeling strange—I'd stay up for days or sleep far too much, be so afraid to go to school I'd pretend I was sick, or be so fearless I'd jump in front of traffic on a dare—I pretended nothing was wrong. I didn't want my father to know, didn't want to disappoint him. I started smoking because it seemed to help, gave me something to focus on when my mind was reeling. I cut myself too, superficially, where no one would see the scabs. It felt good to bleed; it was proof that there was something really wrong with me besides the indefinable muddiness of my mind. When I got to high school and was offered drugs, I didn't do them, though I was tempted. I was too afraid of my brain to monkey with it. I'd be likely to throw myself out a window on my first acid trip.

I thought about death. Thought about death all the time, the way some girls thought about boys, or boys thought about sex.

Once I was pregnant, though, I got better. I felt really good for a while, actually woke up happy in the mornings. I was focused, organized, never tired, got straight As and ate three meals a day, kept my room clean and wrote a dozen short stories, three of which were published in the school magazine. I made all these plans, they seem stupid now, for what I was going to do with my boy. I was going to take him to live in Europe, we'd write children's books together, shit like that. I read aloud to my stomach. I hadn't been so productive and enthusiastic since I was a little girl and I was sure being pregnant had cured me. That my baby was rearranging my neurotransmitters, putting them into balance, and that they would stay that way. I read all these parenting books that said once a woman has a baby she stops worrying so much about herself. That sounded perfect to me.

It didn't matter. No one believed that I wasn't sick. I told my father when I was almost due and he freaked out. He was sure I was psychotic to have kept it a secret for so long, even though the reason I kept it a secret was so no one would think I was crazy. Anyway, he had me committed, and by the time I got to the hospital I was hysterical, and that combined with my family history was enough to get the doctors to medicate me. They induced labor while I was out of it and gave me so much Haldol afterward that by the time I knew where I was, my father had already given him away. He had me declared mentally incompetent so he could take away my baby. One of the nurses told me it was a boy. All I could say, over and over until they had to sedate me again, was: "He's going to think I left him."

After my father brought me home I set the house on fire. Not to kill myself or ask for help, or even to punish my father, all things the psychiatrists at Abenaki assumed. I was just manic and not sleeping and obsessed with the fear that there would be a fire, and worried for the baby who wasn't even there. I set it because it was the only way to stop worrying.

When I'm sick, even sometimes when I'm not, all I want to do is die. The medicine just distracts me, makes me too tired to plan, writing does the same thing. Normal life isn't real to me. What's real is that I want to die—that is my illness— and I'm afraid it will never go away.

And you think if you find your son that will stop? Oscar says.

He looks sad, and doubtful, the way Dr. Miller looks when they talk about this.

Why not? Alba says. I've tried everything else and nothing works. Not medication, not therapy, not writing, not my father's plans. When I read through Mary's letters I thought: maybe my *soul* is broken. All along I've been told it's my mind. Mary said people's souls break and a part of them gets lost and the cure is to find it. For a while I thought it was my mother. But now I think maybe my son is the missing part of my soul.

For a moment they just sit there, watching the yellow-shaded hotel lamp between them, as it dims and brightens in time with the hum of the air conditioner.

What are you thinking? Alba says, and Oscar looks startled. You think I'm crazy, don't you?

No, Oscar says, then smiles slightly. Well, relatively. But I doubt my opinion's of any use to you.

What are you talking about? Alba says. You asked me.

I know. I shouldn't have.

Why?

I'm just not the type of guy people go to for help or advice. His hand wanders up to his shoulder, kneading the joint.

I doubt that, Alba says. You just refuse to help, that's all.

Look, Oscar says, standing up. I think you should get some sleep. Tomorrow you can tell me where you want to go next.

Alba just stares at him.

I'm going out for a while, Oscar says. I'll be back.

And he's out the motel door so fast it's like a cruel slapstick routine and Alba almost laughs.

It strikes her as funny, even as her eyes well up, that she had imagined—whenever they kissed and she felt her numb soul come alive—that Oscar would understand her.

31

Saint Dymphna's Asylum

1942

Dear Peter,

It has been over a year since I took a pen and composed small, secret lines in the back of a book. I'll admit, though it shames me, I intended never to write you again. The insulin therapy, which has been consistent in three-month stretches and one-month recoveries, murdered any urge I had to communicate. I write you now because two things have occurred: I have started dreaming again and I received a letter from the man you call your father.

My dreams—which usually occur during an insulin-induced shock—are not about the women who surround me. I am traveling to the Abenaki village that I

first saw during my fits when Dr. Madden was here. In each dream
I follow one woman through tragedy or illness, and then
resurrection under the care of the village healer. Unlike today, this
place was once a haven of healing; the women patched their
broken souls and were often unwilling to return to the people who
had broken them. They married within the tribe, raised their
children to speak both English and Abenaki, warned them of the
world that would do everything in its power to drag them down.

At the end of each dream I see a blood-red river flowing
beside the ravaged body of the woman who was healed. Often,
they are clutching children whose blood feeds into the same river.
I don't know why they have died—but every one of them ends
this way. Each time I wake from the shock, it takes a good while
before the thick redness clears from my eyes.

Dr. Stockwell has decided that the insulin treatment is no
longer beneficial, as I now wake from each coma screaming about
murder. He seems frustrated by my lack of cooperation. He is in
the process of writing a book about this therapy and apparently I
am his most fruitful subject. His normally prying gaze has turned
accusatory, like a disappointed parent.

It was Dr. Stockwell who gave me the letter. It was formally
typed and far too articulate to have been written by your father
alone. There are sentences that reveal him, however. The letter
moves from a detached compassion, which I assume comes from
his lawyer, to the thinly veiled hatred Michael had alternately
swallowed and exploded with throughout our marriage.

He has divorced me, you see. Because of my prolonged
absence and Dr. Stockwell's diagnosis—he says I am unlikely to
be released any time soon and that I am incapable of maintaining
normal relationships—the court has allowed him to dissolve our
marriage without my consent. He has married another woman,

one I suspect has been around for a while. There is nothing I can do—according to Dr. Stockwell, there are no legal avenues in which I can contest this divorce. My condition has rendered me powerless in the eyes of the law. It is as if, as far as the world is concerned, I am already dead.

Michael and his new wife have been granted full custody of our five children. I will never be allowed to see you or the girls again. At first, I didn't understand this clause—it was hard enough to accept that I could be divorced without agreeing to it—but that I could never see my children, even if Michael was not there, seemed particularly harsh. Dr. Stockwell explained it to me.

Apparently, coming out of my comas, I have continued to relate my life in confused sleep-talk. Dr. Stockwell has notes on a number of my intimacies with Peter, as well as the fear and guilt the affair caused me. He has deduced that the Peter I speak of is actually you. It was based on his recommendation that the court decided I was never to see my children again.

I have just returned to the ward after a week of solitary therapy in a small, padded room tufted with buttons like the inside of a coffin. Apparently confinement is the recommended treatment for women who attempt to scratch their physician's eyes out.

Dear Peter,

Everything is clear to me now—as though I have just awoken from the most powerful dream imaginable, with the answers to every question I have ever sought. I know the history of this land, I have seen the slaughter that this place was built upon. And I now know what it is I am required, destined really, to do.

It began with my final treatment—a process called electroshock therapy, which is something new that Dr. Stockwell is very excited about. I am the first patient in this hospital to receive it—as usual I am serving as Dr. Stockwell's guinea pig.

The machine arrived last week, and the attendants cleared one of the hydrotherapy rooms to accommodate it. Dr. Stockwell stayed late every day testing it out. Though we never saw it, every woman on the ward felt it. There would be an audible click and a loud hum, and the ward lights would dim considerably. Usually a bulb would blow out, and occasionally the entire hospital would plunge into darkness, and it would take a while for the attendants to get the lights running again.

The women on the ward became very nervous. They were sure we were all going to be electrocuted one at a time until the hospital was finally empty. They were right, in a way. Except that the treatment does not kill you—it merely brings you to the brink of death and then back again.

Before breakfast, the head nurse and two attendants came to escort me to my first treatment. They brought me to the humming room where Dr. Stockwell waited by a control box, trying hard to contain the excitement bubbling beneath his serious bedside manner. The attendants helped me lie down on a gurney bolted to the floor. They wedged a slanted wooden board under my back so that I was half-sitting, and tied down my wrists and ankles with the familiar leather straps. The head nurse applied a very cold, foul-smelling jelly to my temples, then pulled some straps onto my head and clamped what felt like metal prongs over the jelly. My terror must have been obvious, for the nurse took a moment to place a comforting hand on my shoulder, and she is not known as an empathetic nurse.

"Just relax, Mary. You shouldn't feel a thing," Dr. Stockwell said in a voice that was less than reassuring. I could not turn my head to see him at the controls. I remember noticing a crack on the ceiling and thinking, *this room was never painted,* and wondering if the electricity would feel like that—a jagged rip through my soul. The head nurse put a gag between my teeth. The humming got louder, there was a jolt, I was at the very edge of excruciating pain, then blackness consumed me.

When I woke I was in a private room. A foul taste burned at the back of my tongue, and my body felt as if it were one long bruise. Dr. Stockwell was there and began babbling before I was fully awake. He handed me a pencil and a small stack of clean white paper.

"You may feel a bit confused, Mary, and your memory may be altered temporarily. I'd like you to write down anything you can remember from the procedure, as well as what you are feeling now. First impressions, you understand. It would be helpful for my research if the patient narrated the experience. Take your time. How do you feel, by the way?"

"A little befuddled," I said. This was a lie. I felt battered but I had never been so clear—my mind was bristling with the memory of my travels.

I am in the Abenaki village. It is just before dawn and it is very cold and quiet. People are beginning to rise in their houses—I hear a baby cry, a woman laugh. Smoke from the morning fires tickles my nostrils. People emerge with the winter dawn—I don't notice at first that it is only women and children. But when everyone is up, as the bustle of morning chores commences, it is obvious that the men, other than very small boys, are missing. I question the soul of a woman nearby to find out where they are. She is worried about her husband, away fighting in a white man's war. The colonists came to them a few months ago and asked for their help against the British. They were promised legal ownership of the land they already lived on. Though the healer advised against it—reminding them of the wars between the English and the French in which so many of their ancestors had been slaughtered—the men decided to go. In the end, even the healer joined them. For a while, teenage boys were sent home periodically with news, but there has been no word for weeks now.

When the soldiers arrive, the women are initially excited; they believe news of their husbands comes along with this bedraggled crew. But these soldiers are from a different company, they are dirty, tired and gruff in their demands for food. The women automatically gather what they can find; they have fed soldiers before. The men sit down, remove their battered boots, and tend to feet nearly black with dried blood. They are angry—the pain in their feet is making them more so—and they snap at the Abenaki women and trade raunchy insults when the women's backs are turned. The women, sensing the hostility, have gathered most of the young children and told them to stay in the healer's hut, where his wife will entertain them with stories. The babies, though, remain strapped to their mother's backs. The older boys refuse to be sent away. They shadow their mothers and grandmothers with wide-eyed bravado, trying to look fierce when within sight of the soldiers.

It is because of the child that I first see her—she is the only one still carrying a child older than a year. I know her soul before I recognize her face. It is the woman from the first dream I had about this village—the white woman who was left in the healer's care by her husband, after she suffered multiple miscarriages.

Once she was well, and able to admit that her losses had resulted from beatings by her husband, the woman had decided not to go home. Her new husband is a gentle, handsome Abenaki, who is often teased for his blatant devotion to her. Their daughter, the child propped on her hip, is almost three. She has dark hair and a fair complexion and large, startling blue eyes. The child's Abenaki name is First Woman. The healer recommended this name because of her unique appearance; he said that she looked like the member of a new race. He has predicted that she will be an important figure in the ever-evolving relations between the two cultures that flow in her blood.

I am not the only one who has recognized the mother. One soldier has let his attention wander from the food and is staring at her—not with hostility or sexual threat, but in utter horror. She has felt his gaze and is trying to avoid it; she doesn't know him at first in his torn uniform and thick, dirty beard. It is when he begins to walk toward her, the tongues of his unlaced boots flapping, that she recognizes the distinct, loping strut that she once found so attractive.

"Catherine," the man says as he nears her, his voice low and hard.

"Hello, John," the woman says. She sounds calm, but the knuckles of her hands clasped under the child's bottom are white with strain.

"I thought you were dead," he said, looking her rudely up and down—at her jewelry, her moccasins, her once elegant dress now patched with scraps of other, cheaper garments.

"I doubt that," Catherine said, speaking through clenched teeth. "Wished it, I'm sure. But I doubt you believed it to be so."

He seems to have just noticed the child in her arms, perhaps because the little girl is giving him her most endearing smile. His expression darkens in a way that makes Catherine step back.

"Is that yours?" he says. He turns his head and spits a long stream of foul tobacco juice at the ground near her feet. She notices the dried blood on his uniform, the twitching of his fingers against the knife in his belt, the far-off look in his eyes. He looks like a man who has seen murder, has committed murder, and has found that he enjoys it.

"No," she answers, stepping back again, but it is clear he doesn't believe her and he follows. The child, in an unwitting, familiar gesture, places a small hand on the pulse point of her mother's neck.

The soldier drives his knife into the woman's abdomen, slurring her name and calling on God for vengeance. She crumples to the ground, and he is furiously kicking at the child when an Abenaki woman sinks a hatchet between his shoulder blades. The soldiers jump to action. Barefoot, driven by adrenaline, at first they merely slash their bayonets wildly. Soon they are driving the blades with such force that babies tied to women's backs are murdered in the same instant as their mothers. Two soldiers block the exits to the healer's hut and set it to flame. When frantic hands make holes in the walls, the soldiers thrust their bayonets into the straw. Blood from the women, children, and a few soldiers soaks through the snow, running in thick streams to the river, which will remain red for hours, even after the whole village lies still.

Later, the scene will be discovered by another company of soldiers also searching for food. It will be assumed that the village fell victim to a merciless British attack. Some soldiers will carry this image in their heads—women and children slaughtered on the doorsteps of their own homes. And they will kill to keep their own wives and children safe, to prevent happening to their own what happened to the strange but beautiful Abenaki women by the wide, peaceful river in the Maine wilderness.

Peter Doherty
85 Squantum Street
Quincy, Massachusetts

August 19, 1942

Dear Peter,

As usual, Sandra has been invaluable in helping me organize. This is the most risky endeavor we have planned, but she has not paused to doubt me even once. I believe she senses my urgency, and knows that my time for healing is limited. She has not asked about anything beyond physical details, but she watches me with a combination of pride and mourning. It is the way my mother once looked at me, during the brief interval between my week away with my uncle and her sudden death.

Our first obstacle was the night guards. The attendants have changed since the onset of the war—the beefy young men have been replaced by older, half-deaf, or slightly crippled employees. Sandra offered to steal sleeping pills from the nurses' station. Once she had them it was fairly easy for her to spike the coffee the night guards drink by the gallon. They were snoring in their chairs by eleven-thirty.

Sandra proceeded to pick the dorm locks with surprising dexterity and a simple wink in my direction. The keys to the outside were procured from a comatose guard. I led the seventeen women who had agreed to join us out into the dark Maine woods.

When we reached the clearing, Sandra delegated the gathering of wood and kindling and soon a large bonfire was blazing. She instructed the women to lie down on the blankets each had brought from her own bed. When they were settled, I shed my nightgown and began to chant, singing the song my uncle had helped me compose so long ago.

My uncle had told me of traveling healers, men who would make the rounds of villages that, for one reason or another, did not have their own Medawlinno. It was often necessary for an itinerant healer to perform a group healing, something that was, according to my uncle, a difficult and dangerous undertaking. The healer often ended up in a coma afterward and had to be nursed for days, sometimes weeks, until he was strong enough to rejoin the world. Such village healings had been known to kill inexperienced or older healers, who did not have the energy required to return from the underworld.

Of course, at the time he told me this, when I was thirteen years old and swelling with pride and invincibility, I planned to perform just such a ritual and succeed at it. But, until now, I had never been given the opportunity. As I sang my way into the trance that would gather these women's souls, I remembered an old argument between my mother and my uncle.

"She is meant to be the leader of her community," my uncle had said.

And my mother had replied: "There is no community for her to lead."

Not until I was in the woods with these women, women exhausted and broken with fear and pain, did I realize my mother had been right. It has taken me half a lifetime to find a community who needed me.

Before I descended to the underworld, the souls of these
women in my hands, I had a vision unaided by trance.
Surrounding the prone bodies of mental patients were the
Abenaki and adopted white women, babies in their arms, not a
wound among them. They were there to lend their strength.

———————

Dear Peter,

All of this finished hours ago, and now I am alone in the musty
library, where I insisted Sandra leave me. I underestimated my
task; the healing has taken me most of the night, and dawn is
approaching. This will be my last letter to you, Peter. My hope is
that someone will find all I have written, and that my words will
make their way to you. I realize how unlikely that is. But I have no
fight left to be heard anymore.

I cannot go back there, you see. The electroshock, while
giving me that powerful dream, has also damaged me, and I fear
that more treatments may cripple me entirely. I have seen too
many souls trapped between life and death to want to be one of
them. Sandra would say I owe it to the other women to stay here
and help them. But I won't be able to heal for much longer, and I
don't believe, though I haven't told them this, that my healing will
set them free. I don't think that it is merely broken souls that send
women to this place—something else is broken that I cannot fix.
Something like the disease that killed my family.

What must you think of me, Peter? I have written these letters
as an attempt to communicate with you, but really, I don't know
who you are. The son I remember is ten years old, with the wide
russet eyes of his Abenaki father and a sensitivity that often
causes the world to overwhelm him. What sort of man are you

now, at nineteen? One whose mother abandoned him, left him with the shame of small-town whispers. Perhaps you are a part of this war we hear so little about; you are old enough to be a soldier. Perhaps you are in Europe or Japan, witnessing, maybe participating in, slaughters like those that have come to me in my dreams. Maybe you are already dead.

This is what I have feared all along, because you have never answered me. I have sent the healer's call out to you more times than I can count—more than all the words in all these letters. Not once have I felt you respond, or even felt that you heard me. Perhaps you have blocked me out, afraid of what hearing voices in your head might mean. Or my instincts were wrong, and you cannot hear me at all. Maybe you are dead and, because of the accursed rules I live by, I am not able to visit you. If that is the case, I will see you soon enough.

I hope, though, that you are alive. I hope that you are strong and healthy and happy. That you fall in love, marry, and have children with Abenaki blood who are allowed to live peacefully in this broken world. I hope, most of all, that you don't have my gift, though there was a time I suspected you might. Without me there to guide you, it will have brought you only sorrow. Even had I been there, I am no longer sure this ability is a gift. How can it be, when it has taken everything I love away from me?

Mostly, though, I am sorry. Sorry both for being your mother and not being a mother to you. I am sorry for marrying a man who hated me and who, consequently, has been unable to express any love for you. I am sorry I cannot be an example to you of how to overcome the tragedy of life, and live in happiness even while surrounded by pain. That is what I wanted to teach you, what I thought of when you were still a baby, nestling your dark, sweet-smelling head in the safe space below my neck. That the love I had for you was stronger than any hatred you would encounter. The only hope I have left is that the lesson is still there, safe in the solid core of your soul, and that you can visit it, whether you know you are or not, in times of despair. This is what has kept me going, the part of my soul that belongs to you. I hope it can find you again in that all too familiar landscape of the dead.

Your mother,

Mesatawe

32

Paperwork

HISTORY OF A MENTAL RESERVATION

NATHAN STOCKWELL, M.D., PH.D.

CASE STUDY

Patient: *Mary X*

Date: *August 21, 1942*

Diagnosis: *Dementia Praecox (Schizophrenia)*

Treatment Prescribed: *Electroconvulsive therapy*

Results: *To my dismay, and the detriment of other patients on the ward, following initial treatment with ECT, Mary's delusions became too much for her and she took her own life. She drugged a number of guards and escaped the ward, then set fire to a deserted pavilion cabin in the woods. The fire spread quickly and a dozen buildings were damaged, all of them unoccupied. While some of my colleagues have hypothesized that ECT contributed to her suicide, I disagree, and plan to continue testing the treatment on other schizophrenics. I will do all I can to relieve others of the insidious disease that Mary suffered. May her soul rest in peace.*

33

Relapse Prevention

WHEN I GOT OUT to the parking lot, I realized I'd left the car keys inside the room. I couldn't bear to go back for them so I decided to walk the two miles to St. Francis. I told myself the air would do me good, though I knew I'd still end up at the bar.

Saint's Tavern was still there, between Ed's Variety and the drugstore, now a CVS. After all these years, the fluorescent bulb in the s was still broken, so the sign read AINT'S TAVERN, which was what it had been called since I was a boy, when my mother was an employee, and my grandfather was a regular.

The interior was dark and thick with smoke, and only three customers sat at the bar. The jukebox was playing Supertramp's "Goodbye Stranger," and one old man, who looked vaguely familiar, was trying to talk over the music.

Yeah, I cut their goddamn buoys if they're near my traps. I don't give a fuck what the regulations are; my family's had dibs on that cove since before these cunts' parents were even born.

At a corner table, a woman in a waitress uniform sat with a boy, reviewing multiplication flash cards.

Language, Ed, she called out.

Ed mumbled something into his beer glass. I took a stool at the far corner of the bar, already salivating at the lineup of bottles; some of the more exotic choices had dust layered on their necks. The bartender, leaning against the cash register, asked me what I wanted without lowering the *St. Francis Sentinel* from in front of his face.

Tequila, I said hoarsely. And a Corona.

I'd been in rehab long enough that I half expected him to refuse me, to ask for a special ID that verified I was a casual drinker. But he poured a sloppy, generous shot of José Cuervo and pried the top off a beer bottle, wedged a piece of lime in its neck, and set them both down on cocktail napkins in front of me.

Oscar? he said doubtfully, and I looked up. Oscar Jameson, right? It's Brian.

Brian, I said. I was having difficulty focusing on him; the beer bottle was sweating.

Brian Moriarty, he said. I snapped to attention, nodded and smiled. He'd been a friend of David's in school. His older brother had been a small-time dealer. Their father owned the bar.

Took over the business, I see, I said. How's your dad?

Liver failure, Brian said, shrugging. He'd often come to school with blackened eyes.

And Scott?

Still around. You here with your brother?

Nope, I muttered. The tequila was waiting in front of me, the shot glass as thick as the cheaply framed lenses David had worn in high school.

He looks good, Brian was saying. He's done well for himself, huh? A millionaire, from what I hear.

When did you see David? I said. I wanted to reach for the drink, but I didn't want him to see my trembling hands.

Brian looked at me strangely. Today, at the dedication, he said. I figured that's why you were here.

What dedication? I said.

The youth center, Brian said. David donated the money and paid for the architect. Built them a brand-new gym, movie theater, and computer room.

That's David, I muttered. Always the hero.

His wife's a babe, huh? Brian said.

Mmmm.

You married, Oscar?

No.

Got a girlfriend?

No, I said. An image of Alba's mouth blurred the drinks. Yes, I said. I'm not sure.

One of those, huh? I've got three boys, if you can believe it. That's my wife, Sally—you remember Sally? Patrick over there's eleven, my oldest. He's the smart one. Skipped a grade, just like David.

Uh-huh, I said. The jukebox seemed to get louder. "Goodbye Stranger" had segued into "Walk This Way" by Aerosmith.

Listen, Brian, I said. My lips were sticky. Did you say that Scott's still around?

Yeah. He just bought a trailer.

He still dealing?

Brian lowered his brow.

Why, you looking?

I might be.

Brian took a moment, sizing me up. He glanced toward his wife and lowered his voice.

I can call him if you want.

Yeah, that'd be great, I said. If you don't mind. I flinched at my high-pitched apology. Brian shrugged and went over to the phone. He muttered into the receiver and then stretched it over to me.

Jameson! Scott's voice, gruffer than I remembered, tickled my ear.

Hey, Scottie, sorry to bother you, I started.

No bother, Scott said. I'm on call for old friends. I can't do it in the bar though. You got a car?

Uh, no, I said. I started to tell him never mind.

I'll pick you up, Scott said. Give me twenty minutes. He hung up.

I handed the receiver back to Brian. He wasn't looking quite as friendly now; he busied himself mopping the other side of the bar.

I looked at the drinks growing warm in front of me. As soon as I downed that shot there would be no turning back. I wanted there to be no turning back. I wanted nothing to exist except the next few hours, the past and the future shelved to somewhere I didn't have to keep an eye on them. I didn't want to think about David. I wanted Alba exorcised from my mind.

Some father she had. She didn't even seem to realize it either. I thought about the times I'd seen him, in his fancy suits with his wide, eyeless smiles. And the way he spoke to her, as if she were nine years old instead of a grown woman. He spoke over her, making his voice louder if she tried to interject. Which she rarely did, even though she was quick to argue with anyone else. His presence diminished her. He probably preferred it when she was sick. He could be her savior.

It was all that therapy that messed with her mind. Resolving relationships. She'd be better off leaving them behind. Stop depending on saviors. They often did more harm than good. Even saints have their own agendas.

You want something else, Oscar? Brian said. I still hadn't touched the tequila.

I'm fine, I said. I pulled the napkins closer.

Still got that bullet in your shoulder? Brian said.

What's that? My hands were shaking. A drop of tequila spilled on my thumb. I wiped it on my lap.

The bullet. From your grandfather's rifle. David told the story to some of the youth center boys. Said the doctors didn't remove it, just left it to work its way out.

Why would he tell them that?

Don't know. He was talking to them about loyalty or something. Said he owed his life to you. That bullet ever come out?

No, I said. It's still there.

I remember that. My dad drove you to the hospital. David was sure you were going to die.

Listen, I said. Can I use your phone again?

Sure. He pulled the phone over and set it on the bar. I asked for the Yellow Pages and looked up the number for Motel 6.

This is Oscar Jameson, I said when the clerk answered. Can you connect me to my room, please?

I can, but your girlfriend isn't there, the clerk said. He was chewing gum.

What do you mean? Where is she?

She took off half an hour ago. Pretty batty, that one.

Fuck! I said, slamming down the phone. Alba's voice was in my head: *You just refuse to help.*

I knew I wasn't going to drink that tequila now. I almost hated her for stopping me.

. . .

David wasn't surprised when I called his cell phone. He's answered stranger calls from me. He came to the bar within minutes, after I called Scott and told him I'd take a rain check. I met David outside; I didn't want anyone else to see the disapproving face I knew he'd have.

But when I got in the car, he merely looked blank. Tired, but absent. I launched into defending myself anyway.

Look, I know you're furious. It's not what you think. I've been trying to help someone—

Beth told me, he said. Where are we going?

St. Anthony's Orphanage, I said. David pulled out onto Main Street, signaling even though there were no other cars on the road.

Bar the same? he said casually.

I didn't have a drink, Dave.

I know.

Really. I wanted to. I even called Scott Moriarty for a fix. But I didn't go through with it.

I know, Oscar.

Since when are you so quick to believe me? I said.

It's not about believing you. Don't you think I know when you're high? I've been checking your eyes for twenty years.

Jesus, I said quietly. Memories rushed at me, fast and ugly like a swarm of bats. My vigilance as a child, watching my father's then my grandfather's eyes. Gauging their progress, predicting their behavior. Seeing if they were dangerously drunk or merely on their way. It had never occurred to me, even with all that Al-Anon talk in therapy, that David had been forced to do the same thing with me.

Jesus, I said again. I'm sorry, Dave.

He glanced at me, looking surprised.

We'll talk about it later, I hope, he said.

Yeah, I said. I guess we should.

Tell me why we're going to the orphanage first.

So I did.

By the time we got to St. Anthony's, it was almost midnight and I was dreading having to rouse the nuns. But as we pulled into the lot, I saw the lights were on in the office Alba and I had visited earlier.

I don't see her car, I said. Let me check inside. I opened my door.

I'll come with you, David said, turning off the engine.

I don't need—I started.

Oscar, David said, smiling now. Think back to Sunday school. Which one of us did the nuns like more?

Gravel crunched on our walk to the door. I rang the bell, hoping it didn't echo through the whole orphanage. A curtain flickered, then Mother Superior opened the door, recognizing me with a look of disapproval.

We're very busy tonight, she said.

She's been here? I asked.

Yes, about a half hour ago. She threatened me, if you want the truth. I told her I'd call the police.

Did you?

Not yet. I don't want her in trouble, but it's clear she needs help.

This is her doctor, I said, gesturing to David.

He didn't flinch, just gave a slight bow and said: Evening, Sister.

Do you have any idea where she went? I said.

I'm sorry, no. She was very upset.

Thank you, David piped up. We're sorry to have disturbed you, Sister.

I followed him back to the car.

What now? he said as he turned the ignition.

I don't know, I said. I was really worried now. She hadn't been taking her medicine. I hadn't bothered her because I'd figured it was her decision. Clearly it was the wrong one.

Go back to St. Francis, I said. We'll check the nursing home. Drive around, try to spot her car. Maybe she went looking for me.

Should you call someone? David said.

I thought of her father and shook my head. There's no one to call, I said.

The nursing home hadn't seen her. The Jaguar wasn't on Main or Pleasant streets, the sum total of St. Francis's business district.

Maybe she's headed home, David said.

I don't think so.

What's wrong with this woman, anyway?

Nothing's wrong with her, I said. She's just unlucky.

We started our third round of Main Street.

Oscar? David said after a while. He sounded excited.

What is it?

We donated books to the youth center today. Beth showed me the ones Alba wrote. They're set in Maine. About an orphan named Sam Waban.

We were quiet for about five seconds. David was already making a U-turn when I said it.

Waban Cove.

The Jaguar was there. We parked on top of the bluff and I could see the glow of a beach fire beneath us. The downward path was slippery and more treacherous than I remembered. I heard David tripping over his expensive shoes and swearing under his breath. When I got to the bottom I ran as fast as I could manage through the dunes, toward the fire, though I couldn't see anyone near it.

I saw her boots, her knapsack, her overalls.

David! I yelled. He was fifty yards behind me and started to run. I looked out at the water; the wind was blurring everything. David reached the fire.

There! he said after a moment of squinted concentration. He pointed to the horizon. I saw a dark shape bobbing in the waves.

I kicked off my sneakers and ran down the tide incline and into the water. It was freezing; diving in I felt like my heart would stop. I swam like I haven't since I was a kid—fast, frantic, only coming up for breath when I checked my direction. I could see her head now, barely above the water. A wave swelled and she disappeared; I swam faster. When I reached her she was coughing, bobbing under without holding her breath. Her lips were as dark as the water. I grabbed her in the hold I learned in Junior Lifeguards and started back to shore.

The way back was quicker; the tide was on its way in. When my stocking feet hit sand, I slung her over my shoulder and stood up. David was waiting.

I called an ambulance, he said.

It was hard to move now, with my wet clothes and Alba's limp, heavy body driving my feet deep into the sand. I fell to my knees and laid her as gently as I could next to the fire.

Alba! I said, wiping seaweed from her cheek. In the firelight, her lips were blue. She was unconscious. I leaned down to listen for her breath, but all I could hear was the wind feeding the flames. I turned my head, putting my lips gently to hers, one hand on her chest. There was a slight movement, a whisper against my mouth. She was breathing, at least. I thought suddenly of that gruff voice that had snared me from the beginning and how I would give up anything to hear it again.

Alba, I said loudly, firmly, as if I were the one in charge. Wake up. You don't need to do this. We'll find your kid, I'll help you, I promise. You were right about me. You've been right about everything. You're stronger than you think. Come on, wake up. Wake up, Alba. You need to be all right. *I* need you to be all right.

She coughed, her back arching, and I turned her head as she vomited water into the sand.

That's it, I said, holding on. That's my girl.

She started to shiver violently; David handed me his leather coat and I wrapped it around her torso.

She looked at me, confused at first, then recognition clicked and she began to cry.

I couldn't find him, she said. Her lips vibrated, blurring her words.

I heard him crying and I looked everywhere but I couldn't find him, she said.

It's all right, I said, wiping sand from her forehead. She had a widow's peak under her bangs I'd never noticed before.

It's death, she stuttered. Death is the place where Mary found them. Found what was missing. Right on the lip of death and she pulled them back.

No more death, I said. You've had enough.

She squinted through her tears, trying to focus on me. I thought you were off getting wasted, she said.

I was, I said. I didn't. I came after you instead.

She shifted toward me, still shivering, and I nestled her head in my lap.

Glorious, she said quietly.

David tapped my shoulder. The sirens were growing louder than the wind.

34

Alternative Medicine

THE FIRST THING Alba hears is Oscar's voice. The second: her father's.

She was researching a woman whose letters she found, Oscar is saying. Some sort of Native American healer.

Jesus, her father says. More of that nonsense. Why did you let her go?

It wasn't up to me. Your daughter makes her own decisions.

Obviously you have no idea how ill she is.

Frankly, I don't think illness is her problem.

You know nothing about it.

I know enough.

Who do you think you are—her father starts, but a third voice intervenes.

I think she's waking up.

Alba opens her eyes. Hi, Dad, she says blithely. Did you take the Concorde?

Of course I did, he says. He pushes past Oscar and David to stand by her side. You're safe now, sweetheart, he says. I'm going to get you out of here. They said you could go home as soon as you woke up.

Oscar? she says, looking past her father. Oscar waves feebly; his smile is wide, uncensored. She gestures to him and he comes around the other side of the bed. Alba takes his hand. Her father glares at him but says nothing.

I want to go with Oscar, Dad, Alba says. He'll take me back to Abenaki. I have some things to talk to Dr. Miller about.

I'll take you, her father says. You're in no condition—

No, Alba says. Listen to me. Her father raises his hands in frustration.

You should have asked me, she says. You shouldn't have taken him away like that.

We can talk about this when you get home, her father says.

You have to stop it, Dad. You have to let me get better.

What are you talking about? her father says. You're confused, darling. Of course I'll help you. We'll tackle it together.

Alba's whole body relaxes against the bed, a detached, almost eerie serenity. Except her hand, which holds on tight to Oscar's. She shakes her head and closes her eyes, turning away.

Baba? her father says.

Later Oscar will tell her that, for an instant, her father's face in the fluorescent light was that of a terrified man, and that Oscar almost felt sorry for him.

.   .   .

Alba ends up spending four more days in the hospital; after an initial dose of Alanzopene, they start her back on lithium and check her blood levels. She's prescribed Klonopin as needed for panic, but she doesn't feel the need. The hospital, a few towns over from St. Francis, is small and meagerly funded; the pink walls of her room are chipping, the television is broken, and the charts are handwritten. But the nurses are kind; one of them asks her to sign books for her nine-year-old son. Her father has grudgingly agreed to go home, but he calls daily. Oscar's brother comes back once with gifts: a leather journal and an expensive fountain pen. Oscar is there every day for visiting hours, three to seven P.M. When the nurses aren't watching, he kisses her back into the rubbery mattress.

On her last morning, she is ready to leave an hour early, dressed in her overalls which Oscar has had cleaned. Her boots are slightly small and rimmed with salt. To pass the time, she takes a walk through the hospital, which has only two floors branching out in what seems like endless corridors. She passes X Ray, Ambulatory Surgery, Oncology, Administration, the Employee Credit Union. She veers off when she sees the arrow labeled Postpartum/Nursery.

The ward is large and bright, more modern than the rest of the hospital. The patients' rooms are arranged in a circle; the center has the staff station and a glassed-in nursery. The only person viewing the babies is a boy with his face pressed against the glass. Alba stands next to him. Inside, four plastic bassinets, perched high atop small metal gurneys, hold newborns so tightly swaddled in flannel they seem to have no limbs. Labels, adhered to the plastic with bandage tape, declare them boys or girls and list only their surnames. Three of the infants have a shocking amount of dark hair; the last one is wearing a hat, a small scrap of stretchy fabric topped off with a knot. This is whom the boy is peering at. His nose is flat against the glass, and he is waving, looking a bit disappointedly at the baby—the pink label says it's a girl—who is asleep.

Is that one yours? Alba says. The boy starts, embarrassed. He uses his sleeve to wipe off the smudge his nose has made.

Yes, he says, mumbling, looking down at his feet. His sneakers are monstrous, plastered with logos. She's my sister, he says, smiling now.

That's exciting, Alba says. How many siblings do you have?

She's my first one, the boy says. My parents had to try a long time to get her.

After you, you mean? Alba says. She wishes he would look at her.

I'm adopted, the boy says, lifting his head, as if this is something he has been taught is worthy of admiration, that should be stated with an indication of pride. My father says I was their first miracle, he says. Emma's their second.

His eyes are gray, almost silver, set wide apart in his face.

How old are you? Alba says.

Ten, the boy replies, looking down again. Did you have a baby? he says.

No, Alba says. I'm just browsing.

He smiles at that, turning back to the glass. Doesn't she look weird? he says. Her face is all smushed.

They all look like that, Alba says. In the beginning.

Sam! a voice calls, and Alba and the boy both turn. A tall man dressed in jeans and a flannel shirt is standing in one of the patients' rooms, holding the door open with his elbow.

Your mom's awake, he says.

And Sam, whose eyes reveal that this is clearly what he has been waiting for, hurries away in his ridiculous sneakers, forgetting to say good-bye.

Epilogue

Alba Elliot
Portland, Maine

Dr Julia Miller
Abenaki Mental Hospital
Manasis, Maine

December 28, 2003

Dear Dr. Miller,

I'm sorry I haven't written in a while. Christmas was
hectic, but fun; I helped Oscar in the bookstore, where
he's the manager now that Bethany has decided to
extend her maternity leave. He went a little overboard
buying toys for David, Jr., who doesn't even have neck
control yet. My father drove up for Christmas Eve; we
had dinner, just the two of us. He's still angry, and won't

listen to any sentence that contains Oscar's name. At least he came. I keep remembering what you said at our last session: "If the only way to please your father is to do what he wants, you'll have to get used to disappointing him." I'm trying.

The first therapist you referred me to in Portland was a drip, but Ellen is all right. I feel weird calling her Ellen; is it because she's not an M.D. but a Ph.D. that I get to be on a first-name basis? I'm taking my meds. I think I feel better on the new dosage, or maybe I just feel better in general. I go to AA meetings with Oscar; he's introducing me to Twelve Step so I can quit smoking. (Of course, everyone at AA smokes, so I'll have to find another venue eventually.) The new book is almost done; after this my agent is buying me some time so I can try something different. A novel, I hope. One for grown-ups.

I've been back to see Peter Doherty a few times. I read to him from his mother's letters, though I'm not sure how much he understands. On his good days he is pretty sharp. Once he looked me in the eye and said: "Did you know that Alba means dawn in Italian?" How he found this out is beyond me. On his bad days he calls me Mama, asks why I left him, why he never hears my voice anymore in his dreams. Oscar can't understand why I keep going back. "Doesn't it scare you?" he said last time. "Don't you ever worry you'll end up like that?" I told him: "Yes. That's why I go."

I'm sending you Mary's letters. I kept them from you this long because I didn't want you to tell me she was crazy. Maybe she was schizophrenic, maybe she was a shaman. Maybe both. Lately, it doesn't seem to matter. All I see are the ways she tried to save herself. In the end, like my mother, Mary didn't succeed because she believed she had run out of choices. I have some hidden away.

With love,
Alba

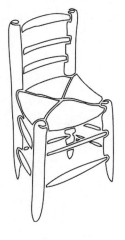

Author's Note

Love in the Asylum is a work of fiction. Abenaki Hospital and its inhabitants are products of my imagination. While the tribe I call Abenaki was inspired by history, it is not intended to be an accurate representation of Algonquins with the same name. Likewise, I took a novelist's liberties in my portrayal of shamanism, asylum protocol, and mental illness. Factual errors, purposeful or not, are all mine.

The following books were the most helpful during my research:

An Unquiet Mind, by Kay Redfield Jamison. (Random House, Vintage Books, 1995.)

Women of the Asylum: Voices from Behind the Walls 1840–1945, edited by Jeffrey L. Geller and Maxine Harris. (Doubleday, Anchor Books, 1994.)

Gracefully Insane, by Alex Beam. (Perseus Books Group, Public Affairs, 2001.)

Surviving Manic Depression, by E. Fuller Torrey, M.D., and Michael B. Knable, D. O. (Perseus Books Group, Basic Books, 2002.)

The Trouble with Testosterone, by Robert M. Sapolsky.
(Scribner, 1997.)

Shamanism, by Mircea Eliade. (Princeton Univ. Press, 1964.)

Shamanic Healing and Ritual Drama, by Åke Hultkrantz.
(Crossroad Publishing Company, 1997.)

Algonquin Legends of New England, by Charles G. Leland.
(Houghton, Mifflin and Company, 1884.)

The Earth Shall Weep: A History of Native America, by James
Wilson. (Grove Press, 1998.)

I'd also like to thank Drs. Judith Robinson and Mark Santello
for answering my practical questions. I am indebted to Dylan
Thomas for the title.